CINDER31LA

FREIDA KILMARI

KILMARI PUBLISHING

Copyright © 2024 by Freida Kilmari

All rights reserved.

No part of this book may be reproduced in any form or by any electronic or mechanical means, including information storage and retrieval systems, without written permission from the author, except for the use of brief quotations in a book review.

No part of this book may be used for the purposes of training or creating generative AI programs without written permission from the copyright holder. No AI has been used in the production of this book.

Developmental Assessment by Hart Bound Editing

Line Edited by Sara Schreiber

Cover Design by Luminescence Designs

Formatted with Vellum

The entire plot was my husband's idea. Please address all ~~complaints~~ compliments to him.

31 DAYS. 3 HOURS. 17 MINUTES.

I HAD 22,280 DAYS TO LIVE. THAT WAS ALL THE TIME I would get, whether I liked it or not. The clock never lied. The brass and steel of my lifeclock embedded in my wrist ticked on despite my mental whirring and purring, and I yanked my blue coverall sleeve down to mask the annoying tick tock of my heartbeat.

Returning my attention to the engine in front of me, I asked, "What've you got today for me, then?" I popped the hood of the steamer open and watched the faulty lines cross where they shouldn't and meet where they should, with nothing transferring. "Hmmm . . ." I rubbed sweat from my forehead with the back of my hand. "Seems you've got yourself all twisted, little buddy. Don't worry, we'll have you fixed up in no time." As if in answer, the steamer chugged and whined, puffing a dirty cloud of old, used air in my face—clearly on its last legs. But I couldn't return it to Old Mags like this; it was the only way she could see her grandchildren over in Prago City.

I spent all afternoon untangling the steam lines, trying to put them back together in a way that resembled the older models, but this thing was built before I was born and I couldn't figure out how to line everything up to the radiator.

"Liquid toffee, El," a synthetic voice croaked out from my desk.

"Ah, sweet toffee." The bitter and sweet mixture always got my heart pumping.

IoN's rusted, bronze body no larger than my head whizzed through the air with his new thrusters, his arms dangling behind as he raced back to the kitchen.

"Careful, IoN! You'll knock something off the shelves if you don't watch those arms."

"Well," he said as he whizzed back out with a can of compressed air, "if you did not pack them full with so many"—he paused and pulled an old project I'd been trying to work on last month from the shelf—"doodads, then I would not have a problem."

He was always like this, moaning and complaining about the state of the garage these days. But with Dad gone, I had to step up and take over the business—my stepmother wouldn't want to ruin her perfect new manicure my earnings paid for—and that meant there was no one to help clean up. The shelves on the metal and wood walls had stopped floating some time ago. I had since given up fixing their thrusters and nailed them to the walls the old-fashioned way.

"Just be careful," I chuckled.

His small, hemispherical body whizzed around the garage, picking up all the tools I'd left lying about this morning after fixing my neighbor's Instacaff mug. Business had been a bit slow recently—or, as my stepmother liked to remind me, nonexistent. The garage used to shine in the middle of downtown's business park on level zero; even some of the rich would come to use Dad's services. "He's the best in the business," they'd say, and I'd coo and wonder at his magnificence. Now, it was nothing but a scrappy old building with a broken sign the sun didn't even reach since they'd built the city's new level twenty-one a couple of years ago. We'd barely had any sunlight reaching us before, but twenty-one's entertainment center blocked out the meager shaft of light that used to flicker our way from 11:00 a.m. until 1:00 p.m. every day. Besides, its white marble and old cog design was an eyesore I could do without. I hated the damn sight of it every time I stepped outside.

"Mom to Cinderella," the radio echoed across the garage, dispelling my thoughts.

I cringed. I hated that name and she knew it, but I was reminded of the warning my stepmother gave me this morning before leaving our apartment: "Cinderella, darling, don't forget to make some actual money today, or I'll be forced to resort to grounding you." She booped my nose, smiled that cruel, frustrating smile at me, and walked to the local spa for her morning massage.

As if grounding me would help pay the bills. I was the only one working!

"Cinderella!"

I snapped out of the daymare that was her plastered-on face and ran to the radio receiver. "Yes, Phyllis?"

"Cinderella!" the radio crackled again, forcing her voice into octaves even higher than her fake personality would usually reach. "How many times must I tell you to call me 'Mom' or 'Mother.'" She sighed over the receiver. "Really, Cinderella, I simply cannot keep telling you."

"Sorry, Mother." My voice retained its usual nondescript tone, hiding anything and everything she might use as leverage over my life. "What can I do for you?"

"Well, now that you've actually asked." She coughed to clear her throat. "I may have a job for you. Someone sent us a letter requesting your assistance at the Dome on level eighteen."

Level eighteen? I'd never even left level zero. Most commoners didn't venture farther than level ten, and even that was only if you had a well-paying job or an invitation to take you there. Level eighteen? I bet I could see the sun from up there. Not the small slithers we occasionally got when you found the right street corner at the right time of day, but real, actual sunlight.

"Are you listening, Cinderella?"

"Oh, um, yes. Level eighteen at the Dome." I tugged my sleeves down again and continued. "What time?"

"Nine tomorrow morning." I could hear the beam in her voice despite the crackling radio. "It should go without saying, but just in case that simple brain of yours hasn't kicked in yet, you must be on your best behavior. Who knows who this might be. This could set me—us—up for life." And by "us," she meant herself and my two stepsisters.

"Yes, Mother."

"Good. Momsy out."

I threw the receiver back in its holder. For the love of Seren, even speaking to that woman put me in a bad mood.

"Here." IoN handed me a bright red candy—the last one from the pack I had been saving for a bad day. "You know," he said, "you should try to request private funds."

"I can't. You know this already." How many times must I repeat myself to this stupid steambot? "Since Dad died, Phyllis owns the garage until I turn twenty-one. Until then, she can do whatever she wishes with the money it earns."

4

"But that is far from fair, El."

I laughed. "Since when did I ever get a slice of the word fair?"

IoN did his best steambotic impression of a sigh, but, like usual, it came out all crackly.

"Still need to upgrade your voice. If I can save enough for the latest model upgrade, you'll be able to moan, sigh, and even make crying noises."

He laughed but twisted his top hemisphere—his attempt at a head shake. "I do like the idea of being able to sigh back at you sarcastically, but it is not worth the money. Save it for something more important."

I grabbed his arm and pulled him to face me. "You are important."

"I am just a steambot." He crackled a sigh again. "I am not real." He floated into the kitchen once more, which was where he went to sulk, and I returned to the crossed lines in the steamer old enough to be my grandma.

I twisted and pulled, realigned and remixed, until eventually —after swearing more times than I cared to admit and sweating more than a miner in the midday heat—I had the old steamer running again. Even the fumes seemed cleaner as they chugged out of the exhaust pipe at the rear.

"There you go, buddy. Good as new."

IoN laughed from behind me. "You like talking to us, do you not?"

"Well, you, engines, and the garage are all I have. So, yeah, I like talking to you." I turned around. "Besides, you and I both know you're more than just an engine. Whatever my dad did to you, he made you into something I've never seen before."

"So you keep telling me." IoN floated away again, content at avoiding the conversation. "You just might not know about things like me yet. It is not like you trained in engineering school or anything," he called out from the garage's back room.

"Low blow," I mumbled to myself. But he was right. I hadn't been to engineering school, and it was one of the primary reasons business was so bad. Well, that and the whole Phyllis removing Dad's "Needs Must Policy," where you could pay whatever you had if the work was necessary to your survival. But even then, no one wanted to pay money to the girl who turned in Green to the police for a free meal—even the girl trained by my father. If I could just gather enough money for a year's worth of tuition, I bet I could fast track through the course and graduate in no time. "Fat chance of that," I mumbled. A year's worth of tuition cost more than I'd made working here in the last five years.

Just one more year to go, and then I'd be twenty-one and I could do with this garage whatever I wished. I could even get my own place and live without Phyllis breathing down my neck every moment of the day. Or maybe I could sleep here?

The lights outside the window glowed a dim orange, having changed from daylight yellow moments earlier. "Time to lock up and get this steamer to Old Mags." I looked into the back room for IoN and found him already in stasis, fixing himself up for the next day. "Good night, then." I flicked my hand in a small wave and tore myself away.

I sat in the driver's seat, powered it up—relishing in the clean engine purr that followed—and drove it down the street and around a couple of corners. The houses down here were all old stone, metal, and wood, with makeshift repairs dotting almost every surface. Even the businesses were made of much the same stuff. Raggedy kids played on every corner, old-fashioned steambots ran from house to house—almost in as many numbers as humans nowadays—and various blackened people wandered in and out of the small hatches in the ground that led to the mines. Although you couldn't tell due to lack of light, the moss and shrubbery that grew here was dense, covering every spare inch it could as it seeped into cracks like Phyllis's face powder; the derelict church down the way had so much of the stuff growing over it, I swear it was more greenery and cracks than stone.

But on every wall you could guarantee there would be a poster advertising news or reminding people of the law. The one next to Mags's house had been the typical *Meddling is a Punishable Offense* for a few months now, reminding everyone, regardless of how desperate, not to interfere with your lifeclock. I couldn't imagine ever being that despaired that I'd risk being taken. But it happened at least once a year, more during times of famine.

The steamer hovered a few inches above the ground, and as much as I wanted to take it higher to better navigate the busy streets, I couldn't. This thing didn't even have thrusters. It was made of those old steam hovers they'd used back in the beginning of the industrial revolution—First Cycle, year 34X, if the textbooks were to be believed.

According to the history books, Palatina used to be a bunch of single-level towns and villages, but when our ancestors discovered steam power, everything changed. Suddenly, we could power fake lights, radios, engines, and all manner of things no one had ever dreamed of before. As time moved on and the population grew, we discovered steambotics, and now our streets were littered with bots, old parts, and Seren knew what else in the upper levels.

Mags said Prago City was built in levels too, but I'd heard tales of flat villages and towns.

Maybe one day I'd get to see them.

From this angle, those upper levels all looked so clean and white. I could see some of the crisscrossing bridges and streets they used to navigate. The houses and apartments and businesses were all piled on top of one another to create higgledy-piggledy towers that got more elaborate the farther up you looked, until eventually you couldn't really see any of the detail. People down here never got to go that far up, so I'd never met anyone who knew what they looked like.

I dreamed of seeing them someday.

The door with the yellow-speckled moss was Old Mags's house. Her real name was Maggie, but the kids had dubbed her Old Mags, and I'd never heard anyone call her by her real name before. Well, there was a police officer who had tried one time when I was eight, but she gave him a piece of her mind. That was the first day I'd ever seen Old Mags yell. She was badass for her age. Not that anyone knew what her age was, of course, but she was the oldest person I'd ever seen.

It was taboo to talk about your age and how many days you had left to live—even to your family and friends. Most people kept their lifeclocks covered, with long sleeves common on modern-day dresses and shirts. I rolled the sleeves of my bright blue coveralls up when in the garage, but everywhere else, I kept them rolled down. The tick-tocking wrist I'd been stuck with since birth caught my eyes, and I yanked at my cuff —again.

I hated even thinking about it.

What would it feel like to know you were going to die tomorrow? It must be horrible. I'd heard about people trying to off themselves before their time was up, to retain some semblance of control outside of the clock, but it never worked. They'd survive or be badly injured or someone would save them. The clocks never lied.

Mags's little apartment was around the next corner, but when I turned, several policebots surrounded the kid from the corner shop who always wore the pink ribbon in her hair despite her otherwise grungy clothing taste. Elise Cappenholt, along with her little sister, survived the famine that swept floor zero three years ago.

"Miss Cappenholt, please remain calm. We are here to remove you from the property for crimes against Seren."

Crimes against Seren? That could only mean one thing. She messed with her lifeclock.

"No! I didn't do anything wrong!" She thrust her arm out at them and sobbed. "Look! Look, it's still intact. I didn't do anything."

"You will be questioned by Minister Farro, but until then, anything you say will be recorded as evidence. Do you understand?"

"No, please! I have a little sister. She's only five. I'm all she has."

One of the policebots clasped its cuff arm around her wrist and yanked her forward. "Please follow me."

"No!" She kicked and screamed, but there was nothing she could do. There was nothing anyone could do. "Please, no!"

Another policebot cuffed her other wrist, and they lifted her off the floor and wheeled her down the street as she screamed, "Elsie! Find Mags!"

The policebots were just following orders, but it was hard to view them as anything less than evil when the only time they did anything was to force more misery onto our people.

Outside the corner shop stood a small child in a simple brown dress cinched at the waist; she held a pink ribbon in her hand as tears flew down her face and sobs echoed around the desolate street where people stood in mournful silence. No one moved as she wailed on the doorstep of a business she now owned at the mere age of five.

I hopped out of the steamer, scurried over, and knelt in front of her. "Hi, Elsie. My name is El. Would you like me to take you to Mags? I was just heading over there." I held out my hand in offer.

She placed her tiny hand in mine. When I plopped her on my lap in the steamer, she curled up and sobbed into my dress the rest of the way down the street until she fell asleep.

I stopped outside Old Mags's front door and went to knock, but her smiling face greeted me as it swung open before I got the chance. "El!" Her face fell when she saw little Elsie wrapped up in my arms. "Oh dear. Has something happened?"

"Elise was arrested moments ago."

Her eyes widened and a wan smile crept across her face. "Here. Let me take her off your hands." She wrapped Elsie in her arms, and the little girl buried her face in the old woman's neck as Old Mags took her to the spare room upstairs, where she allowed any child who needed a space to stay. When she had no doubt tucked the child into bed and soothed her crying, she came back downstairs with a somber face. She grabbed me in a bear hug tight enough to crush bones. Pulling away, she looked behind me to see her steamer, and her eyes widened. "You managed it." She let me go and inspected her steamer. "You . . . fixed it."

"Yeah, those old steam lines caused me a lot of hassle, but I figured it out."

She whacked me on the back, her gray hair and crooked nose beaming. "Good on ya, girl." She opened her garage door, which was just wide enough to allow the old steamer to pass through, and beckoned me inside. "C'mon. I just put a spot of toffee on."

Ah, toffee. Pretty sure I'd never turned a cup down. Solid toffee existed too, but it was almost impossible to get ahold of this far down. I remembered my father buying me some for my birthday one day when I was little. It was sweeter than the steaming cup of liquid toffee in front of me—usually mixed with some kind of coffee bean and had a strange texture—but, if Seren allowed it, I wouldn't scoff at a chance to taste the solid kind again.

"Tell me how you've been, girl," Old Mags demanded. Her usual gruff way of asking how I was always brightened my day, but recently, thinking about a summary of my life only made me grimace. "That bad, huh?"

I tried to smile, but I wasn't sure it worked. "Same old, same old." The last of my energy left me in a slump of my shoulders. "Even when I do manage to get ahold of that garage in a year's time, I won't earn enough to get by. We're only okay now because Phyllis is still claiming the dregs of Dad's death fund."

She grinned and patted my shoulder. "It'll all work out."

"You always seem so sure of things."

She chuckled, her toffee threatening to spill over the side of her mug. "Everything usually does work out. You just gotta have faith in Seren."

I didn't even know if the god, Seren, existed, but if He did, then I hoped He'd heard my prayers. "If I could just get a year's worth of lessons at a top engineering school and graduate on a fast track, I'm sure more people would be willing to at least try me." The moment Dad passed, it was like the entire floor gave up on us. On me. No one wanted to even give me a shot, despite having seen me assist Dad for years prior. Dad used to have customers all the way up to floor twelve, but not me. The other floors might as well not exist for all I see them. "I'm nothing like Dad."

"Stop that," Old Mags scolded. "You're just a little rough around the edges." She placed her mug down on the small tower of cogs she used for a side table and wrapped me in her arms. "And you know who else was a little rough around the edges at your age, girl?" I shook my head. "Your father."

"Really?"

"I remember when he was as unsure about life as you, crying over not having any chances, the first time a girl dumped him, and even when he was unsure about engineering school."

"He was unsure about school?" I sniffed, holding back the tears. "I thought Dad had always wanted to be an engineer?"

"Oh, he did. But he was full of doubt. His father wasn't particularly nice about him having grand plans and wanted him to settle for what he had, and your father often let that get the best of him. But he believed in himself." She smiled at me, and I forced myself to grin back, even if I wasn't feeling it.

Believe in myself . . . I could do that. Maybe.

I looked up at the ceiling with a frown. "Do you think she'll be okay?"

"She has a shop she can run, and I know a family who'll take her in and keep her fed for a few years until she's old enough to be on her feet. I think she'll be just fine."

"It's lonely being an orphan." I stared at the floor as the words tumbled out of my mouth unbidden. "Friends help."

"I'll make sure she has plenty, don't you worry."

"Thanks, Mags." I got up to leave, but she grabbed my arm.

"Don't even think of leaving without payment, girl. I won't allow it."

"I can't take money from you." She was the only reason most of the orphaned kids down here got fed. "You're like family."

She waved my concerns away and grabbed a coin purse from the side. "Here." She patted me on the shoulder. "Same as your dad used to charge me." She winked and laughed at my shocked face as she showed me out.

31 DAYS. 1 HOUR. 48 MINUTES.

JEMEENA STOOD IN FRONT OF HER FATHER, WHO LOOKED at his plate with such empty eyes, laced with disappointment so deep in the cracks of his wrinkles that, for the first time in her life, she saw her father speechless. He wasn't giving her a command, telling her what to do, offering more lessons in this or that; he simply looked at her from across the breakfast table with his soul on display. She could see the pain he usually hid so well.

Her lifeclock, unwrapped from its usual gold cloth, seemed to tick louder than the others in the room. It was probably just her imagination.

Everyone's eyes kept flitting back to it with a different variation of the same emotion in them: Mother looked like she might be on the verge of tears but was holding them back with a barricade of politeness; Father looked stern but haggard, as though the years of trying to do something about the issue hanging around like a fog had forever changed him; both of her brothers, though trying their best with light-hearted humor, kept having moments where the inevitable clearly burst their carefully crafted bubbles.

"Father?" Jemeena asked, breaking the silence.

He looked up from his breakfast with a questioning gaze.

"I was wondering if . . . I could be removed from duties for the next month. I would like to see the world." It was a lie, of course, but if she told them the truth, they'd be in a difficult position, choosing between the law and their daughter. "There are things I would like to do now that the end is nearing."

Her father looked at his wife, who allowed a single tear to escape, and a sound of disapproval left his lips. "Jemeena, I would prefer if you stayed close. Stayed at home."

"The request was a formality. I'll be leaving in the morning. I do not wish to spend the remainder of my days trapped on the royal floor of Palatina like a bird in a gilded cage. I'll spend them not as a princess, but as a free citizen of Clepsydra."

"I cannot stop you if you truly wish to leave," Father admitted. He could, of course, stop her with guards and confining her to her chambers, but she didn't think he had the heart to do so. Not anymore. "You are free, then, to explore the kingdom as you see fit." He looked at her with those green eyes, as though he had more to say but didn't know what words to put to the sentiment. Finally, he settled on, "I am sorry, daughter."

Jemeena's youngest brother, Zalto, shoved his chair out and stood, frustration overflowing the boundary of his control. Without a word, he stormed out of the room, slamming the chamber door closed behind him.

Her other brother simply looked at her, a brief moment of pain in his eyes before he closed that well shut. "Explore the world, go on a romantic adventure with some girl, watch an endless number of those stupid plays you like, see Prago City one last time like you've always wanted to?" He stood and walked over to Jemeena, kneeling in his white suit, and removed the ostentatious top hat she had always despised. "I wish you the best of luck, sister, and an ungodly amount of happiness." He grabbed her wrist and flipped it over, taking one last look at her lifeclock with a shake of his hand. "Seren, I am sorry."

There was a hidden weight to his words Jemeena didn't want to acknowledge. That perhaps there was something he could do, if only he deemed her more worthy than the law preventing him from meddling. He left with as much grace as he always walked—a swagger she usually rolled her eyes at, but today she simply watched for what was perhaps the last time. She would miss that stupid idiot's swagger.

"Where will you go?" Mother asked her.

"To Prago City maybe, or perhaps to the west. I've never seen the outlying towns."

"You'll take Hera, I suppose?" Father asked, his usual disdain for his daughter's closest friend barely present. "At least you'll have a friend there at the end. If you wish to come back, you are more than welcome." He had barely eaten his breakfast, but he, too, departed, leaving just Jemeena and her mother in a room of tension thick as fog.

"I hope you find what you're looking for, dear. I really do."

30 DAYS. 2 HOURS. 34 MINUTES.

THE NEXT MORNING I WAS UP BEFORE THE OUTSIDE LIGHTS turned yellow, and I could barely stop yawning the entire trip to the garage. I wanted to open up shop before I left for the Dome; IoN could take any orders and messages for me. The business couldn't really afford to shut for Seren knew how long this meeting would take. A day of work lost was a potential new customer not gained. We couldn't lose those right now.

Newspaper in hand, I unlocked the cogged doors with the brass key I kept around my neck and dragged my feet into the kitchenette in the back room at the ass-crack of dawn—much to the surprise of IoN.

"What are you doing here so early, El?"

"Wanna open up shop before the meeting," I mumbled around a cup of steaming toffee as I threw the paper on the side. The headline read *New Zimeon Invention Takes Convention by Storm*.

IoN whizzed around the kitchen, making me some boiled eggs for breakfast by the looks of it.

"You don't have to make me—"

"It will do you some good." IoN whirled around to face me.

"You need to eat three meals a day to remain healthy. And eggs are good for a human's serotonin levels."

"Yes, Dad." He was always like this, trying to get me to eat more, sleep more, smile more. I guessed IoN . . . cared. That fact alone started the usual line of questioning: How could IoN care? What kind of strange internal cogwork did he have to make him able to learn? No steambot could learn; they could only do what you tell them to do. No steambot, that was, except IoN. Dad had made him when I was a child, and although I'd fixed his external parts as needed over the years, he wouldn't let me fiddle with his internals. Steambots had no rights, since they were not capable of emotion, but every one of them had to be registered with official paperwork; since Dad didn't want anyone knowing about IoN's differences, he is, technically, illegal.

So I kept IoN in the garage where he could cause the least amount of suspicion. The last thing I needed was an illegal bot who showed signs of advanced technology on the premises. They'd shut the garage down for good—no questions asked.

"Keep an eye on everything for me today. Take any orders, answer the radio, and take messages." I steeled myself as I prepared myself to say the next thing. "And remember, act like a regular assist bot. None of"—I gestured to the way he was watching himself in the mirror, curious—"this."

"Yes, El. I know." He spun around as the eggs finally boiled. "I know how much this garage means to you. I will not be in the way. Promise."

"I also don't want you to be taken away, IoN. You're important too." No matter how many times I told him, it never stuck.

At least this time he didn't bother answering. He just peeled my eggs, plated them up, and handed them over. "Here. Eat."

Breakfast was . . . well, it was breakfast. Eggs were the cream of the crop down here, and the only reason I got to eat them was because Old Mags kept a small farm of chickens in her house. She gave eggs to me, but they were only allowed in the garage because she didn't like Phyllis and the girls eating them. Safe to say Mags wasn't a Phyllis fan.

I spent the next hour doing some basic calculations for the garage and wondering how the hell we were going to even pay the 650-coin rent this month, much less afford to eat. If Phyllis could stop taking so much for her stupid spa days and the girls' ridiculous wardrobes, we wouldn't be struggling so much. Mags paid me a good one hundred coins yesterday, which needed to go toward paying the rent, but other than that, we didn't have anything else right now.

If I didn't get any more work this month, we were screwed.

I was just about to start work on an old project—an old steambot previously used for picking apples back when we got enough sunlight down here to grow them—when a light knock on the garage door stole me from my mind.

A faint "Help" sounded, followed by a "Please."

I rushed to the door and yanked it open, but I wasn't prepared for the beauty standing in front of me. Long black hair in carefully waved tresses flowed over an elegant turquoise dress with various intricate layers of lace and beading decorating the bodice. Even her face was an immaculate presentation of golden skin, green eyes, red lips, and eyelashes longer than any I'd seen. Not that I usually spent so long staring at a woman's eyes. This one was just breathtaking.

"Thank you," the girl said, hand on her chest as she took several rapid, raspy breaths.

Instead of asking if she was okay, however, I continued to

stare dumbfoundedly at her, wondering what someone so noble was doing here on floor zero, let alone at my garage.

"Hello?"

Crap. She'd caught me staring. My pale skin blushed like a tomato, and I ducked out of her sight, waved her inside with a "Come on in," and walked into the kitchen to brew a cup of toffee. I threw an intense glare at IoN, who bobbed up and down—his best attempt at a nod—in understanding: Act like a normal bot.

We didn't know who this girl was.

She followed me into the kitchen, and I spun to meet her piercing green gaze. "You're welcome," I said. "It can be a long walk from the elevator station."

"Yes, well . . . I probably should not be this far down, anyway."

Just as I'd thought: She was from a higher level. Did she know what the sun looked like? This was my chance to ask.

"Hey, do you know what the—"

"Where am I?" she interrupted with curious eyes as she examined her surroundings.

I'd never really cared before, but I was suddenly ashamed of all the dirt and grime this room contained, and I couldn't even remember the last time I'd cleaned. IoN had probably cleaned it at some point. Right? "Er . . ." I mumbled, "sorry about the mess." I grabbed a spare chair from under the table and gestured to it. "Here." I plopped down in the one next to hers. "You're in the Tinker Hut. Were you not searching for an engineer?"

Her eyes widened as she sipped her toffee. She looked down at the liquid in her mug and frowned but quickly replaced it with a stone-wall expression. I knew that expression; it was the one I used on Phyllis when I didn't want anyone knowing how I really felt. She didn't like the toffee.

"Sorry," I mumbled. "You're probably used to better stuff." I didn't know what level she was from, but she wore things I'd never seen, like bracelets in a golden material and her shimmery cloak I still didn't understand. Plus, her skin was golden, and you only got that from regular exposure to sunlight.

"It is quite all right." She coughed into a handkerchief she had pulled from her cloak pocket and didn't stop for a good thirty seconds, and I swear her golden skin paled. She waved my concern away and said, "Just a little dusty down here."

I asked IoN for a glass of water, and he whizzed back moments later with a clean glass of water for our guest.

She took it with a thank you aimed at me, and I hid the scowl that tried to form. I was so used to treating IoN as a person, it irked me when someone treated him like some regular machine.

Not the time, El. So not the time.

"If you don't mind, miss. What are you doing down here?"

She raised her eyebrows at me.

I laughed. "It's obvious you're not from here."

She frowned. "I put on my worst clothes and everything." She frowned, genuinely upset about her failings.

"Whatever material your cloak is made from, I've never seen it before. Nor whatever that golden stuff your bracelet is made of."

She raised her eyebrows in amazement. "You've never seen silk before? Or gold?" She fiddled with the small, delicate thing dangling around her wrist and the key that joined it together in a complicated clasp.

I shook my head and shrugged. "Sorry."

She chuckled under her breath and apologized. "Sorry, that was terribly rude of me. I am just laughing at my failure to know the people of this city." She looked me straight in the eyes. "I promise I was not laughing at you."

I waved away her concern. She clearly hadn't ever ventured

lower than floor ten before, so who was I to judge. I'd be just as out of place at the top.

"El," IoN said as he floated near my head. "Your nine a.m. appointment on floor eighteen at the Dome is in one hour."

"Thank you, IoN."

He floated away again.

"I am sorry for intruding." She stood up and went to leave but clutched her chest tight as she wobbled on her feet.

I grabbed her by the waist and sat her back down. "It's okay." I needed to make that meeting, but I couldn't just kick her out. "If you promise not to steal anything, you can stay here while I'm out."

Her eyes widened. "I couldn't possibly—"

"You're in no condition to be going anywhere. Is there someone I can get for you while I'm out? It's the only chance I'll have to leave floor zero." I looked at the ground, not wanting to admit how embarrassed that fact made me.

She shook her head. "I'm here looking for someone. It's important."

I got her to her feet and rested her on the sofa in the back room. "Well, who are you looking for? Maybe I can help?" I ruffled the ends of my dress straight. "I've lived here my whole life. I know everyone on this floor."

As her body convulsed into another coughing fit, I winced. This girl wasn't well. Was that why she was down here on floor zero?

"I'm looking for a legendary engineer. I used to hear stories about him when I was little." She blushed. "It could just be a fairy tale, but I . . . I'm out of options." Her eyes met mine, and those green orbs struck something inside me.

This girl needed help, and IoN was right, I wanted to assist her. My father had always said, "If not you, then who?" He had helped anyone who needed it, and he did his best for them—a lot like Old Mags in a way. I couldn't watch this clearly very ill girl be tossed to the curb.

I gestured for her to continue.

"There is this bedtime story my mother told me about an engineer who worked on floor zero, but he worked for anyone who asked, and he had legendary skills. Rumor had it he could give steambots personalities." She coughed again, her hand clenching her side. "Preston."

I blanched and choked on my toffee. Dad. She was talking about Dad. But he wasn't some kind of legend. Was he? Not that I'd heard of, anyway.

"Have you heard of anyone like him?" She looked at me with such conviction. "I am a little desperate."

"I'm sorry, but Preston died five years ago."

She gasped as tears slid down her face. "But, but, but . . ." The few tears quickly turned into small streams and those into rivers as they ran off her chin and onto her beautiful cloak. "This is so unfair!"

I was going to regret asking this, but I couldn't stop the words from tumbling out. "Is there anything I can do to help? I'm El, Preston's daughter, and the person now running his garage."

She shot up from the dingy sofa and had to pause to cough once again. "You . . . you're the daughter of the legendary engineer?" Her eyes widened with disbelief.

"He was just a good engineer to me. I don't know about all that other stuff." I helped her lie back down. "Sure, he had customers from some of the higher floors, but that's just 'cause he was good at his job. He wasn't some magical engineer capable of advanced technology like that." As I said it, my eyes flitted to IoN with suspicion. Maybe there might have been some truth to the legend. But I couldn't risk telling her that. Who knew who she really was? "Is there anything I can help with?"

The girl looked to her wrist, where her lifeclock was covered by some shiny yellow cloth. "I was wondering if you know how to fix a broken... lifeclock."

I hissed as I threw a hand over her mouth. "You can't just ask that down here!" I inched my hand from her mouth, making sure she wouldn't ask again. "We're disposable. If one of us went missing, no one would notice."

"Hence why I looked down here." She grabbed my arm in a vice-like grip. "I can pay you. As much money as you'd like. So long as you keep silent."

I yanked my arm out of her grip and frowned in her direction. "Messing with a person's lifeclock is grounds for execution, or at the least, permanent imprisonment."

"I know." Her green eyes pleaded with me, and I fully looked her up and down. Her body was thin, wasted, and she looked... sick. "Please. I will pay you anything. Get you and your family living on a higher floor. Anything you want."

"Anything?"

Her eyes widened and she smiled. "Anything."

"Think you can get me into engineering school on a fast track program?"

Her laugh deepened, and she had to catch her breath. "That is all you want?"

I shrugged. "It's really all I need." It was far from all I needed, but I wasn't about to tell a stranger of my financial situation.

"Then, we have a deal." She pulled her hand out of her cloak and offered it to me.

I shook her hand and grabbed my multi-tool from the workshop. "Let me have a look, then."

She unwrapped her unusually colored piece of—silk, was it?—and handed me her wrist, wincing as I touched the sensitive skin wrapped around the edges of the mechanism buried in the body. The brass cogs turned at the edges, going deeper than my eye could see, and the clock slowly ticked her heartbeat. However, it was the clockfaces in the center that gave me pause, because their hands pointed in directions not often seen in someone so young. We were taught how to read the hands at a young age. Three clockfaces, each representing a different figure, ticked like a regular clock with a series of numbers around the edges: The first was for years, the numbers around the edges extending up to 120; the second for days, the numbers extending up to 365; and the final for hours, with only twenty-four available on every clock.

Hers didn't take as long to read, though, because the first clockface was obsolete.

She only had thirty days and one hour to live.

"Please," the girl with the raven-black hair begged. Her voice cracked with emotion as tears leaked from her eyes. "Please, fix it."

"Fix what?" I asked. "It's not broken." Everything looked functional. Hell, the insides were shiny.

Her polite resolve snapped, and her sculpted facial expression spun into one of agony and anger, her lips downturned and her brow furrowed. "It must be broken!" she screamed. "I can't die in thirty days!" She fisted her hands as they shook and she wobbled on her feet. "Please..."

"What you're asking," I said as I guided her back to the sofa, "isn't possible." I sat next to her and grabbed her hand in mine. "It's not possible to alter a person's internal clockwork, and even if you try, it never affects the number shown or experienced. Plus, opening a lifeclock and trying to alter one is forbidden by the Temple of Seren."

It was steambotics rule number one: Never interfere with a lifeclock. This girl, this dying, sick girl, was begging me to do so nonetheless.

"I'm sorry." I put a comforting hand on her shoulder. "I can't help you."

Her shoulders shook as she sobbed. Leaning into me, she rested her head on my shoulder. "It is not fair."

"I know," I whispered.

"Cinderella!" Phyllis called from the workshop.

"Crap," I cursed. "Please"—I turned to the crying girl in my arms—"stay here. Don't be seen." I plastered on what I hoped was a reassuring smile and sprinted into the workshop.

Phyllis could not get wind of me keeping a stray in the garage. Seren only knew what she'd do to me as punishment.

"Cinderella! Look at you!" Phyllis ranted at the state of my coveralls after having potted about in the dusty garage this morning. "You're a mess." She yanked a kink out of my hair and dusted me off. "Get dressed, for Seren's sake. The meeting's in an hour."

Phyllis looked around the workshop disapprovingly. Her gray hair—"it's supposed to look like that"—shined with fake vigor and her corset locked her curves into place in a way that couldn't be comfortable. The brown and gray dress she'd chosen was her finest casual outfit—I knew, because I'd been there when she'd spent the entire month's earnings on it. It cinched her waist in the right places, fell in the right waving, tufted way her dresses always did, and trailed at the back to give her a more noble appearance. She'd even had her hair done—somehow.

She didn't sit anywhere, just looked at me expectantly.

I rushed to throw my dress on—a simple gray and white piece that fell to the floor in pleats and bunched at the waist, leaving me looking haggard and underweight. I threw a comb through my hair and did my best to get the knots and dirt and grime out, but I was pretty sure I was just moving it all around.

"Move aside," Phyllis said and yanked the comb out of my hands.

My mother used to do my hair for me, style it into beautiful golden locks that made me feel like a princess, but this was nothing like those long-lost times. Phyllis tugged, pulled, and scraped until my locks obeyed her every demand and sat in a loose bun on top of my head.

Phyllis chucked a pair of earrings at me. "Put those in."

The earrings in question were one of my stepsister's, Lapis, and I knew that because she'd scalded me with a hot pan the day I looked at them a second too long. Back in those days, her jewelry collection was her prized possession that I was not to look at, touch, or go near.

I took a deep breath and shoved them into my ears, letting the white cogs dangle from my lobes. Lapis was going to flay me alive later, and Phyllis was going to do nothing about it—as usual.

"IoN," Phyllis shouted into the echoing room, "come along."

He whizzed out of the back room and into the workshop. "Yes." He beeped. "Following mode activated."

Great. Now I had to leave that girl all alone in my garage with no way of keeping an eye on her. She could die or leave and let looters steal everything.

This was going to bite me in the ass, wasn't it?

30 DAYS. 0 HOURS. 28 MINUTES.

THERE WEREN'T MANY WAYS YOU COULD GO UP OR DOWN the level system, since most houses didn't allow you to travel to the levels above it, but there were government-controlled elevation buildings you could use if you had the proper paperwork.

"Come along, Cinderella." Phyllis grabbed my hand and yanked me down the next street that widened the closer we got to the corner building ahead.

It was one of the only buildings that got any decent sunlight, and its gray brick and bronze metal were free from any sort of moss, cracks, or other floor-zero appearances and structures. I felt less at home the closer I got.

IoN whizzed by my head, his arm brushing my shoulder every now and then in comfort when Phyllis wasn't looking, but he remained otherwise empty of himself.

Why did Phyllis bring IoN with us? She hated the steambot, thought he was a waste of money. I had a bad feeling about this.

As I stepped through the building's grand revolving doors, I looked behind me at the crumbling street and nearly gasped. The girl was following us. Well, that made me feel less guilty about leaving her alone, at least. Her golden skin was paler than before, and I swear I saw a speck of blood on her chin from all the coughing. Whatever was wrong with her, she was going to die from it. In thirty days.

"What are you staring at?" Phyllis scolded. "Stop being such a dither-dather and come along."

"Yes, Mother."

She guided me to one of the terminal booths where an old steambot sat behind a high desk in the shape of a giant cog wheel chipped at the edges. I got the feeling it wasn't due for repair anytime soon. Nothing got repaired down here.

"Papers," the bot stated.

Phyllis handed over the two invitations that came with the letter.

The bot took the papers and stared for a moment before his eyes flashed yellow. "Please proceed to elevator eleven."

"Come along." Phyllis grabbed the papers and followed the signs to elevator eleven.

I trotted along behind her, trying to discreetly check on our tail who'd managed to skip past the guards and follow us up the dingy, busy path made of broken cobblestones. The building might look fancy on the outside, but it was just as rotten as the rest of floor zero.

We traversed the main path that led to all of the central elevators, passing smaller pathways that led to more specific elevators and destinations on the higher levels. Everything was dark this far down the main street, and even with the lights flickering on the walls in their swirling, bronze holders, it was getting harder to see with every step.

The next offshoot to our left flashed a sign as yellow as all the others: *FLOORS 11-20*. Taking a deep breath, all three of us rushed down the much smaller path with the only sound being the whirring of IoN's thrusters as he kept pace with Phyllis's monster-walking speed. She shot off down the path in such a frenzy, even her hair was starting to fall out of place, and I briefly wondered if she was scared of the dark. That thought made my lips curl up. Imagine that? A level zero resident afraid of the dark. The idea was almost laughable. If I thought hard about it, though, I couldn't remember a time when Phyllis didn't have some sort of light on. She even slept with a pink light she clipped to the edge of her bedside.

Perhaps she really was scared of the dark.

I tucked that nugget of information away in the recesses of my mind as I looked behind us once more, but everything was too dark to make out more than a few feet of space. I hoped she was okay.

I felt for the girl. I really did. She had only thirty days to live, and by the looks of it, they weren't going to be pleasant final moments. It was a shame; I didn't even know her name.

The path opened into a wide, double-doored space filled with the same eerie light as back on the main path. On either side sat a steambot of some kind—ones I'd never seen before, but they seemed to be some kind of conductor.

"Please," the one on the left said, "step inside the elevator." It flicked a switch on its left, and I marveled at the sight that unfolded.

A massive mechanism swallowed the room, where a pillar in the center held a glass dais currently resting upon the concrete floor. Various pipes joined the walls and the pillar together, like a spider web of engineering I tried to track with my eyes but didn't have the time to figure out. How did this thing work? Did it lift us to higher floors somehow? Was this also powered by the steam mines? It had to be.

I followed Phyllis up the two steps on to the dais with my mouth agape and my eyes wide.

I'd never left floor zero before, but I'd made Dad tell me all about the other levels he'd been to—over and over again until he'd order me to bed. The memory of him standing above me with arms crossed and a smile on his rugged face while I lay tucked in a blanket and begging him to tell me more had me as gleeful as a child once again.

Phyllis regarded me with much the same disdain as always, though I thought I saw the hint of a bemused expression in the depths of that scowl somewhere.

I stepped onto the dais with caution; I knew what could happen if even one of the internal mechanisms were faulty. Once we were safely over the line roughly painted onto the glass floor, I ummed and ahhed over the cogwork beneath our feet. You could see everything from here! The way the cogs all piled together to create one perfectly working machine whose only aim was to lift the floor—with the people on—up to the higher levels. It was simple engineering really, but it was still beyond even my imagination. I could fix things, but creating? That was left for great inventors, like the great Zimeon—he was behind the latest steamer designs. Oh, what I wouldn't give to meet Zimeon over a steaming cup of toffee.

"Please stay behind the line and hold on to the handles provided," the other steambot announced.

IoN settled himself onto the floor behind me while Phyllis and I grabbed a metal railing circling the central tower at waist height.

"Lifting to floor eighteen."

As the bot pulled a lever near the gate, the entire central

mechanism at my feet lit up in dim oranges, reds, and greens, and each cog turned, triggered the next cog and then the next and then the next, until the mechanism reached the central tower and the whole thing began buzzing and hissing as steam flew through its metal piping.

The floor rose a few centimeters and latched onto a thick metal pole surrounding the dais, which detached itself from the wall, and we began ascending. It was a slow ascension, but since there were no walls to prevent us from simply falling down the gap between the dais and the exterior tube, I guessed that was a good thing. I bet it could go faster with some glass walls and a seating system for the passengers.

It took about ten minutes to ascend to floor eighteen, but those ten minutes revealed more about the other floors than I'd ever learned from other people: The walls got cleaner and whiter the farther up we went, and as we gained height, the cogwork and lighting systems attached to the walls of the elevator tube got fancier. I wasn't sure what I expected, but it left a sour taste in my mouth. They had money to throw away on fancier machines and lights and elevators, but not enough to feed us down on floor zero?

The thought made me sick.

"Welcome to floor eighteen," another bot—identical to the pair on floor zero, if slightly shinier—said. "Please remain behind the line until the elevator completely stops."

We waited for the whirring of the machine to end before crossing over the line, down the steps, and through the similar-looking archway. That was where the similarities stopped. Unlike floor zero, where barely any light lit the tunnels and paths, floor eighteen was pristinely white, with bronze cogs stained the same color as the girl's bracelet built into the marble walls similar to the ones in floor zero's temple—or maybe they really were gold cogs.

We walked through tunnel after tunnel, following the exit signs that marked the way every few feet, until we reached the foyer at the front of the building. The foyer had security guards—real, live people—checking bags and pockets before allowing anyone to pass to the floor beyond. Everywhere I looked there were people dressed in corsets, dresses, and skirts, and they were caked in so much makeup and hair product, I doubted they looked anything like their real selves. No dirt marred their features, no bones stuck out from malnourishment, and their corsets amplified their curves rather than bunched what little they had.

Even Phyllis looked uncomfortable with our surroundings, though she tried her best to hide it with courtly detachment and a polite glance at everyone we passed. No matter how hard she tried, her polite actions were getting her nowhere. These people took one look at us and sneered at our cheap clothes, imperfect faces, and hair, and then walked on, their heeled boots clicking against the marble floor.

Phyllis walked all three of us up to the nearest security line, and we waited to be seen by one of the men with the bored, uninterested looks on their faces.

"Next!"

Phyllis gave him her purse, which he sifted through before checking her pockets and person and announcing her clear.

I looked at him as I stepped forward, and he frowned.

"Bag?"

I shook my head.

He asked, "Pockets?"

I raised my hand and gestured to the rims of my dress, where two pockets lined either side.

After rummaging around both and finding them empty, he shifted me along, but he stopped IoN and scowled. "What model is that?"

Err . . . "He is an Internal OxiNexus, sir."

He blinked at me. "A what?" His black mustache wrinkled as he frowned.

"An Internal OxiNexus. He was designed by Preston, my father." Pride filled me as I straightened my shoulders. "He's one of a kind, sir."

"Well," he said with a gruff scowl, "do you have his paperwork?"

"Paperwork?" Crap. "Not on me, no."

"He simply cannot come onto the floor—"

"Excuse me, sir?" Phyllis tapped him on the shoulder. "If you wouldn't mind examining our invitation, you might find his presence requested."

What? IoN had been invited to the meeting too? I looked at him and let out a withheld breath. Something about this didn't feel right. No one this far up should have even known IoN existed, much less required his presence.

The guard examined the invitation and his eyes widened. "Oh, okay then." He let us pass without any hesitation, but as I looked back, he looked at IoN with more curiosity than I was comfortable with.

Phyllis scowled at me like usual, fiddled with my dress, and tucked a stray strand of hair back behind my ear before allowing us to leave the building. When we did, the gentle breeze caressed my cheeks as something strange tingled every inch of my skin.

Sunlight!

I took deep breaths of fresh air mixed with the smell of something sweet baking. I couldn't get enough. The walkway we were on was large with plenty of people traffic, but the steamers on this level flew high in the air—well out of everyone's way. There were so many kinds: chug engines, balloon risers, and even a few fender fins with their wide, angular wings and open tops.

I sprinted to the edge of the path, ignoring Phyllis's shouts of protest, and peered over the side. We were so high up, I couldn't even see floor zero, and Seren, there were so many lights, advertisements, and signs floating in the air, attached to buildings, and even nailed to railings.

New Zimeon Engine Design Unveiled

Donuts, 10 Coins a Dozen

See the brand-new entertainment center!

See New Floor 21: Tours Available

They were allowed on floor twenty-one here? I thought only the royals and their families and servants were allowed that high. Well, it was an entire floor, and I guessed everyone there had to make a living, but I thought they were all rich enough not to have to work.

"Cinderella!" Phyllis grabbed my hand and yanked me into the nearest line of people walking down the street. "Stop gawking and start walking. We'll be late."

"Yes, Mother."

Phyllis tried her best to navigate the busy streets and various signs of level eighteen, but we eventually got lost and had to ask a nearby vendor for directions. Luckily, we weren't far and eventually made it with minimal sweating and scuffing of our dresses— much to Phyllis's glee.

"Now, Cinderella," she said with a grimace, "please behave in there. And let me do the talking." She patted me on the head and looked as if she were going to say something else but decided against it.

"Yes, Mother."

The Dome in question was a giant structure made of bronze and some black shiny stuff I'd never seen before. It was easily the biggest building here, having to be held up by at least ten building towers. Flashing on the front doors was a sign that read *Zime Industries*.

"Wait, Zime Industries?"

"Yes."

They were owned and run by Zimeon, the legendary inventor. What would they want with me?

"But what—"

"Oh, really, Cinderella. Would you just stay silent for once in your miserable life?"

I snapped my mouth shut and stifled the whine of disapproval that threatened to escape. I just wanted to know what this was all about. The closer to our meeting we got, the more I suspected this wasn't a regular job. They had their own engineers. Why would they need me?

Upon entering the doors that were the height of ten men, Phyllis directed us straight to the reception desk. There, a woman greeted us with a warm, practiced smile. "How can I help you today?"

"Hello," Phyllis began. "We have a meeting scheduled for nine this morning."

"Uh-huh," the receptionist said as she took out her book. "And what's the name, sweetie?"

"Cinderella Ferning."

The receptionist's eyes widened with shock for a moment, but she quickly covered it up with that same smile. "Of course." She waved another employee over and said, "Could you please show our guests to meeting room twenty-three?"

The blonde-haired, thin-waisted woman beamed at us in that practiced way that seemed to be all the rage up here and beckoned us forward. "Of course." She directed us down hallways, up smaller elevators, and through so many twists, turns, and doorways, I was lost before we'd even begun. Eventually, she stopped outside an engraved metal door: *MEETING ROOM 23*.

29 DAYS. 23 HOURS. 12 MINUTES

INSIDE, THE ROOM HAD LITTLE LIGHTING AND A GIANT, Tshaped table in the center with about a dozen chairs surrounding it. No windows in sight. I was pretty disappointed in the contrast to the rest of the fancy building. They probably didn't bother putting us—two people and an unregistered steambot from level zero—in anything fancy. Oh well.

It was just a job proposal.

The room was currently empty, so we stood by the door and waited until the other door at the far back of the room swung open and six people poured into the room. These weren't just any people; they were the executives of Zime Industries. The people Zimeon himself entrusted to run his company while he was busy inventing.

What was going on?

They sat in an arc at the back of the table and gestured for us to sit on the opposite side. "Please, take a seat," a gray-haired older gentleman said. He wore a fancy suit that had far too many frills poking out of the collar and sleeves to be taken seriously. "Miss Ferning." He looked directly at me as he addressed us.

Satisfaction curled my lips as Phyllis stiffened beside me at being ignored. IoN sat himself on the table in front of us, causing every set of eyes in the room to home in on him.

"This is the Internal OxiNexus?" the same man asked, his eyes matching the curiosity of the room.

"Y-yes—" I stammered.

"Yes," Phyllis replied. "It was invented by my late husband, Mr. Ferning." She placed a hand on her heart and feigned sympathy for a moment.

Watching their looks of pity made my teeth grind.

"We are sorry for your loss, Mrs. Ferning, Miss Ferning," the man to the left with brown hair and golden freckles lining his reserved face said, "but we thank you for meeting with us here today."

"I'm sorry," I interrupted, "but what is this about?"

The gray-haired man flinched. "You have not told the girl?" He looked at Phyllis.

Phyllis shrugged. "It is not her decision to make. I own the garage and everything Mr. Ferning owned."

The gray-haired man looked at me with pity. "We are here today to discuss the financial terms of the sale of the Internal OxiNexus."

IoN moved ever so slightly in my hands—his only indication of a reaction.

What? But . . . Phyllis couldn't do this! She . . . "I am sorry, Mr. . . . ?"

"Mr. Bunting," he said.

"Mr. Bunting, but IoN isn't for sale. My father left him for me after he died to help out in the garage."

Mr. Bunting looked confused for a moment and waved his hand toward one of the gentlemen at the end of their line of important people I had no business interacting with. A blond man, no older than me, threw a file down the table. Mr. Bunting flicked through for a moment and frowned. "I am sorry, Miss Ferning, but that is not listed in his will. Meaning, just like the rest of your father's possessions, they belong to the will's sole beneficiary." He gestured to Phyllis. "Your stepmother. The decision lies with her."

I snapped my attention to Phyllis, who looked at me with her general level of disdain that I was sure was the only mood she was capable of expressing.

"The decision has been made."

"No!" I grabbed IoN's body with tight, rising anger. "I won't let you sell him."

"Cinderella!" she scolded. "You will do as you're told." She leaned forward and hissed, "We need the money, and who's fault is that?"

Tears fell down my face in fierce streams that I batted away. "No," I edged out, my usual placid expression all but a distant memory. "I won't let you destroy everything my father worked for." IoN was his pride and joy, his assistant when creating and fixing other bots, and his friend when Mom died.

"The decision really isn't yours to make, Cinderella. I own it." She rested her hand on top of IoN's head, but I yanked him away and looked at her with as much fire as I could.

I looked at the men across the vast expanse of corporate table and pleaded with them to leave us alone. If they took their offer off the table, Phyllis couldn't sell him.

The gray-haired man, however, just looked at me with pity and resolve. He wasn't going to change his mind no matter how hard I begged.

Fine.

I picked IoN up off the table and cradled him in my arms as I turned to walk away.

"Stop!" one of the CEOs shouted—the first time I'd heard any of them raise their voice. "Stealing a steambot is a crime in Palatina, Miss Ferning."

I stopped three inches from the door and something in me crumpled. "I'm not stealing anything, because IoN is mine."

"El?" IoN spoke. "It's okay." He whizzed into the air and faced me. "This will be for the best, I promise."

I shook my head. "No, it won't." I'd be all alone. Every member of my family finally gone: Mom, Dad, and now IoN.

"Shhh." He wiped a stream of tears away and rested his other arm on my shoulder. "This will mean you can afford that year in engineering school you always wanted."

The room gasped and murmurs rose like vultures circling their prey.

IoN's mouth—the rectangular hole that acted as a mouth, anyway—lit up in a bright green, a sign he was happy.

I thought he was trying to cheer me up, but seeing him be himself only made it harder, and rather than be a fully functioning twenty-year-old adult who had fended for herself for the past five years, I broke into a heap on Zime Industries' cold metal floor and cried for the first time since Dad had died.

The door in front of me opened and clicked shut in an almost whisper, and I looked up to find a familiar silk cloak and shining black hair falling to a slim girl's waist.

"Enough." She pulled her cloak's hood down from her head. "However much they are paying you for IoN, I will double it." She looked at Phyllis as she said this, then turned to help me off the floor. "I protect my employees."

All six men who had previously been lording over us rushed to their feet and bowed. "Princess Jemeena."

Princess . . . ? But how? Wha—?

The girl—Princess Jemeena—grimaced, and I got the feeling she was trying to silently apologize for her earlier deception. She turned to face the board of Zime Industries with a face like stone. "Now, gentlemen, if you don't mind, myself and Miss Ferning have important business to discuss."

This entire time, Phyllis, who was still in her chair, opened her mouth to speak on several occasions, but she seemed lost for words but for stuttering, "Princ-Princess? But I . . ." She turned to me with wide eyes and a genuinely impressed look of surprise. "How?"

I scratched my head and shrugged. I honestly wasn't sure either.

Princess Jemeena dusted off my dress and linked her arm through mine. "We bid you good day, sirs." She led us through the door, around all the twisting hallways, down all the small elevators, and out of the building, all the while ensuring IoN stayed with us.

"Umm, Princess?" IoN moved ever so slightly in my arms.

She turned to me. "Please, call me Jemeena."

"Jemeena, are you sure that was a good idea?" I asked as we got to the elevator building and passed through security without a hitch.

She giggled and led us through posh hallways, passing gilded lights and signs in languages I'd never heard. "No one will argue with the next in line to the throne." She let go of my arm the moment we were alone. "Do not worry about a thing." She looked away, despondent for a moment, as though her world were ending and there was nothing she could do about it.

42

That was when it hit me: Her world *was* ending.

Princess Jemeena, next in line for the throne, was going to die in twenty-nine days.

I stopped dead in my tracks underneath a flickering orange light. "Princess . . . you're—"

"I know," she interrupted. "But, please, not here." She looked all around us as though spies were watching. But then, she *was* the princess; who knew what kind of enemies she had.

Her black hair swished in the wind as she turned on her heels and power-walked down the hallway that led to a fancier version of the elevator I'd used coming up.

"Where are we going?"

She stopped before the dais steps and grimaced. "To floor fifteen." After walking up two stairs, I realized why. She was out of breath. She'd probably used most of her energy helping me back in the meeting, then she'd charged all the way here.

Damn it, I should have made us take a hover or something. "Here." I offered her my arm. "Let me help, Princess."

"I do not need you to help me because of some patriotic obligation."

I stifled a laugh, but she shot me a glare that could cut glass. "Sorry, Princess—"

"Jemeena."

"I'm sorry, Jemeena. It's just . . . no one below floor five is overly patriotic."

She lowered her gaze as her cheeks burned red. "I understand."

"Do you?" I asked as we finally made it up the steps and behind the safety line.

Princess Jemeena looked to one of the steambots instead of answering me and said, "Floor fifteen, please."

He repeated, "Descending to floor fifteen. Please remain behind the lines and hold on to the handles provided."

We both held on, but I kept one hand on her arm, just in case. As the lift descended, she struggled to keep her balance and I whispered to myself, "Yep. Definitely needs some seating and glass doors."

Jemeena laughed and shook her head.

"Floor fifteen. Please remain behind the safety line until the elevator has fully descended."

Once the elevator floor had locked into place, Jemeena took my arm and guided me down some less fancy but still clean, pretty, and clearly expensive hallways until we passed security and exited the elevator building's doors into the midday sun.

"Wow!" I gasped. The floor in front of us opened out into a large expanse of green grass that baked in the afternoon sun. "What is that?" I pointed to the . . . whatever it was, then looked up to notice a giant metal statue the same height as the floor in the shape of birds flying out of a stream of water.

Jemeena laughed and stepped up beside me. "It's a garden." She looked puzzled for a moment before asking, "Have you never seen one?"

I shook my head. "We have a few fields on floor zero that used to provide food, but as they build more and more levels, we get less and less sunlight. Most are pointless now."

"But no gardens?"

I shook my head again.

"That's so sad." Her moment of care took my breath away as the watery gleam in her eyes shined on the backdrop of green, and her mouth twitched down in a frown. "Everyone should be free to explore nature."

I couldn't help but snort. "Yeah, well, nature is nonexistent for us, unless you count the moss."

"Well, technically, moss is a part of nature, but, no, I don't count it as one of its many wonders." She sighed and grabbed my arm again. "Come on, I need to take you back so we may converse."

She led me down vast open sidewalks, past larger gardens she called parks, and even through the open market in the floor's center. Eventually, she stopped outside a large house without much sunlight that left me a little disappointed.

She chuckled when she saw my fallen expression. "It's underneath the palace." She gestured above us, and there it was, the palace that sat atop many building towers and got moved with every new floor built. "We stay in the same few towers on every floor. I think there's even a royal embassy on floor zero."

"Really?"

She looked at me and shrugged. "Supposedly. But we're not allowed down that far, so I've no idea."

Not allowed? They were royalty. I thought they could do whatever they wanted, go wherever they wanted to go. But looking at her less-than-happy expression as she ushered us through the golden door, I thought maybe that wasn't the case.

Beyond the door was a foyer in an off-white marble color that seemed so out of place in our dark, dingy world—even on floor fifteen—that the brightness of it all took me by surprise.

"What is it with you rich people and the bright colors?" First Zime Industries and now this. Seren, this was getting ridiculous.

Jemeena grabbed my arm and huffed and puffed for a moment, laughing until she was bright red in the face and her lungs were coughing up a storm.

I was about to help her to a seat when a bustling lady with

gray hair and a scowl shot out of a nearby door—one of over a dozen—shouting, "Princess!" She ran up to her and guided her to a seat. "Where have you been?"

"I . . . was . . . trying to—"

"She was on floor eighteen with me, attending a meeting with Zime's board." I bowed slightly to the lady. "I apologize for keeping the princess longer than necessary."

Jemeena looked at me with a smirk on her face and swallowed a laugh at my pathetic attempt to match her social graces. One stern look from the gray-haired lady had her stifling a further laugh.

"That'll be all from you, Princess." She turned to me. "And you"—she pointed at me—"I should have you arrested for kidnapping."

Dread filled me.

"No, wait, Lila," Jemeena said. "I was there by choice. I promise." She batted her lashes at this woman and made her face look as adorable as possible.

Seren help us.

To my surprise, it worked.

Lila looked at me with disdain but said, "Fine. You might as well stay for a spot of lunch." She looked at IoN, who was cradled in my arms, and asked, "Is there anything we can do for your steambot?"

I looked at Jemeena, who gave a firm shake of her head. "No, thank you. But a cup of toffee would be much appreciated." I bowed my head once more and watched the lady bustle out of the foyer through a door.

"Come along," Lila shouted. "The sitting room's this way."

I offered an arm to Jemeena, but she shook her head and followed without assistance.

She must be feeling better. I followed behind, feeling out of place in a royal household in my pathetic dress.

"So?" I asked Jemeena the moment Lila, who I'd learned was her lady's maid, left us.

Jemeena coughed to clear her throat and looked at me without her usual mask in place. "So." She put her cup of toffee on the table and looked sheepishly at the floor. "I am sorry for dragging you into this."

I shook my head. "I should be thanking you. Without you, I would have lost IoN." I squeezed his body in my lap, where he lay comfortably.

"About that . . ." She gestured to my cup of toffee, which I had yet to pick up. "I heard what your steambot said while I was standing on the other side of the door."

I avoided her gaze.

"It's okay," she reassured me. "I won't tell."

I breathed a sigh of relief as my shoulders relaxed.

"But IoN can feel emotion, can't he?"

I nodded again, not trusting my voice.

"That means the stories about the great engineer Preston are true. He can create life."

"Create . . . life?"

She brushed her hair away from her tanned skin, which had returned some of its color after this morning's adventure, and tucked it behind her ear. For a moment, I was dumbstruck by this girl's beauty. It was as though sunlight itself poured from her every cell.

"Well," she said, "he created IoN, didn't he?"

"I remember him doing it."

"Really?" she asked, suddenly more interested.

"I'm sorry." I sipped my cup of toffee and groaned. Seren, this stuff was good. "I was just a little girl at the time. I can't use whatever my father did to create IoN to help you, even if I wanted to."

"I thought that might be the case."

"Look," I said, "I'm truly sorry. I am. But I can't help you. I simply don't know how." I placed my teacup with the pretty pink flowers back on the table. "But I sympathize. I do." I grabbed her hand. "If I were you, I'd live my best life for the next twenty-nine days. Do everything I ever wanted to do."

"Everything you ever wanted?"

"Yeah." I pulled her off the chair she was sitting on and spun her around, watching in joyous satisfaction as she laughed. Pulling her to a stop, I asked, "What do you have to lose?"

IoN floated behind us, awake and doing his usual whizzing through the air that he'd done every day for the past week since I'd upgraded his thrusters. "Princess Jemeena?"

"Yes?" she asked once she'd sat back down and gained her breath back.

"Preston left some paperwork behind that might be of some assistance to you." He flew up to her and pressed an arm into her shoulder. "I do not wish to get your hopes up, Princess, but he recorded everything he did while making me."

I shot up out of my seat and gasped. "Really?"

IoN moved up and down, nodding.

"Why didn't you tell me about this sooner?"

"I was instructed not to."

"By who?" I asked, my hands balling into fists.

"Preston."

"So," I started, just to clarify, "I've been wondering what about you is special so I can better protect my only family member, and all this time you've been ignoring my questions while sitting on the very answer I seek?" I sat back down, a calm facade, and placed my folded hands in my lap.

"Yes," IoN answered as though he hadn't just admitted to lying to me for the past several years.

"So you can lie?" the princess interrupted.

"Yes," IoN repeated as he turned to answer her question. "I am capable of lying if it does not disrupt any orders from my creator." He looked at both of our cups of toffee and did his best impression of a sigh, but, as usual, it came out crackly. That module upgrade moved up my list of priorities every day.

"Sorry," I apologized to Jemeena with a wince. "I've been meaning to get his voice upgraded, but funds have been . . . limited."

"I understand." She looked at me with sincerity. "I can help, if you like?"

"No, you can't," I said. "And that's the problem." I got up and paced the room, eventually stopping at the large bay window that overlooked the city. The palace sat at the northern wall of Palatina, so all of these towers could see most of the city. "I bet you can see everything from the palace."

"One would think," Jemeena said as she sat beside me, "but that high up, you miss out on half the population." She curled up next to me on the window seat. "It's easy to forget about problems when you can't see them."

"How far down can you see?"

"To floor twelve, at most." She played with the tassel of one of the cushions. "And even then, only from the lowest vantage point of the castle."

I cringed. But what else did I expect? They hadn't cared enough to help us lowlifes for a long time. "Is that why they keep moving the castle higher up? To avoid looking at the poverty that spreads farther up the levels every year?"

She nodded. "And I cannot even help." She sniffed, and I got the feeling she was going to cry again. "I won't live long enough to try."

I grabbed her hand and rubbed circles over her palm. "That you care at all is a vast improvement."

She chuckled. "It's my mother's doing. She cares so much for the people, but with my father on the throne her voice is silenced. Just like everybody else's." She looked up at me, and I was once again mesmerized by her vibrant green eyes. "Not everyone up here is vain and ignorant. There are those who wish to help."

"It's kinda hard to believe."

"I don't doubt that."

"Listen," I said, "come by the garage tomorrow. You can at least look at the paperwork Dad left behind."

She squealed in excitement. "Really?" Her eyes lit up, and I found myself wondering if this was what she would look like without the threat of death looming on her imminent horizon.

"I don't promise it'll help, but you can look. If it'll make you happy."

"It will."

I looked at her, confused for a moment, wondering why she continued to fight a lost cause, but she answered my question before I could voice it.

"I can't stop trying. The throne is my birthright, and my brothers will just continue the work of my father. He's not an evil man, but he's not the most inclusive, either." She looked away from me. "He's just a tad short-sighted is all."

28 DAYS. 22 HOURS. 48 MINUTES.

The next morning I met stares, looks of bewilderment, and scowls of disapproval from all at the breakfast table—to which I was invited for the first time in five years.

"Cinderella, I must ask," Phyllis started, and I internally groaned, "what work are you doing for the princess?"

Lazuli snorted as she reached for her water glass. "As if. There's no way Cinderella knows the princess. Who would even speak to someone as grubby as you?" Her brown hair fell in awkward waves down her back, and I grimaced at the ridiculous amount of pink eyeshadow she'd used.

"Yeah," Lapis said. "No way."

"Girls," Phyllis said. "I was there too. Or did you forget?" She scowled at them. "She really is working for Princess Jemeena."

"But . . . but," Lazuli said, "that's not fair!" She stamped her foot and pouted like a child. "How come she gets to prance about with royalty?"

"That's enough, girls!" Phyllis shouted. "Go finish getting ready for this afternoon's pageant on floor three."

Every floor held an annual pageant for women and men to

meet and be paired up by their parents for marriage. Phyllis had been trying for the last two years to get both girls up a floor or two—in vain.

Once the two of them had left, she looked at me and waited for an answer. "I'm sorry," I responded, "but I signed a confidentiality agreement. I cannot talk about the work she assigned me."

Phyllis looked at me in defeat. "Just remember to be polite and don't forget to negotiate a solid payment for us! She's royalty, she could pay us thousands if she wanted. Do not settle for a three-figure sum, Cinderella. Do you hear me?" She licked her lips, as though the thought of all that money solicited the same reaction as a kid in a candy store.

Disgusting.

"Yes, Phyllis."

"Mother!" she shrieked. "Call me mother!"

"Yes, Mother." I ran out of the room before her limited politeness exploded and shed its mask to reveal the beast within.

By the time I'd walked around the corners and down the barely lit streets, the sun had risen. Or, at least, I assumed so, because the lights had turned to their usual daylight yellow. I paused outside the garage door, contemplating what the day would hold.

By the end of today, I'd finally know what secrets my father had been hiding all those years.

I'd never seen a bot like IoN before—a bot who cared. As though part of his machine makeup gave him a personality. But that was impossible. Wasn't it?

"Get it together, El," I muttered to myself as I took a deep breath and opened the loud metal shutters. "It's just IoN." There was nothing I could learn that would change anything.

"El," IoN said the moment I closed the door. "We've already begun, but—"

"Already begun!" I shouted. "What? Why?"

"Sorry," a gentle voice crooned from the center of the workshop. "It was my fault. I persuaded him." Princess Jemeena sat on the dirty floor and had cluttered the space with papers, diagrams, schematics, and a whole host of other complicated mechanisms and tools I hadn't seen in years.

"Dad's things," I whispered.

Princess Jemeena flushed as she looked from my bewildered face to the mess scattered around her. "I-I-I am sorry." She stood and leaped over the pile, dodged a particularly precarious pile of instruments, and skipped to a stop a few feet away. "Now that I think about it, I should not have dived into your father's things without permission." She bowed her head in apology. "I am deeply sorry, Cinderella."

I cringed at the use of my full name. "Er . . . it's okay. Well, it's not, but you . . . you're fine." Damn it. What was it about this girl that made my insides flutter and my words fail? "And, please, call me El."

She looked at me with a raised eyebrow.

"No one but Phyllis calls me Cinderella, and it's ruined my name for all future use." I laughed but it was true. The way she screeched it while my mother and father used to use it with such adoration made my blood boil.

"Not a fan of your . . . stepmother?" She used a higher pitch on that last word, ensuring she was correct in the relationship.

"She's awful."

IoN added, "Truly evil."

"An evil stepmother?" Jemeena said with a laugh. "It is like we're in some kind of fairy tale."

I laughed alongside her, and for a moment, everything was right. There was no looming royal death, no moneyless peasant, no evil stepmother . . . no dead father. But reality always crashes down, and this time, it did so with a knock on the door.

I looked at Jemeena, then at IoN, and realized I should probably be the one to answer. Out of the three of us, it mattered least if I got caught doing something illegal.

The garage door swung open before I could reach it, and I blanched, yelling at the princess to hide.

"Do not be stupid, El," she scolded. "No one down here will recognize me."

Oh, right.

The flickering light of the garage I'd been meaning to fix for days illuminated a small, familiar figure with shaggy brown hair and clothes that barely fit his rapidly growing frame.

"Bobby Helsham," I chided. "What are you doing here at such an early hour?"

"Sorry, El, but . . ." Tears rained down his raw, red face, and I panicked. "It's Ma. She's . . ."

"Heeey," I soothed as I grabbed him from the floor and held him in my arms. "Heeey, it'll be okay."

"No," he mumbled into my neck. "No, it won't. They said she's gonna die."

I stiffened. Bobby Helsham was the six-year-old boy from the corner everyone knew because he was always out doing odd jobs, like carrying shopping home for the elderly, for a small amount of money. It was just him and his mother, and she'd been sick for a while. We all suspected the worst, of course, but she wouldn't let anyone check her lifeclock. She always had it covered.

I placed him down and wiped his tears with my blue sleeve. "There," I whispered. "That's better." I grabbed his hand and pulled him to the back room. "Come sit down." The sofa slackened under our weight, and I groaned as I added it to the ever-growing list of things that needed fixing or replacing. "Why don't you tell me all about it."

He crawled up to me and sat between my legs, head buried into my chest as he cried and sobbed some more.

I didn't know what to do, but I stayed and rubbed circles into his back. Nothing I could say would help if she really was dying, but having someone around would be useful. Maybe I could offer him a job here afterward?

I scoffed. With what money?

Bobby sniffed and pulled his head off my chest, wiping his snotty face with the sleeve of his raggedy jumper. "The doctor said she's gonna die in a few days." He hiccuped. "She's been sick for years, but..."

"We all thought she'd get better." I said it, but I didn't mean it. We all knew her time was coming.

He sobbed into his hands. "And now she won't!"

"Heeey." I rubbed his arms in gentle strokes and pulled him in for another hug. "I know it doesn't seem like it now, but everything will be okay."

He nodded, but he still cried. "But I can't... stop crying."

"It's okay to cry. When Dad died, I cried for three months nonstop."

"Really?" He perked up.

"Yup."

"But you never cry."

"Everyone cries. Once in a while." I turned to the door where IoN and the princess hovered. "IoN, make Bobby a cup of toffee and a sandwich, would you?" I looked the kid up and down. "I bet you haven't eaten in a while?" The question was rhetorical—you could tell by looking at the bones jutting out of his chest that it'd been days since he'd eaten.

"Mom's been real sick. Couldn't leave her bedside."

I nodded in understanding.

Princess Jemeena sat on the other side of the sofa, and Bobby turned to look at her. "Who are you?" he asked.

If I didn't know she was the bloody princess, I wouldn't have cringed, but I knew and so I did. I mouthed, "Sorry," but she didn't care. At least, she didn't act like she cared.

Instead, she frowned at him. "I am sorry about your mother, Bobby." She held out her hand. "Hi, my name is Meena."

He sniffled and grabbed her hand. "Name's Bobby." He shrugged and grumbled, "Thanks."

"You know," she said, "I think your mother would love that you have friends to turn to." She met my eyes as a tear slipped down her cheek she quickly brushed away. "That even in a time as hard as this, you're not alone."

"Mom would love El, but she's not been right in the head for the last two years, so El's never gotten to properly meet her."

Jemeena looked at me with a quizzical expression.

"No one really understands what's wrong with her, but she sees things, then she gets a bad flu-like virus and is bedridden for weeks."

"This last one's been bad." He shuddered as he cried again. "Been coughing up blood."

The princess cringed. There was nothing we could do. If her time was up, no amount of medicine or tinkering with the lifeclock would help. You couldn't mess with time.

"Did you want us to come back to your mom with you?" I asked. "Or would you prefer to stay here?" The choice was his, and I wouldn't take it away from him by forcing him to watch her die. I could always leave him here with Jemeena while I sat with Mrs. Helsham.

But Bobby, the brave little boy that he was, said with a weak voice, "I want to be with her, even if she does . . . die." The last word was said with a sob, and he started crying uncontrollably again.

"Shhh, it's okay." I returned to rubbing soothing circles on his back and holding him tightly as he clutched at my coveralls. "We'll go together."

His head lifted and grabbed my hand.

"Come on, then."

IoN grabbed the sandwich and drink he had made and followed along with the princess, and we all traveled the crisscrossing streets of floor zero to Bobby Helsham's small apartment. We took a left at Old Mags's moss-covered door, took a right at the small apartment I shared with Phyllis, Lapis, and Lazuli, walked past the dilapidated old playground and the dumping ground where everyone put their used stuff to see if someone else could make use of it, and eventually found ourselves outside the door with the peeling red paint, dusty windows, and rusted bronze knocker.

Bobby grabbed the key from his pocket and let us all in. The smell hit us immediately. It reeked of mold, decay, and dust as weeks' worth of dirt plastered every visible surface. Bobby, however, noticed none of it and rushed through a door just off the lounge.

I turned to Jemeena and whispered, "You can wait outside if you'd like. Or IoN can escort you back to the garage."

She shook her head and took the drink and sandwich from IoN's grip and stepped forward.

IoN whirred in front of me and settled into my arms. "You cannot help her, El."

"I'm not here for her. I'm here for Bobby."

We walked through the same door Bobby had run through and found a small cheerless room that had a bed with ragged sheets littered with mysterious stains, a small barrel acting as a nightstand, and a tossed-through pile of clothes in the corner. Mrs. Helsham lay on that bed in that half-asleep way people did when they were ill.

Or dying.

I picked Bobby up and placed him on my lap as we sat on the floor beside her bed. Her wrist dangled just outside of the sheets. I grabbed it and unwrapped her lifeclock. I took a quick glance and then flipped her arm over and wrapped it back up, hopefully quickly enough that Bobby hadn't seen.

"She only has a few hours," he sobbed. "I checked yesterday."

"Here." Jemeena sat on the floor beside us and handed Bobby his drink and sandwich. "You should try to eat something."

Bobby took the plate and started nibbling on the crusts, but his gaze was fixed on his mom's face as she slept in a fitful daze and struggled to breathe. While he ate absentmindedly, we all sat in the pregnant silence and watched her labored breathing.

"She used to take me to the playground," he mumbled. "The one around the corner, before it got too dangerous to play in."

"I bet that was fun," Jemeena said, a distant edge to her voice.

"She was fun. We'd walk all the way to the square and dance to the violin man who played by the fountain." Tears ran down his face, but they were silent, lacking the harsh sobs from earlier, and he continued sharing memories, eating the food, and watching his mom die until, eventually, two hours later, her breathing stopped altogether and he wept into the crook of my shoulder until his eyes had run out of tears and he fell asleep.

"What now?" Jemeena whispered.

IoN flew into the air and turned to us. "We should find somewhere for him to live for now, then alert the authorities that she's passed."

"I'm going to take him to Mags. She'll know what to do."

By the time I had taken Bobby to Mags, who had taken him in with a promise that she would handle everything, we were exhausted as we made our way back to the garage, but Jemeena wanted to keep looking through Dad's paperwork. We worked until the exhaustion ate at our bones. Jemeena looked more determined than ever, fueled, no doubt, by the death she had just witnessed.

"Maybe we should call it a day?" I handed her a cup of toffee, but she declined and instead made herself a cup of mint-leaf tea.

"I don't want to, but I don't think I can work for another minute." She flicked off her heeled boots and rested her feet underneath her legs on the sofa. She sipped her tea and looked at it with surprise. "Seren, this stuff's good."

I laughed and sat next to her. "Dad used to love it. I never had the heart to get rid of it. I never saw him in this garage without a cup of the stuff." I stuck my tongue out in disgust, remembering the last time I'd tried some, hoping my taste buds had changed.

"He had good taste." She looked at me. "I am sorry about your father."

"Thank you."

IoN whizzed into the room and shouted at full volume, "I have found something!"

"What?" I rushed to my feet and followed him into the workshop, Jemeena hot on my heels. "What do you mean you found something?"

Jemeena wrapped her arms around IoN and squealed. "Thank you, thank you, thank you!"

IoN removed himself from her arms, dusted himself off, then flew to a series of papers he'd pinned to the wall. "Read these."

Jemeena and I squinted at the scratchy handwriting, starting from the top left and working our way through.

Test 392, he wrote. *I've played with the calibration settings and reversed the time polarity, so I'm hoping this is it. Eleday's time is nearly up. This has to work.*

"Mother," I gasped. "This must be from just before she got sick."

The steam lines connected and both lifeclocks glowed then made a whirring sound as the hands on the clocks spun faster than I could track. A small burst of white light appeared, and the steam lines disconnected themselves. It caused us both to fall backward and gasp deep breaths.

Result: Test 392 failed.

Eleday's lifeclock—the paper had been smudged here, where the ink had gotten wet—*lost time. Perhaps meddling is not something that should be done after all. She now has a mere fourteen days left with Cinderella, and I don't know how to fix it. But I will try.*

The papers came to an end, and I looked at IoN with tears in my eyes. "He was trying to reverse Mom's time, wasn't he?"

He moved up and down, nodding, and said, "He never managed it though."

"I can see that."

Jemeena chimed in with, "But he was nearly there." She put a hand on my shoulder. "He somehow managed to find a way of stealing someone's life." She frowned and looked at IoN. "That is why he made you hide this away."

"Why?" I rubbed the tired tears from my face.

"El," she said as she faced me, grasping both sides of my face between her hands, "imagine if this information got out? What would people do when desperate to save loved ones? To save themselves?"

My eyes widened, understanding the implications. "This could change everything."

"The rich would live forever and the poor would barely live at all." She took a deep breath and began cleaning up the objects and papers scattered around the floor. "This cannot get out. Not even if it means saving my life."

"Now, wait a minute." I gestured to the stuff lying everywhere. "This is all safe here." I grabbed her wrist and yanked her toward me. "We can keep looking."

"Correct," IoN said. "Your father was looking for a way to reverse what he had done until the day your mother died. It was his only mission. His singular drive."

"That was why he was barely around back then, right?"

IoN nodded. "He traveled all over the land looking for answers. But she died before he could find them."

"So," I said, "if we track his progress, we might be able to pick up where he left off?" I spun around to face Jemeena, grinning. "There's your hope, Princess."

27 DAYS. 19 HOURS. 14 MINUTES.

The following day, we were once again rifling through Dad's paperwork when Jemeena piped up. "There's a receipt here." She waved a scrap of old paper crumbling at the edges. "It's signed by someone called Green." She wrinkles her nose in confusion at the name and looks at me expectantly. "Well, Miss I-Know-Everyone-Down-Here?"

Green's a black-market dealer on floor zero and the second son of Minister Farro, but I wasn't sure I should tell the princess of the city that. I grabbed the receipt out of her hands and looked it over, shocked Dad would deal with Green of all people. He hated people who did things unofficially, always complained that those kinds of people made it harder for everyone to get official work and to persuade the king to allocate us resources. I ran a stressed hand through the unkempt strands of hair nesting around my head.

"Do you know them, or . . . ?"

"Yes." I looked at her face, then at the golden cloth covering her lifeclock, and sighed again. "Okay, I'll take you to see Green, but on one condition."

"Anything."

"Don't report anything you see. Green's an important part of how floor zero works, and while it's less than legal, it's the only way some people feed themselves." I did not hold Dad's prejudice, especially after how hard I'd had to fight to remain on the legal side of this business.

"Deal. I promise to keep all floor zero secrets." She placed a hand to her heart and looked to the ceiling. "Lunch, then we leave?"

Lunch? Right. "Er . . ."

"Or we can go tomorrow, if you have things to do."

"Princess," IoN said, his crackly voice echoing throughout the space, "we don't have anything for lunch. Sorry. It has been a tough month."

"Oh. That's okay. I'll take us up a few floors and treat you."

She was . . . buying me food?

I shrugged. "Sure. I'm not gonna look a gift horse in the mouth."

"Don't feel guilty. I have more money at my disposal than sense. I donate loads, but the crown's funds are as endless as the city's."

Turning to IoN, I cringed. "Sorry, buddy, but I think it'll be best if you stay here."

He turned away from me but said, "It is okay."

"Huh?" Jemeena asked.

"They asked for his paperwork last time when crossing security, and I don't want to risk it. He's the last family member I have left."

"I can look after the garage while you are gone, El, so it's in the best interests of everyone." He floated into the kitchen at the back.

Leaving, Jemeena put her cloak back on as we left—a brown cotton one this time like most people wore down here in the colder months. She tugged the sleeve down her wrist, covering the golden cloth, and we took a slow walk to the lift. Where, lo and behold, she had paperwork to get me on any lift at any time.

"You have no idea how valuable that paperwork is. I wouldn't go waving it about," I mumbled as we stepped onto one of the normal lifts.

"How do you get to the upper floors without paperwork? I thought most citizens needed them?" she asked.

As the lift elevated us a few floors, I explained, "We don't. Access to paperwork is controlled. We can only go higher by invitation, like to a pageant or ball or meeting with a noble."

"You're stuck here?" she asked incredulously. "Nobles can just buy it."

"So can we. But that paperwork costs a year's wage down here."

"Oh, right." She looked sheepishly at her feet as we arrived at floor fifteen. "Come on. The least I can do is take you to my favorite diner."

"Right, but this time, we're taking a hover."

Her lips pursed, but she blew out a frustrated breath and gave in, stepping onto the marble floor and removing her cloak. Her shoulders rolled back as her face neutralized, transforming her into what I now realized was a princess persona—a face she used when dealing with the general public.

Was I not considered part of the general public? Or was she just comfortable enough to remove her mask? Maybe it was because she could. I couldn't talk to anyone about what I was doing with her anyway.

Stepping onto the steel platform of the two-person hover, I

grabbed the steering rod in front of me. This was a 2000X model, with better suspension between the thrusters and the platform so it rode smoother. It also used a different fan system from previous models that slowly let the airflow lessen, so braking was smoother and momentum could be increased and decreased at the rate the driver required, increasing control.

I flew us across the streets, following Jemeena's directions, and marveled at the light shining from the sky and all the small gardens pocketed on street corners and outside cafés, each with varying statues and seating arrangements.

"Take the next left. It's the hole-in-the-wall restaurant at the end."

I took the turn, exiting the line of hovers I was in, and entered a near-deserted street with buildings towering on either side close enough that the light didn't reach us. Parking in front of the restaurant she pointed to, I hopped off and steadied myself on solid ground. "That was fun. Thank you."

She waved away my thanks and ducked into the small door in the corner that barely looked like a building, much less a restaurant. She held the door open, and I followed.

My eyes flew across the room, taking a cursory glance at the place the princess frequented. It didn't look like much. More of an old corner food place you'd find on floor zero, if a little more modern and less run-down.

"I know it doesn't look like much," she whispered, "but the food here is amazing, and there's no one around to recognize me."

Ah. She could be herself here without worrying about keeping up the princess mask. Without having to wave away concern for her coughing, which she was doing the moment we sat down and caught our breaths.

"You okay?"

"Just ignore the coughing." She looked at the menu with a familiar gaze, flying over the items available and no doubt knowing what each one was. "I recommend the eggs."

I got eggs at home thanks to Mags though. "What's a cooc-on-ut creepe?" I knew neither of those words.

"It's like a thin pancake made from coconut flour. It's sweet."

Sweet sounded good. Sweet was expensive and therefore a luxury back home, so I rarely had it. "That sounds good."

"You can order more than one thing. If you want to try a few different things."

"I'm good. Thanks."

The food arrived fifteen minutes later, and I had to force myself to eat slowly and not gorge myself, aware that it'd been a while since I'd eaten anything more than a single slice of bread in one go. I'd be sick if I weren't careful.

The princess was also eating slowly, taking pauses to cough, struggling to eat without losing her breath. It was then, watching her do her best to live with what few days she had left, that I realized she was maybe pushing herself beyond what she should for the small hope that I might be able to cure her. That I could fix her.

But I couldn't.

She had to know that, but she was clinging to the hope, the one-in-a-million chance, that Dad's notes held any sort of answer, and that hope bubbling inside her, fueled by the desperation to live and the fear of death, was keeping her going, like the last ember of a fire.

If that fire was to roar again, I had to find more fuel to feed it, but I didn't know if such a thing existed.

BACK ON FLOOR ZERO, BACK TO THE SUNLESS STREETS AND the mossy walls, Green was on the other side of the city and there was no way Jemeena could walk that far. I'd need to borrow Phyllis's or the girls' hover. I didn't want to take Old Mags's steamer.

Ugh. This was going to be a not-so-fun morning after all.

Back in the garage, IoN greeted us with cups of steaming toffee and mint-leaf tea. "Welcome back. How was breakfast?"

"I tried coconut crepes, and they were amazing, IoN!"

"I am glad you had a good time."

"I'm sorry you couldn't join us." I looked at the floor, shame covering my features in a heated blush. "You deserve to see the upper floors too."

"I am just a steambot," he repeated for what felt like the thousandth time. "I have no need to see or experience things."

Jemeena looked at me, then at IoN, and placed her cup back on the table. "Look, I know I'm new to you, IoN, but it seems you're more than just a bot, and if that is the case, then you have every right to a life. You wouldn't expect us to live without experiencing things, would you? What makes it so different for you?"

IoN looked at her in silence, having no rebuttal, let alone an explanation, and then proceeded to my desk and picked up the tattered notebook and pen I used to log jobs. He handed them to me—he didn't have the hands to write. "Telith wanted you to look at his wife's pressure cooker."

"Really?" I had a new customer.

"By the end of the day, if possible."

"Sure. Can do." I placed his job in today's space with relief. "A new customer is always good news." Suddenly I'd gone from so barren I was bored to not enough hours in the day to get it all done. Looking at Jemeena, I explained, "I'll do it at the end of the day."

"Are you sure? I know you need the mo—"

I waved her question away. "You're more important. Besides, a fast track on an engineering program is greater than any amount of money."

"Right." She looked away, noticed my dad's pile of old paperwork, and started digging through, going over what IoN did yesterday.

"I'll be back in a minute. Just stay here."

Head stuck in the papers, she nodded slowly, her hair in black plaits spun into buns on her head today.

I ran out of the garage and took a breath, steeling myself for what I assumed would be a frustrating conversation with Phyllis. Our small apartment was three right turns and a left away, behind the brown wooden door with the broken knocker that looked like a desert deer I begged Mum to buy when I was four.

Luckily, Phyllis was not attending the pageant on floor three as she had a hair appointment with our neighbor at four, which meant she was still sitting in the living room, reading a daily paper when I walked through the door.

Her beady eyes peeked over the top of the page, surprised to see me. Feet in a bowl of warm water, she placed the newspaper on the arm of the sofa and looked at me with tired eyes. "What is it, Cinderella?"

"I need to borrow one of the hovers for the afternoon." She went to immediately say no, but I interrupted. "I'll bring it right back. It's for my work with the princess."

She groaned, her voice as crackly as IoN's for a moment before she cleared her throat and smirked. "If you clean the stove tonight, I'll let you borrow the girls' hover."

"Thank you!"

She threw the key she'd dug out of her pocket at me. "Don't let it run out of water, or I'll have plenty more things for you to clean this evening than just the stove."

"Yes, Phyl—Mother."

I ran out the door and yanked the crank around twice to open the apartment's garage door, listening to it whine and creak with a wince. The shelves at the back were filled to the brim with Dad's old stuff in boxes, overflowing crates, and split packages that I'd shoved there for fear of Phyllis throwing them out to "make space." It's a two-bedroom apartment on floor zero, we didn't have space to make.

But in the center of the crowded garage were two hovers—one for my stepsisters and one for Phyllis. They'd cost a pretty penny that Phyllis had taken right from Dad's death fund, of course, but they came in handy from time to time. When they let me use them. I hopped up onto the one with more wear and tear in the handles and shoved the key into the hole, starting her up.

She glided a few inches over the concrete floor, disturbing various patches of moss and dirt, and handled the corners with some level of ease. Not quite as well as the one on floor fifteen, but still easier than walking the two miles to Green's with a wheezy princess.

Back at the garage, IoN displayed surprise, and the princess looked at me gratefully, which I took for the thank you it was. "Phyllis let you borrow that?" IoN asked.

"When I told her it was for the project with the princess"—I curtsied toward Jemeena—"she let me have it, no questions asked. Are you ready, Your Highness?"

She dusted herself off, threw her shoulders back, and practically floated to the hover, a bemused smirk on her face. "Thank you, kind citizen."

We both chuckled, hers turning into a cough halfway through, so I had to find a clean handkerchief I could give a royal. I ended up grabbing a clean cloth I used for dusting IoN after cleaning him. Oops.

"I will hold down the fort and keep reading through these notes," IoN said from his place on the floor. "Be careful."

"Will do!" I called as I whizzed us out the door and down the myriad of streets it took to get to Green's unit. We passed the church, the kids' playground that used to be a field we grew fruits and vegetables in, and so many houses that used to home friends and neighbors who had since passed that, for a moment, I forgot how to breathe as Jemeena asked millions of questions about almost every building.

We eventually got there, both of us intact and the hover not even half empty of the full tank of water it had when we left.

I scowled at Jemeena as she flopped her cloak's hood down, then I yanked it back up. "Not here. Here you're just an old family friend visiting from floor two."

"Okay." Her guard flew up instantly, her hands tugging her sleeves down to make sure her golden cloth was covered. "What is it Green does, exactly?"

"He's a black-market dealer."

THE INSIDE OF THE GRUBBY WAREHOUSE ON THE EAST SIDE of the city was much like my garage: Dusty, full of bits and bobs scattered across the space, and smelled as one might expect from a black-market dealer who barely saw the light of day. But the moment I stepped in, a light turned on overhead, illuminating the space. Hovers, steamers, and different trinkets covered the floor, all in various states of repair—far more than I'd worked on in my entire engineering life.

"Nice to know where all Dad's customers went," I mumbled to myself.

"Indeed, Cinderella," a familiar voice echoed from a workstation above us in the corner. "What brings you here?"

"I have a question to ask. Privately."

"If this is a marriage proposal, I'm afraid you're too late. Pinkett's daughter already beat you to it."

"I'm not here to . . . Really? You and little Pinkett?"

Without answering, he sidled down the ladder and grinned, extending his hand to me, then to Jemeena. "And who do we have here?" He looked at Jemeena suspiciously, wary of strangers.

"Just an old family friend," Jemeena said from beneath her hood. "Visiting from the floor above." She even managed to remove the proper sound of her voice and make it a bit more casual, but it wasn't brilliant.

"A friend of Cinderella's is a friend of mine." He grinned at her, and she smiled back. "What sorta question you got for me?" His green hair, for which he was named, was slicked back behind his pierced ears, and the brown corset he wore sat under the bust over a black shirt whose sleeves were rolled up to his elbows. "I'm a bit busy."

"Yes, I can see," I said through clenched teeth.

"Come on, Cin . . . You can't still be mad about all this, can ya?" He gestured to the booming business behind him—to the workers he'd hired, to the multiple jobs he had going on—and smirked. He knew damn well I was mad, but he shrugged with a simple, "Business is business."

Sure, if business was throwing your old acquaintances under

the nearest hover. For the love of Seren, this guy made my blood boil.

"I need to know what my dad bought from you."

His eyes widened a fraction as his fists clenched. He grabbed our wrists and yanked us behind a door that seemed to lead to a storage room. "You can't just ask questions like that in public. Someone might overhear."

"Why not?" I pressed. "What did he buy that was so threatening?"

Green looked from left to right, then back to left, and finally settled on us with a frown. "He bought a lifeclock."

Jemeena and I gasped, but it was me who asked, "But that's . . . very illegal." Punishable by desertion in the desert. "Why did he need it?"

Green shrugged. "He never said. And even if he did, I wouldn't tell you." Placing a heavy hand on my shoulder, he looked me in the eyes. "Whatever follow-in-your-daddy's-footsteps bullshit you've got going on, stop it. It's dangerous. If you need the ego or the money that badly, I can pass a few customers your way."

I yanked my shoulder from beneath his hand. "I don't need your charity." Grabbing Jemeena's wrist, I stormed outside, hopped back onto the hover, and sped us home before my mind could catch up with the information.

26 DAYS. 22 HOURS. 42 MINUTES

THE CLOCK ON THE WALL TICKED SIX-THIRTY A.M. THE next day, which meant I had thirty minutes to get ready for church. I rushed the rest of my breakfast, tugged down my sleeves, and left the apartment doors open as I turned left. Every Saturday, it was always left.

The streets in the dim daylight were a little better than at night, so I stepped on fewer piles of slippery moss, which had caught my balance by the toe on more than one occasion.

The two kids from the house around the corner sprinted under my feet, and I paused to let them rush by, their screeches the only sound as everyone made their way southwest. Mandy dipped her head at me as she chased her boys, her dirty blonde hair piled atop her head in crisscrossing plaits.

After a few more streets, and with few minutes to spare, the church loomed in front of me. Its spirals twirled into the church on the floor above us, the overlapping pathways shadowing much of the stone features. It was the derelict nature of the building—the moss growing up the sides, the ivy cracking the stonework, the wooden door that could barely be called a door anymore—that sank my heart upon every visit.

Dad used to say the building was beautiful once—a paragon of floor zero unity—but as more and more levels were added, fewer funds were given to the lower floors, and now the only parts of the city's singular church building that matched the reverence people once held for it were on the upper levels.

Following the line of people into the church, I headed for my designated seat between Phyllis and Mrs. Nab, the elderly lady who lived in the basement apartment below us. Her seat used to be Dad's. Beside that used to be Mom's, but Mrs. Nab's granddaughter sat there now, her high ponytail ruffling down her dress's peach corset. This seat, however, the rickety one I knew how to sit upon without getting a numb butt, with the cushion whose left side was plumper than its right, had been mine for as long as I could remember.

A whispered silence fell over the crowd, echoing its way up the open-topped chamber. I snuck a quick glance up, and the hole where the ceiling should be made way to the levels spread out above us in all their glory, layer upon layer of them as they rounded the hollow space we occupied the bottom of. Jemeena would be sitting at the top somewhere, as obliged to attend church as I was, but I couldn't see that far up. Floor one, however, I could see, and they sat in their usual chairs, dotted in concentric rings around the open hole in what I supposed was their floor but our ceiling.

Phyllis coughed and glared at me. "Look forward, Cinderella."

Forward. Always forward in church—never up, never back, never down—though no one could tell me why. The custom seemed to permeate everyone's thoughts as we all stared at the same spot in front of us.

At Minister Farro. Floor zero's Minister of Seren.

Every floor had a different minister, but they all said the same thing at the same time, a well-rehearsed speech that differed week to week.

Minister Farro's graying hair was hidden beneath a silver cap that stopped short before falling down the sides of his head, and the corseted vest sat neatly on his chest over a dark green shirt whose sleeves fell into frills at the end. As always, he looked impeccable. The usual silver buttons adorning his clothes, as well as silver studs in his ears and the usual silver collar around his neck, marked him as a minister of Seren—the only people in Palatina allowed to wear silver.

His eyes crinkled as he looked out at us all, determination on his face. "Welcome, children of Seren, and thank you for once again joining us for a weekly sermon." His hands outstretched upon welcome, a genuine smile on his face. Despite church not being my favorite activity, Minister Farro was a kind, elderly gentleman who had offered much counsel after Dad passed, and I would hate to think badly of the man. He fed the young orphans out of his weekly rations provided by the church, often creating stews for the sick and the elderly who had long since passed their ability to fend for themselves. "Let Seren's light wash over you, even when light is otherwise hard to find, and let His belief in you become your belief in yourself, even when times are hard."

Believe in myself? That sounded just like Mags yesterday, almost as though her words echoed out of Minister Farro's mouth.

"While faith in Seren and all that He teaches is important, faith in yourself and in others is equally so. For without faith in yourself and your community, Seren's work and creations—being all that we are and all that we see—ceases to function," the ministers echo.

If I listened carefully enough, I could make out floor one's younger-sounding minister. I couldn't see him from here, but apparently you could sneak a peek from some of the seats farther back. He had black hair with a small beard covering his chin and wire glasses that sat on his nose, if general chatter among Phyllis's pompous friends was to be believed.

"Challenges are normal in life, set in front of us by Seren to help us grow, to help us shape the world, for He wants us to have a hand in His own creation. To help shape what He made. He provided the foundations upon which we, His creations, must build."

By the end of the hour-long sermon, I had learned two things: that I needed to remain faithful to myself and that I needed to stop sulking. So long as I kept my head above water and continued to do my best, things would fall as they were meant to. Hopefully. With enough luck.

DAD'S SCRIBBLINGS WERE ILLEGIBLE IN MORE PLACES than not, even IoN had a hard time deciphering most of his words. We'd been sifting through the rest of his things for the three hours since church had ended, and we'd created a road map of his travels here on floor zero.

"So," Jemeena said, "the first thing he did was purchase an old lifeclock from a black-market dealer here on floor zero and start fiddling with it."

"I wish we still had the lifeclock he was working with; maybe I could see what his thought process was. Where did he go wrong?"

I scratched at my head, befuddled as to where to start next. "Are you sure it's not in that box, IoN?"

IoN's crackly sigh sounded, probably frustrated with my asking again, but he went and looked nonetheless. "There is nothing but scraps and pieces scattered at the bottom. A few coils, some steam lines, and a silver cog."

"That's a shame," Jemeena said. "It would have been useful."

I snapped my head up and stared at IoN. "Wait. What did you say?"

"There are coils, some steam lines, and a cog at the bottom of the box?" he asked in question.

"No, you said a *silver* cog." I jumped to my feet and rushed over to the box. "Most cogs are made of bronze and copper, and the upper levels have platinum ones, but silver cogs are found in only one device in the entire city."

"Silver is reserved for the Ministers of Seren and other religious wares, but I don't . . ." She trailed off, not understanding my meaning.

I rifled through the box, scraping cardboard with dirty and broken fingernails, my hair falling out of the curls Phyllis had insisted upon before church. "Silver cogs are *only* found in lifeclocks."

IoN whizzed over, looking at the bottom of the box that I'd scraped clear. I carried it all over to where I was sitting on the floor with Jemeena. I really should get the princess a damn chair. I tumbled all the pieces from my overflowing hands onto the floor, where they jangled to a heap between us.

"You think he took it apart?" Jemeena asked.

"I think he took apart a black-market lifeclock to save himself or anyone else getting into trouble."

IoN whizzed above our heads, a green light shining from the

slot of his mouth. "No one would bother to look through a box of random parts in a steam engineer's garage."

Jemeena's eyes widened as she looked at the pieces, uncertainty shining in her eyes. "Clever Preston."

"Clever Dad." I fiddled with the pieces, uncertain where they all went. I knew the basics, that the steam lines connected to the cogwork, and that was what kept time, eventually showing us the number of hours we had left to live on the clockface, but beyond that . . . we weren't allowed to delve that far. "He must have figured out how they work, otherwise, he wouldn't have been able to make any changes to his or Mom's."

"You don't know how they work?" she asked.

I was deep in thought, trying to figure out what the steam lines connected to, so IoN answered for me. "It's illegal to alter the mechanics of a lifeclock, so no. No one does. Or, no one we know." He flew into the kitchen for a minute and came back with more peppermint tea for the princess. "Preston used to say that engineers who messed with lifeclocks were often taken by the church, never to be seen again. Rumors say they were executed."

A huff escaped my lips at that, just catching the end of their conversation. "More than likely taken to Vine Valley Prison."

"I promise I've never heard of any executions." Something clicked, and her eyes went wide. "But there are regular passenger dirigibles that leave the city a few times a year, and not a regular transport dirigible for the wealthy, either." She looked at the floor, red covering her ever-paler cheeks. "Father used to tell me they were lucky citizens going for an adventure around the world when I was little."

"He probably just didn't want to talk about dark subjects with his child," I reassured, then looked up at her. "All fathers do that."

"Right." She looked skeptical as she fiddled with one of the bows on her dress.

I took her hand and squeezed gently. "Father used to tell me that we were soldiers working for the great king, having been given orders to work in the mines beneath the city. That, without us, the city couldn't exist and we were doing Seren's work."

Her eyes lit up a little as they met mine in the dim light of the garage, and her confusion made my chest tighten and my hand squeeze hers a little harder.

Wait a minute... "The mines."

"Huh?" My interruption seemed to only further her confusion. "What?"

"The mines. That's where Farro's son works."

"El..." IoN warns. "I don't think—"

"If there's one person who knows how lifeclocks work and who might be willing to share that information, it's the son of floor zero's minister."

Jemeena's eyes widened in understanding. "But they're not supposed to tell anyone the secrets of Seren. It's forbidden."

I smiled, wicked ideas playing across my mind. "Do you want some floor zero gossip, Princess?" I jumped to my feet and brushed the dust off my dress.

She followed. "Sure."

"Five years ago, when Minister Farro's son was due for inscription into the Church of Seren, his mother, Farro's wife, died. No one saw it coming—not even her son, because they never uncover their lifeclocks."

"It's forbidden for a minister and his family to show their lifeclocks, lest it cause civil unrest," she recites, as though she had memorized the book it was written in.

"In a show of grief and despair, the minister's son shunned

the church, his father, and the entire institution. He doesn't even attend church. His seat at the front remains empty. Which, for most people, would be enough to get them arrested, but everyone knows Minister Farro pays the police off, begging them to leave him be. That he's grieving and in pain." My eyes rolled of their own accord. "Of course, he's just protecting his son, but still."

"So, if anyone would know anything and be willing to share, it would be Minister Farro's son."

"Yup. And he works in the mines."

There were many entrances to the mines, but the one closest to the garage was, luckily for us, a mere three streets away. As we approached the gated steps that led underground, the dirty sign saying *Mine Entrance* glowing a faint yellow under the artificial light above it, the air grew hotter and drier, like the moisture was being sucked out it.

The mines were what kept the city running—Dad wasn't lying about that—but they were staffed by the lower three floors because it was the only work that kept food on the table for most. Dirty, dangerous, and unregulated places, the mines were the end for many. Dad described them as "necessary evils." The mines produced steam power for the entire city, even the palace on floor twenty-one, by converting seawater from the ocean to the southwest to high-pressure steam, which was then forced up pipes lining every building. The pipes rotated the shafts in our electrical appliances to generate power. Sometimes, some devices did this themselves on a smaller scale, like the hovers, which you had to keep topped up with water. But in terms of powering the city? That was done manually by the good old people of floors zero, one, and two. Maybe even a few from floors three and four, if they were unlucky.

Descending the steps, I turned to the princess with a grimace. "I think you should use your scarf as a mask down here."

She unwrapped the scarf from around her neck and turned it into a makeshift mask through which it must have been hard to breathe. Beneath the scarf was her corset, which was lined with more gold around her breasts. The gold showered down the rest of her outfit, eventually trailing into what I thought might have been something meant to mimic what little I remembered of starlight.

"It's a beautiful dress."

She cleared her throat. "Thank you."

Shaking my head clear, I shrugged my cloak off and handed it to her. "But it stands out like the sun."

She wrapped herself up, doing her best to protect her identity down here. "I've never seen the mines before."

I couldn't tell if what was hidden in her voice was excitement or fear or a mixture of both, but we were going to find out because we descended the stairs into the levels below the city.

The dry air scraped across my skin the moment we descended to the first level, and for a moment I was thankful I had given my cloak to the princess. The heat required to make high-pressure steam made the temperature hotter than anywhere else in the city, but it was also a blessing during winter.

On this level, metal tubes ran through the ceiling to all the houses, and they would continue up through the levels until they reached the top, where the excess steam would be let out through ventilation shafts at the top of the buildings. So all that happened here was keeping an eye on the pressure gauges, ensuring good pipework, and management working in some offices.

To find the minister's son, however, we had to descend farther. Specifically, down to level three where they turned the water from the floor below into steam to send up the pipes. So we descended another two sets of stairs before the heat engulfed us and we could barely breathe.

I turned to Jemeena, who was out of breath and struggling. "Maybe you should wait up top with IoN?"

"No." She yanked the scarf from her mouth and sniffed, then replaced it. "I want to see what's down here for myself."

On we went, exiting the staircase onto level three where miners huddled in groups around tanks, funneling fuel into the vats below at timed intervals. The men and women were sweaty with faces blackened from coal and charred from heat caking the dust into their skin. You could always tell a miner apart from the rest of the floor because they never quite got their faces clean.

I wasn't sure where our target was and would have to start looking systematically, but these levels went on for miles, mirroring the entire city floor, and I would soon have a fainted princess on my hands if I continued.

"Maybe we could ask for help?" she suggested and turned to the nearest pit. "Excuse me?"

"Wait, Jemeena—"

"We're looking for someone."

A grumpy, pale, malnourished man turned around and huffed. "Look, Miss, I'm tryna' work, and—"

"I know," Jemeena said, "and I'm sorry to disturb you, but this is really important. Do you know where we can find the minister's son?"

The man's eyes widened and he shook his head. "Sorry, but no." He turned back to the sealed pit that was a raging inferno of fire a few feet below him, and swore as he wiped a bead of sweat away from his face.

"Do you not have masks?" she asked.

I laughed. He laughed. But she looked at us like we'd grown two heads, so the man explained, "You get what you bring with you."

"There's no protective equipment at all?"

He shook his head.

"Well then, you can tell me where the manager is after you're done telling me where the minister's son is. I'll make sure that's rectified." He snorted in disbelief and got back to work, but Jemeena wasn't done. She lowered her cloak to show the gold on her corset dress and lifted the sleeves to show off her bracelets. "I am not from this floor."

He turned back around, frustration edging his features, and his eyes widened at the gold he'd probably never seen before. "Just who are you?"

"That doesn't matter right now. Tell me what I need to know, and I'll make sure you get masks from now on. Deal?"

"All o' us?"

"All of you."

He looked at me for a minute, but I just shrugged, then he looked back at the princess and held out his hand. "Deal."

She shook it without hesitation and looked at him expectantly. "Well?"

He looked to his left, saw no one there, and then said, "The minister's son is on the level below us. He's usually two lefts from the staircase over there." He pointed to a barely there door in the wall behind him. "And the manager is in office twelve on the top floor."

We thanked him and moved on before we got him into trouble. The stairs were narrower here, less even, and they were wet, slippery, and easy to fall down, so I held her hand and told her to be careful. There was no light to see by as the stairs spiraled into darkness, and the heat of her hand engulfed mine, which felt like it was pounding along to the beat of my heart.

"You okay?" I asked as we reached the final step.

"Yes. Thank you." She didn't let go of my hand straight away but instead stared at me in what little light trickled through the slits between the wooden boards making up the door behind us. "You've been amazingly helpful, Cinderella." I cringed at the name, and she noticed, so she corrects herself. "El. Sorry."

"C'mon." I yanked us through the door, where she dropped my hand and stood beside me, mouth agape in wonder. I'd been down here once or twice with Dad, but it'd been a while.

A gaping hole in the wall wider than ten men opened into the ocean, waves crashing against the rocks, a roaring thunder in my ears. The water flowed into the pool in the center of the space via a manmade trough. Men used buckets bigger than their heads on a rope and pulley system to send the buckets down into the water and then up through holes in the ceiling, where they were deposited into the large vats above the vent holes the miners filled with fuel. The buckets were then sent back down the other side into the water to be filled up again.

It was cooler down here but more dangerous. High tides and waves meant people often got swept out into the ocean, never to be seen again.

"Do you see him?" Jemeena shouted above the roar of the ocean.

Looking around, I pointed to a blond man a few feet around the corner from us, turning a crank to keep the pulley system going. "That's him."

"Then let's go." She grabbed my hand and dragged me over there, but she turned to me just before stepping into his space. "Don't tell him who I am or what we're doing. Please."

"I won't." I stepped up to the blond man. "Carden, how are you?"

"Cinderella? Wow. It's been a while, hasn't it?"

Jemeena looked at me, surprised, but continued to listen to the conversation.

"How long has it been? Five years? Damn." A hand tugged through his hair, sadness in his eyes. "I'm still sorry that he's gone."

"Me too. But listen, I'm not here for that."

"Then what are you here for?" he asked, brows furrowing. "Because I can't help out at the garage again—"

"It's not that. I have a question. But it's not . . ."—I looked around—"allowed."

"Seren, Cinderella, just ask me whatever you need to know."

"How do our lifeclocks connect to us?"

His eyes widened, scanned the area, and he yanked us around another corner and into a quiet nook. "Why the hell are you asking that?"

"Not important. Do you know or not?"

"Why would I know that?"

We were in a very small corner. The princess was pressed up against my side, and I was doing my best to place as much space between the minister's son and myself as possible.

"Because you're Minister Farro's son, and you've been through the training. If anyone knows, it's you."

He dragged a rough hand down his face as he grimaced, glanced at us both, and then slumped in defeat. "Do you know how much trouble I could get in for this? You realize I could be executed, right?"

I was almost certain Jemeena could prevent that—assuming I

actually managed to defy the laws of basic biology and save her life—but I couldn't mention that. "I do."

"You must be desperate if you're asking." He glanced at my lifeclock, and a sad grimace overtook his face. "How long?"

He thought it was me. "Twenty-six days."

He met my eyes in shock, his hand clenching into a fist. "It connects to our bloodstream, where it measures various factors, and then it uses the magic of Seren to determine the date. It's never wrong."

My arm tightened around the princess. "So the steam lines connect to our blood supply?"

He nodded. "I don't know any more than that. Sorry."

I turned us both around and marched us away, but just before we could leave, he grabbed my wrist and yanked me back. "If you get caught, I'll deny helping you."

"I know, Carden."

The blood? Magic of Seren? But . . . I didn't understand. Did blood run through the lifeclocks somehow? And if it did, then how did it measure our time?

Before I had time to ponder this further, Jemeena had dragged me to the top mining floor and to the door with the barely visible one and the two that was dangling on its last screw.

"Wait, Jemeena, this will mean someone will know who you are."

Her hand hesitated on the door handle, her fingers clenching into a tight fist that vibrated with what I could only assume was contained rage. "But I could help."

I placed my palm gently over her fist and squeezed. "I know you could, and maybe you'll get the chance to." If people found out who she was, who knew what they'd do in exchange for a ransom from the richest family in Palatina?

"Not if I die first." She turned to face me, her mouth still covered by the scarf, but her eyes shined in the dark underground room. "If I weren't working so hard on fixing myself, I could help fix floor zero, but I don't have the time to do both." She held up her cloth-covered lifeclock and looked at it like someone looks at a dead loved one—with reverent fear and a sadness about their helplessness. "Maybe I shouldn't be wasting time on myself. Maybe I should be helping with what little time I have. Though, I can't really do that while my father sits on the throne."

"Jemeena . . ." I exhaled deeply as I uncurled her fist from the door handle and pulled her into me. "No one on floor zero would hate you for saving yourself. Not a single one of us."

She buried her face in my shoulder, and a few sobs leaked out before she pulled away and took a deep breath. "I'm okay. Besides, when you save me, I'm going to spend every second of my new future reforming the lower floors as payment."

Great. Now floor zero's future was in my hands too.

Back at the garage, Jemeena removed the cloak and scarf, folded them, and left them on the chair, but it was the person sitting next to them that had my gaze fixed in that direction.

"What do you want, Lapis?"

She folded her arms across her perfect cleavage. "That's no way to greet your sister, is it?"

I shrugged, not caring. "Either tell me what you want or get out."

"I need another few hours at the garage tomorrow."

I rolled my eyes but said nothing as I grabbed a cup of toffee and sat in front of Dad's notes again, trying to make sense of all the new information.

"Pleeease? Faryl will be here this afternoon, and he wants to meet tomorrow, but you know Mom would just die if she knew."

"Fine. But I'll be here working because we're on a deadline, and you can't go poking around our project." I'd have to separate us from them somehow, otherwise they'd figure it out, and I was sure Jemeena wouldn't want that.

"Deal." She squealed in excitement. "Thank you, thank you, thank you."

"You know," I said as she was leaving, "one day you'll have to tell Phyllis. Whether you like it or not."

"Yeah, I know." She didn't meet my eyes as she left with much less energy than before.

"Who's Faryl?" Jemeena asked.

"Her boyfriend. He's from Prago City, but he's equally poor. A scrapper." He collected scrap pieces from both inside Prago City and out in the desert and then sold them to engineers like me. "He's not a bad man, but Phyllis would throw a fit if Lapis didn't at least try to get onto a higher floor."

"So they've been using the garage as a secret rendezvous for . . . how long?"

"I think it's been two years now."

"Wow."

IoN whizzed by, his mouth hole lit up in yellow. "I wish she would use somewhere else, rather than risk getting El into trouble."

"She has nowhere else, IoN," I reminded him, because he could be unfair sometimes. "Besides, her and Lazuli have been much nicer to me since the arrangement started. They only tease with words now. They used to make me do all kinds of horrid things, like clean their underwear and run errands for them all around the city."

"As opposed to running you ragged, now they're just cruel," he said, and I knew he would have used a sarcastic voice if he could. "You'd do well to learn to stand up for yourself."

"Yeah, well . . . I could also do with a decent hot meal and a new sign for the garage door, but we don't always get what we want."

Jemeena had been rummaging through Dad's things while IoN and I argued the repetitive argument—old and worn, but still not used up, it would seem. Just when I was ready to retire for the day, Jemeena leaped to her feet and yelled, "Look here!" Then bent over and coughed, catching her breath. She waved the piece of paper around beside her.

I grabbed it and looked down at the ticket. "A ticket for one to Eto Valley on a carrier dirigible."

"Maybe he went there next?" IoN asked while fetching a glass of water from the kitchen for the princess. "Maybe he was just as clueless about how this worked as you and he sought answers outside of the city."

Jemeena had caught her breath and flopped onto the sofa with shaky hands. She wiped her mouth with her handkerchief and folded it back into her pocket. "Maybe he wanted to ask questions he couldn't here."

IoN pulled out a leather-bound book that looked as dusty as an old sock and handed it to me. "I didn't think anything of this when I came across it, but it might shed some light on what he was doing in Eto Valley."

Opening the book, I realized it was a diary. Everything Dad did in the last two months leading up to Mom's death, and then, in his grief, it ended—he was unable to pen a single other word.

"Page twenty-five," IoN said, then settled down on the floor next to me.

Dad, ever the organized one—clearly it skipped me—

numbered every page, and so I flipped to page twenty-five. "It's some kind of notes about a conversation with a person named Varissa, but some of it's written in code or another language or something. IoN, can you read this?"

He hovered over my shoulder. "It talks about a specific plant rumored to be watered by Seren Himself that has the power to change certain . . . properties. I'm not sure what this bit is." He runs his claw-like hand over the final paragraph.

"A plant?" Jemeena asked. Her eyes widened in surprise as her mouth fell open. "I think he's talking about the herbilore plant."

"The what?"

"It's an old legend. It's supposed to grow at the feet of Seren and offer the person who picks it a single wish."

"A wish is not mentioned in these notes," IoN argued before looking up at the princess.

"I know, but legends are often slices of history all mixed up in magic and stories. Maybe there's some truth to it."

"Maybe. But at the feet of Seren? Where is that?"

Jemeena shrugged. "No idea, but I know one person who will." She tapped the diary. "Varissa."

26 DAYS. 3 HOURS. 08 SECONDS.

When I returned home from walking Jemeena to the elevator building, I told an unhappy Phyllis I was leaving for a few weeks. Phyllis was so angry her face turned an entirely different shade of red and she snapped two fingernails from clenching her shaking fists too hard.

"What do you mean you're leaving?"

"The princess and I are going on a little road trip to gather some parts"—the lie we came up with to tell anyone who asked—"but I'll be back in a couple of weeks."

"A couple of weeks?" she asked as she put the teapot back on the stove. "What in Seren's name would take that long? We're an island, for Seren's sake."

"It's confiden—"

"Confidential, yes, you've said." Pouring a steaming cup of tea so large I worried she'd turn it into a lake, she said, "You cannot go, Cinderella."

I took a deep breath and exhaled with some force. "I was not asking for your permission, Phyllis." I placed a hand over hers, and she flinched. "This is my personal job. I'm not working for the garage right now. I'm twenty years old, so you only have control over Father's garage and will, not me."

"But, but, but—"

"Good night, Phyllis." I gently clicked the kitchen door shut and trotted to the bedroom I shared with Lapis and Lazuli.

"Cinderella!" they called out in unison.

I shivered in repulsion as I emptied my lungs of breath and opened the bedroom door. "Yes?"

They patted the space in between them on a bed, but the very thought of sitting between their overly perfumed bodies made my nose in protest. Instead, I sat on my bed opposite.

"What is it?"

They looked at each other, a perfect mirror image, and said, "We want you to take us with you."

Thinking they must have been joking, I laughed, but upon seeing their frowning, upset faces, I realized they weren't. "You can't be serious? No. Absolutely not." I spun around and crawled into bed.

"But," Lazuli said, "we want to get some of that softening hair dye they only make in Prago."

"Oh, please take us with you," Lapis said. "We'll stop bullying you?"

I chuckled. "Your bullying hasn't bothered me in years. Now stop being so stupid and go to sleep."

Lazuli threw a pillow at me—at least, I assumed it was her, since she had always been the pillow thrower. "At least pick us up some while you're there," she grumped. "Red and purple."

I yawned and whispered, "I'm not even going to Prago City." Stealing the pillow she threw, I added it to the lumpy flat thing that usually adorned my bed and snuggled down for the night, but a crinkle under my ear kept me awake. After I could hear the rhythmic sounds of their sleeping breaths, I pulled out the paper in the pillowcase. *Dear Faryl.* A love letter to her boyfriend.

How disgusting.

I unfolded the pages and scanned them under candlelight, but it wasn't a love letter at all. She was trying to convince him to let her live with him in Prago City, to not force her to wait any longer. She was struggling, and clearly I had misunderstood what snippets of conversations I had overheard between the two of them. He didn't think he was good enough for her.

I looked over at Lapis's sleeping form on the bottom bunk and smiled. She just wanted to begin her life. Who was I to get in the way? If we ended up in Prago City, I'd deliver the letter myself.

THE NORTH GATE WAS A DUMPING GROUND FOR LEVEL zero. It was the only open space we had, so we used it to store everyone's old stuff for others to make use of. Waste not, want not, and all that jazz. Walking through it, however, never failed to remind me of the reality of living on floor zero. All the dirt, the crime, the crappy mixture of great compassion and great apathy— you could find it all in the dumping ground.

I hated coming here.

I grabbed IoN tight against my chest and yanked on the straps of my pack to keep it close as I hurried past piles of broken furniture, tattered clothes, and worn toys as fast as possible.

The north gate stood tall and imposing in the distance at ten floors high, the mold, moss, and grime sparser the higher up the concrete I looked. The gates themselves were a complicated contraption of cogs, steam lines, and pistons that worked seamlessly to keep any unwanted enemies out and the people in. A person needed the proper paperwork to get outside the gates, or be high enough in the food chain to forgo the security checks altogether, and I was hoping Princess Jemeena had thought about my lack of papers.

The security that manned the gates was extensive, and there was no sneaking past them. Trust me, I'd tried. When Dad died, I was distraught and wanted to get away from Phyllis, so I tried to leave. Safe to say I was arrested for kicking an armed officer in the junk, and Phyllis wasn't too happy having to pay my fines. This time, the guards considered me with wary eyes, but they mostly went about their business of talking crap and checking their weapons.

I waited patiently, hoping Jemeena was on this side of the north gate, because there was no way I was getting out of here without her. I didn't have to wait long before a girl with flowing black hair and knee-high boots, all wrapped up in a silk cloak that billowed in the breeze, stormed my way.

"Princess," I said, bowing my head lightly.

"Pshh"—she whacked me on the arm—"we passed title politeness when I cried in your arms right upon meeting you." She laughed, but the tinge of red smattered across her cheeks told me she still hated that memory. "Call me Meena."

"Meena?"

She shrugged. "I was just using it as an alias, but I like it."

"Meena it is. So, Meena, do you have a plan to get me past the guards, because I have no travel paperwork."

She looked at me with utter bewilderment for a few moments before doubling over and cracking up. "Oh, El, you are a funny one." She slipped her arm through mine and dragged us to the gates. "A princess does not need travel papers." She shook her head and yanked her hood down.

"Princess," the guards all said at once, stumbling over themselves. "What are you doing on this floor?"

"Leaving the city on an urgent errand. Please open the gates. Our escort waits on the other side."

"Very well," the one at the front said as he rose from his bow. He turned to the slew of guards behind him and yelled, "Open the gates!"

The guards sprinted to their stations and each cranked wheels and handles in a complicated series of movements like a rehearsed dance. The doors hissed, groaned, and heaved, but the cogs eventually started turning, the pistons moved with increasing fervor, and the steam lines chugged power from the bottom to the top.

Then, the first crack of real light hitting floor zero washed over me. For a moment, I forgot all about the princess's oncoming death, IoN's mysterious personality, and the orphan status that hung over my head like a stubborn raincloud, and I breathed in deep at the sun that stung my eyes. I turned back to look at the dumping ground dappled in light that breathed life into an otherwise lifeless air.

"It looks so . . . bright," I whispered. "Less dirty, more like . . . home." And it was true. It did. Without the endless darkness that pervaded the entirety of floor zero, it looked almost lively.

"Things usually do when you take an honest look at them." She turned me around. "Come on. We do not want to be late." She walked on ahead.

"Late?" I asked as I jogged to catch up. "Late for what?"

"Our escort." We walked through the gates, and she gestured to the giant dirigible hovering a few hundred feet above ground, running and ready to fly.

"We're flying in a dirigible?" A gentle buzz of excitement powered through me.

I tried hard to contain it, but I think she might have spotted it anyway because she laughed and said, "You didn't think we were walking around the island, did you?"

"I assumed we'd get a steamer to take us," I mumbled. "But this"—I gestured to the giant white dirigible in front of us—"is miles better."

"There are perks to being hired by royalty, you know. Including having the princess escort you wherever you need in her personal, private dirigible."

"Well, then sign me up for future jobs, because I could get used to a life like this."

We both laughed as we walked to the entrance platform lying flat on the dusty ground. It connected to the dirigible by a pole that ascended the moment we secured our hands to it.

"This is just like the elevators!" I shouted above the high winds the engine gave off. "It's amazing! Look at the cogs and how they move something this huge . . ."

"You are such a nerd, El," the princess shouted back, but she coughed and hacked up a small smattering of blood into her hand.

I tore a piece of my coveralls' sleeve off and wrapped it around her face, hoping it would keep the desert's dust out of her fragile system. "There!"

She nodded, still struggling not to cough. She'd turned pale despite the morning sunlight glowing up her tan, and I worried she wouldn't make it another week out here. Instead of wondering myself to death about it, I yanked her right wrist and lifted the golden silk wrap off.

Twenty-five days still left.

Relief washed through me despite the needlessness: Nothing can change a lifeclock's numbers.

Once the platform had floated all the way up and locked into place, I looked around. The dirigible was huge on the inside, but it wasn't particularly homey. This was what the princess had chosen? I thought royalty would choose something a bit . . . I don't know . . . plushier?

"It's an airship, El," Jemeena said while holding back another cough. "It's not a cruise liner." She held a hand to her material-covered mouth and grimaced.

"What's a cruise liner?"

"It's a ship for the air that carries hundreds of people, and—"

She coughed up a storm once again, and I had to catch her when she stumbled. "Stop talking for a moment." I pointed in all the directions we could go and asked, "Which way to your accommodations?"

She pointed to a corridor lined with steel walls and leaned on my shoulder.

IoN woke up and headed that way, scoping everything out for us, no doubt.

I plodded along after him, half carrying Meena and half dragging her. "Come on," I whispered. "Work with me here. Do not make me bridal carry you the entire way."

She muffled a giggle and began putting one foot in front of the other, guiding her body's movements a bit more.

"There you go."

IoN whizzed back toward us. "It is not much farther."

"Okay, thank you," I said. "Could you open the door for us, please?"

I gripped her waist tighter and took more of her weight after IoN flew off again, but she kept trying to hold herself up. "Stop trying to resist help, you moron. Let me help you, or so help me Seren, I will not hesitate to bridal carry you all the way to your room."

"You shouldn't . . . talk that . . . way to a . . . princess."

"Since when have you cared about your royal status? Now stop being so stubborn and accept help from a friend." Friend? At what point did she move from client to friend? When did I start looking at her like she's someone I want to remain close to? When she saved IoN, when she cried in my arms upon first meeting, or when I saw her on my dusty garage floor looking through Dad's old junk and realized she looked good in my life?

She stopped struggling at that and let me hold more of her weight, but she was eerily silent—not even looking at me.

"Everything okay?" I asked. "You know, besides coughing up half a lung?"

"Err . . . yes," she wheezed. "It's just . . . you see me as a friend?" She paused a few feet from the doorway IoN hovered in and had another coughing fit, doubling over and bracing her back against the wall.

"Of course," I whispered, rubbing her arm. "Why else would I agree to go on an almost pointless cross-country trip with a stuck-up royal?" My voice dripping with sarcasm, I winked at her.

She lifted her head up and met my gaze. "Oh, I don't know. I thought maybe you were here for all the interesting technology you'd get to use." She'd gotten some breath back and could now at least talk in full sentences, even if they were sounding weak and breathy.

"Well, there's that too."

I got the princess into her cabin—which was larger than my entire apartment back in the city—and forced her into bed to rest.

After all that desert sand, she needed it. I left IoN with her in case she needed anything, then headed out to explore the dirigible.

I thought it odd we hadn't been greeted upon arrival or something, given that one of their passengers was the princess, but I was sure if I could find the command deck, I would be able to see what was going on.

The dirigible was made of a lattice of corridors that crisscrossed all over the place, with the only kind of signage a complex series of numbers I could make neither heads nor tails of. After about five or six twists and turns and lefts and rights, I was well and truly lost. I'd even descended some kind of staircase at one point, but it just led me to more crisscrossing corridors.

I occasionally passed a servant or worker, but they all seemed much too busy to deal with me. Plus, I probably just looked like another engineer to them. What I wouldn't give to see the engineering deck of this thing. I bet it was hug—

"Excuse me?" a rough voice said from behind me. "Do you need some help?"

I spun to face him and found myself gazing into steel-colored eyes that matched the ship.

"Err . . . I'm a little lost."

"I can see that." He crossed his arms over his chest. "Need to get back to your station on the engineering deck?"

"Oh, no." I cleared my throat. "My name is Cinderella, and I'm here with the princess. I was trying to find someone to greet or get some direction to the command deck."

He blanched and stuttered, "I-I'm so sorry." He bowed his head at me—which made me feel ridiculous—and said, "Come with me, Lady Ferning. We'll get you to the captain in no time." He held out his arm for me to take.

I took it and let him guide me back the way I had come and up four flights of stairs before knocking on a plain door.

"This is the command deck," he whispered. "The captain and flight assistants are inside."

The door swung open revealing a surprised woman with a captain's cap atop long brown tresses that trailed down to her waist. "Yes?" She wore a brown leather jacket that had seen better days over a corset accentuating her waist, tight, brown trousers, and she had straps to hold various things to her person.

The mysterious man who had guided me here cleared his throat and announced, "This is Lady Ferning. She was lost and looking for you."

"Oh!" The captain beamed and flushed red. "I'm sorry, Lady Ferning, I was not told you had both boarded." She threw a stern glance at someone behind her but then returned to me. "I am pleased to make your acquaintance." She held out her hand.

"Thank you." I shook her hand. "It's nice to meet you."

She ushered me inside, and my guide turned to leave.

"You'll have to excuse the princess; she was feeling unwell upon boarding."

The captain's eyes snapped to me. "Is she okay?" Her brow creased and her lips frowned. "I know of her illness. We're . . . friends."

"She'll be okay."

"Well, welcome to the command deck, I guess." She pointed to a plush seating area over on the right behind the important control centers. "That's where we allow our guests to join us up here."

"Of course."

I headed that way, but she grabbed my arm. "Please, let me introduce you to the flight crew first."

"Oh, of course." I bowed my head slightly. "Forgive me, I'm not from these upper circles."

"So I've heard," she said in an odd tone of voice. "C'mon!"

She guided me down the few steps to the central command deck and introduced everyone from left to right, starting with the crew commander. He was a portly fellow with a rotund middle and graying hair, but when he turned to say hello, he only grimaced and went back to taking notes and making various announcements over the radio. Next were the dirigible's military commanders: a pair of twins with bright blonde hair. Lilly was in charge of offense while Layla was in charge of defense. Together, they protected the airship and its passengers in all kinds of situations. Truthfully, they reminded me of Lapis and Lazuli; I bet they would make excellent military commanders after the proper training. And, finally, the captain's second in command, Yolot—a dark-skinned man who spoke with an accent I hadn't heard before.

"And that's where I sit"—she pointed to a seat in the center of the semicircular deck—"at the helm." There were a complicated series of buttons and levers in front of her chair, but she seemed to know what she was doing.

It was all so overwhelming. I wanted to ask a million questions about how the dirigible worked and what protocols were in place for errors or things going wrong, but no matter how many times I tried to force the words out, my mouth remained devoid of them.

"I can see you need a moment." She guided me to the lounge area behind the central command deck and sat me down. "Tea?"

"Toffee, if you have it?" I still stared at the deck in front of me in awe. "This is all so amazing."

She sat next to me with a steaming cup of toffee, which I took from her. "Yes, the dirigible is a wondrous feat of technology, isn't it?"

I swallowed my first sip and breathed in contentment. "It's just . . . I could never imagine designing something like it—or fixing it, for that matter."

The captain placed a hand on my shoulder. "It's fixed by a team, rather than one person. And this model was designed by Zimeon at Zime Industries." Her brown hair bounced as she laughed at my face. "I know, he's brilliant."

He'd tried to steal IoN, so how brilliant was he really? Well, objectively speaking, his mind must be a wondrous place—shame about his lack of morals. "More than brilliant," I responded, a hint of that wonder still evident in my voice.

It didn't go unnoticed by the captain, who smirked at my obvious embarrassment. "Yeah, you'd lose that wistful look in your eyes if you met him. He's a real trollop."

"So I've noticed."

She laughed some more and gripped her hands together on her lap. "The princess and you are pretty close, no?"

"We've known each other less than a week, but . . . yeah, I guess we are kinda close."

Her eyes widened with shock. "Less than a week?"

"Yeah . . . Why?"

She spluttered a moment and her cheeks turned red. "No reason."

"Oh, c'mon, spill it." I put my cup down and folded my arms over my chest. "Don't leave me out of the loop."

She looked at me with raised eyebrows. "It's nothing, honestly. I just thought you'd known each other longer with the way she talks about you."

"She talks about me?"

"Yes. Says you've got a brilliant mind."

"She . . . said that?" About me? "But I've not done anything."

She gestured to me. "You must have done something, because the princess is not an easy person to impress."

But she was impressed by me? I was no one—a small-time barely engineer on level zero with no money and no friends. I wasn't worthy of her impression.

The door to the command deck opened, and the woman in question walked through with freshly painted makeup and newly curled hair, looking like the princess she was always supposed to be. "So," she said, smirking at the two of us, "this is where I find you both." She came and sat down after giving a brief hello to the crew—who all bowed. "How are you?"

She looked genuinely concerned, and I didn't quite know why. "I'm fine, thank you?" I raised my eyebrows.

"I was just worried you might have gotten lost without me guiding you."

"Oh," I said, blushing. "No, er . . . I mean, I did. But some crew member found me and escorted me here, where I met our captain and crew." I hid my face behind my teacup and internally scorned myself for stumbling over a simple sentence.

"Ah, well that was lucky." She got up and poured herself a cup of mint tea before sitting back down on the captain's other side. "I was worried you might not have found your way around my airship."

"*Your* airship?" I looked at the dirigible in a whole new light, but I could see it now. How this dark, mysterious piece of machinery belonged to her. It wasn't fancy or full of pompous social rituals. It just was.

"Yes. I had that giant oaf design it for me." She gulped her tea with gusto before adding, "Cost me a pretty penny too." She gestured to the captain. "Captain Hera here is a good friend of mine."

The captain looked crestfallen at the term of endearment. Who could be annoyed at being friends with Meena?

"She looks to be a very capable captain, Meena." I angled to look at Captain Hera, but the look of hatred that flashed across Hera's face before the practiced smile came back into play had me halting all pretenses of social decorum. "And at the very least a lovely . . . person." My voice dropped at the end, and even I winced at the hesitation that filtered through. I shot up out of my seat. "If you'll excuse me. I'm going to get some rest before we depart."

"Oh," Meena said, disappointment flashing in her eyes, "very well. Your quarters are right next to mine. IoN's there now."

I turned to them both and bowed. "Thank you for your hospitality."

What the hell was that?

I charged straight to my room, just about remembering all the twists and turns from earlier, and lay on the silk sheets in the nicest space I'd ever set foot in, much less called my own—even if only temporarily. The wooden armoire across from the bed had vines carved into it and an ornate mirror that reflected my visage perfectly; the rugs covering the metal floors seemed denser and had a more complicated pattern than I had seen before too.

Captain Hera had done nothing to offend me, yet I was hesitant and rude. I needed to apologize the first chance I got.

In the meantime, I'd rest here until the dirigible took off. I wanted to watch our ascent from the command deck with the big windows, Hera be damned. I bet the world looked amazing from up in the air. I hoped I didn't get motion sick. That would spoil the entire trip.

I shook my head. I shouldn't keep referring to this as a trip. It was important that we followed in my father's footsteps, since the princess's life could rely on it, but this was the adventure of a lifetime for me, and I wasn't going to miss a single moment.

Previously unattainable knowledge was just on the horizon. I could feel it. And I planned to grasp it with both hands and never let go.

"Are you feeling all right, El?" IoN asked. "It has been an eventful week. It's okay to feel overwhelmed."

"I just . . . This is everything I've ever wanted." I sat up and rested on the headboard. "The answer to every question I've ever had. The chance to make friends. The chance to hold more knowledge than any engineer in our city."

"And that is causing you concern?" He hovered by my face for a moment before settling into my lap.

"What if I mess it up?" I fiddled with one of his antennae, which he used to see all of his surroundings and not just the things in front of him. "What if I'm not good enough?"

"El, you do not need to be in your father's shadow your entire life. You're allowed to be yourself. You are allowed to make mistakes and grow. In fact, it is the whole point of the human existence." He pointed at the numbers represented by the hands of my lifeclock. "All this means is that one day you will die. It does not stop you from living."

The door creaked open. "Is that really what you believe, IoN?" the princess asked.

I shot up and IoN hovered, neither of us knowing what to say. "I am sorry, Princess. Forgive me. I did not know you were there."

She waved a hand at him as she walked in. "Don't be so silly. Both of you." She shot me a stern glare. "You are allowed to be yourselves in front of me, regardless of this." She pointed to her own lifeclock. "It does not change who I am."

"Very well, Princess," IoN said. "Then, if I may . . ." He floated over to her. "Yes, I really do believe that the number means nothing. It does not change how you live your life; it only states a fact you already know: One day you will die."

"In twenty-five days, to be exact." She sat on the edge of my bed not three feet away, but by the look on her face and the distance in her eyes, she might as well have been a hundred miles away.

I couldn't imagine the pain of knowing you were going to die in under four weeks. The fear she must be feeling.

I crawled across the bed and sat next to her. "Want to talk about it?"

She opened her mouth but closed it. Eventually, she tried again. "One would think you grow used to the idea of dying young. I have known my entire life that I would not make it to my twenty-first birthday, so I thought I would not be scared. That I would meet death with honor and grace. As a princess should." Silent tears slid down her cheeks and her shoulders shook. "But instead, I can barely sleep, eat, or function because I am so scared of leaving my family, my city, and my friends"—her watery green eyes pierced through me, and I shuddered—"behind."

"I can't even imagine, Meena." I wrapped an arm around her shoulders and pulled her close. "But even if it's just for twenty-five days, I'm right here."

A sea of people surrounded this girl every day, and yet she always looked lonely. How many friends did she honestly have? And how many of them were genuine?

Sitting on the finest bed I had ever parked my butt on, in a room bigger than our entire apartment, I made a vow I knew I could never break. "I won't let you die alone, Meena." I took a deep breath and grabbed both sides of her tear-stained face. "No matter what happens, no matter how hard or difficult it might be, I will not let you die alone."

"Y-y-you . . . Really?" She looked at me with such fearful reverence I worried she might die of some kind of emotional attack before she managed to make it through her last twenty-five days. "I . . . Thank you."

I grabbed her hands and pulled her into me. Her arms wrapped around my chest as she breathed into the crook of my neck, taking a deep breath. "No need to thank me, Meena. Ever." I rubbed circles on her back. "Not for this."

We stayed like that until she eventually dried her tears using a handkerchief I was sure would pay for a week's worth of food back home. "I am quite sorry, El." She bowed slightly and said, "I did not mean to impose upon you."

I tapped her on the shoulder and scowled. "Don't do that."

She flinched. "Do what?"

I gestured to her rigid posture and emotional mask and said, "That. Don't hide it all and shut yourself away in the process." I grabbed her hands. "Not with me."

She sniffed one last time. "Okay." She shot me a devilish grin. "So, spill it." She looked at me with a stern eye. "What happened back on the command deck?"

I groaned and fell back onto the bed in a huff. "I know. I'm sorry. I'll apologize the moment I see her again. I promise."

She laughed and shook her head before lying down next to me. "That was not what I asked."

I groaned, unsure how to answer. "I don't know. She just looked at me like I'd spat in her perfectly steamed teacup." I shuddered at the memory of that expression. "And I got . . . defensive."

"Over what?" She looked at me with a shy expression on her perfect face, and I got the feeling she already knew but wanted me to say it out loud.

I didn't know if I could. Not yet. "Um . . . I don't know." I shrugged. "She just rubbed me the wrong way, I guess."

Meena looked disappointed and stood. "Come on, El. Let's go watch the dirigible's ascent."

I jumped to my feet and let out a squeal of excitement. "Yes, yes, yes!"

"You are like a child today." She shook her head, but I could see the glee behind the scolding. "But you'll see Hera there and can apologize." She shot me a withering look that could cut glass.

I shivered. "Yes, Princess." I even bowed my head a little. "Let's go, then!" I grabbed her hand and IoN, then dragged them both back toward the command deck. "I really wanna see the ascent."

We traveled at a reasonable pace, despite my legs clearly wanting to sprint there. I knew Meena couldn't run, not so soon after the desert dust had affected her lungs.

"Meena?" When she looked my way, I asked, "What is wrong with you?" I waved at her lifeclock. "Besides dying in twenty-five days," I whispered, not wanting anyone to overhear me.

"It is a lung condition that affects my breathing. They've been slowly collapsing my entire life. Only one is fully functioning now."

Damn. Her lungs were collapsing? "That's why you get so out of breath and cough up blood occasionally?"

She nodded.

"I'm so sorry." I moved us on, determined to not let this change our friendship.

We'd only known each other a few days, but this woman was

the closest I'd ever had to a friend as an adult—other than IoN. It was a shame she would die in twenty-five days. What *would* I do then? Shit. What would I do? Go back to normal? As though nothing happened? No. That would be . . . impossible.

Meena walked up to the command deck's door and pushed it open without knocking—perks of royalty, I guess—and walked to the deck's lounge. Captain Hera sat at her station, barking commands to the rest of the crew, and they followed without hesitation or question. She was . . . powerful.

"She's incredible," I whispered as I sat beside Meena.

"I know." She chuckled. "She really knows how to take charge." Meena blushed a deep crimson.

"What," I started, "is that about?" I raised my eyebrows in that gossipy way she did whenever she wanted juicy information from me. Oh, how the tables had turned.

"N-nothing," she stammered.

"Really?" I looped my arm through hers. "That why you look like a ripe tomato right now, huh?"

She blushed harder, and I laughed. She was too much fun to mess with.

"We used to . . . casually date when we were younger." She cleared her throat. "But it was a long time ago."

"Not still an . . . item?" I inquired.

She shook her head. "Not in years, no."

"El," IoN said from his place on the table, "we are about to rise, I believe." Just as he finished his sentence, the entire machine and all of my surroundings vibrated as steam power ran the engines throughout the dirigible's lower levels.

"Oh my Seren," I gasped. I stood and ran to the edge of the lounge, getting as good a view as I could.

Commander Hera looked over at me. She tried to yell something, but I couldn't hear. Instead, she waved me over. I didn't think twice. I ran to her and leaned in to listen. "Wanna watch from the best seat in the house?" She gestured to the captain's chair.

I shrunk. I couldn't sit there. "Oh, I couldn't possibly—"

"Shush." She grabbed my wrist and twirled me around before pushing my shoulders into her chair. "I can do my job standing up." I guessed this was her way of apologizing.

The dirigible lifted off the ground with a grumble, and the feeling of floating enraptured me as we rose higher and higher into the sky. The desert below us was soon nothing more than a wash of golden sand amid a world of blue wonder. I stood and walked to the window wall that marked the front of the command deck and pointed to the city beside us. "It's so small," I said as the twenty-first floor disappeared beneath us.

Small hands wrapped around my waist from behind as Meena whispered, "This has always been one of my favorite views."

"Really?"

"Everything seems so small and trivial from up here: the city's level system, the social division, the people. Even the castle."

I breathed it all in and let out a shudder as our home city flew out of view. "It's all so . . . beautiful."

"The world's a big place." Meena twirled me around to face her. "One day, I hope you get to see more of it."

I grabbed her hand and pulled her into a hug. "We'll do it together."

"I would like that very much."

24 DAYS. 23 HOURS. 17 MINUTES

THE FOLLOWING DAY, MEENA WOKE ME UP WITH A promise of breakfast and a surprise. I didn't know what this surprise entailed, but Meena's eyes sparkled as she hopped from foot to foot. The smile practically jumped off her face.

"C'mon." She yanked me out the door the moment I was dressed. "I don't want to miss a single moment."

We dined for breakfast in a small hall with enough seating for six people, but today it only had three: Meena, myself, and Hera. Hera looked at me with a gentle curiosity while Meena chatted endlessly about what might await us in Eto Valley, leaving out the real reason we were going, of course, but I indulged her.

"Apparently it's flat, with no levels whatsoever, and resembles a town of old."

"Really?" I asked.

"There are a few flat towns," Hera said. "I've seen a couple on my travels, but the two cities on the island are, of course, up-leveled." She looked at Meena with a question on her face, and Meena nodded in encouragement. "Jemeena has asked me to show you around the engines today, so you can see how they work for yourself."

I placed my fork back on the table a little too vigorously and grinned at Hera. "Really? That would be okay?"

"Sure. But I'm only escorting you there. I'll leave you in the engine master's capable hands after that. He'll probably know more than me anyway."

I looked at Meena with gratitude and whispered, "Thank you. I'll just grab IoN and then we can go."

"Okay, but be quick," Hera said. "I'm a busy woman."

I sprinted to the room, told IoN about it, and grabbed him before heading back. "It's gonna be so cool. We're going to get to see everything!"

"It will be interesting."

He settled into my arms in his usual position before we entered the dining room, and Hera escorted all of us down a few flights of stairs to the engine rooms. "We are here." She waited until the door opened. A portly man stood on the other side, wearing a floppy hat and more grease than I'd ever seen on a person. Hera bowed to Meena and tipped her hat at me, then left.

"Hello, Miss Ferning, Princess Jemeena," the man standing in the doorway said. "Welcome to the engine room." He gathered us inside and shut the door before starting our tour. "This dirigible has four engines, being that it's smaller than other larger passenger models, but it takes over a dozen workers to keep her in the sky." He walked up to a giant metal contraption that was so large, I couldn't see it all without moving around it. "This is engine one. We like to call her Merida. She has water pumped from the tank below"—he stamped his foot on the ground twice—"which is then rapidly heated by use of coal to create steam, which powers the various mechanics onboard. The entire ship is laid with pipes that can carry steam to anywhere onboard."

"Do you use the Baryman Method to keep everything cool and safe, or do you need to use another system for something this large?"

"Well, we start with a basic BM, but we do have to modulate things to adapt them to a complex system, such as the pipes in the metalwork of the ship itself, which use a ventilation system to let the hot air escape at every meter."

That was clever. Could they use something like that throughout the mines? Maybe vents that let out on the ground floor to keep the miners cooler and safer?

He showed us every nook and cranny, answered every question I had, and even took us down to the tank below so I could watch the water being siphoned up into the engines. It was magical, and, despite probably being bored out of her mind, Meena was with me for the entire day. Eventually we had to retire for the afternoon and prep ourselves for dinner, which was a laid-back affair of cheeses, breads, olives, and spreads that we ate while chatting.

---

18 DAYS. 16 HOURS. 31 MINUTES

WE HAD BEEN TRAVELING FOR SIX STRAIGHT DAYS, THE dirigible having managed to stay in the air the entire time other than to refuel at a town en route, and I had not, to my utter relief, gotten motion sick. Meena and I had spent most of the time chatting about Dad's research, the trip he took, and comparing notes on how much we knew about our destination. One thing we both agreed on was that no one other than us three should know about our real purpose, not even Captain Hera.

Meena didn't like lying to her friend, but it was necessary. Who knew a person's real motive when possessed with the knowledge of the potential altering of life time? I had apologized thrice since that first day about my behavior toward the captain, but she shrugged it off and ignored me—whenever Meena was around. Whenever it was just the two of us, her charm and friendly attitude diminished a little; she returned to the cold-shoulder mannerisms I had first pegged her with.

I didn't know what I had done, but I was determined not to let it ruin this trip. In a few hours, we would land at our destination: Eto Valley. According to Dad's notes, this was where Varissa was, and according to Meena, it was a small village community made of a collection of smaller villages and towns that had grown laterally over the years, instead of vertically like us.

Despite trying numerous times, I couldn't make out Dad's scribblings about what had happened in Eto Valley, but we were hoping this Varissa person could tell us—assuming they were still alive.

A knock at my chamber door had me scrambling to gather all the paperwork I'd spread over the bed in the past hour. "Just a minute!" I shoved everything under my pillows and scampered to the door.

A short gentleman wearing a servant's uniform and slicked-back black hair greeted me with a small bow. "We will be descending soon, Lady Ferning."

"Than-n-n-k you." I bowed back, and he turned on his heels and departed back down the corridor.

It was weird being treated like a noble, and I still blushed and stumbled over myself whenever someone bowed or called me lady, but it was . . . nice to be respected. At least, it was nice compared to the daily name-calling, ridiculing, and bossing around that I was used to. But I was only here for eighteen more days, and then it was back to normality.

"El!" Meena shouted to get my attention from her chamber doorway next to mine. "You with me?" She tugged the sleeves of her dress down over the golden material she always had wrapped around her lifeclock. "It's time to descend."

"Err . . . right." I shook my head and stepped outside. "Coming, IoN?"

"Yes." He whizzed ahead of us, and soon it was just us walking toward the disembarkation deck on the lower floor.

We had exited the desert late yesterday evening and had since descended into the grassy valley that sat at the base of the Eto Mountains. The valley, surrounded by shrubbery and small patches of woodland that looked to be as boggy as level zero was dark, was flat with a river that ran through the houses and into a small lake at the center.

"This is Eto Valley?" I asked myself. It wasn't much.

"Yeah . . . They live a simpler life out here."

A rattling sound came over the radio speakers at the front of the disembarkation deck. "Please step onto the boarding platform," the captain spoke. "We have reached our destination." And just as she finished her announcement, the dirigible met solid ground and my legs became heavy and stiff.

Meena and I stepped onto the small platform due to descend any minute and grabbed the railing that surrounded the central mechanism and each other.

I handed Meena a piece of material I'd ripped from one of my shirts and stitched into a mask that would help with the dust outside. "Here."

She looked at me. "I should be fine outside of the desert, but thank you."

I shrugged. "Can't have you dying before we finish our trip." Not that that was likely, unless her time suddenly descended. Rare, but it happened from time to time.

The dusty window that showed us our surroundings was hard to see through, but I could tell that Eto Valley had a starkly different way of life from us. They had sunlight touching everything I could see, and nothing was taller than one or two stories. It was . . . refreshing. Like the stories Mom used to tell me of what it was supposedly like before we discovered steam power, when we lived in one-story towns made entirely of stone and wood. Every bit of the ground floor—the only floor, I guess—was covered in broken pieces of pavement, stone, and metal, and tufts of grass and weeds poked through at every inch. It was like nature was taking back her planet, and the people here just let her.

Meena held on tight to my arm, her grip like ice on my otherwise balmy skin—the desert had been scorching hot, even inside the safety of the dirigible—and I looked at her with worry. Although her lungs had recovered from her earlier trip across the sands, she hadn't. I could tell by the way her skin was paler than ever. She was unsteady on her feet, even though she tried to cover it up and act okay, and she was losing weight. I could see the bones of her shoulders more prominently than ever.

I was worried. Worried we wouldn't be able to complete this trip before she died and worried about what would happen when she did die.

I shook my head. I could deal with that when it came. For now, I wanted to try to save her life.

The platform lowered just as the door slid open and we descended into Eto Valley. The first thing I saw was green. Everywhere was covered in green. Not the kind of rotting moss that saturated the walls of floor zero, but bright green grass and ferns and flowers that dotted every spare surface they could find, and if they couldn't find one, they made one; some of the plants even grew out of the sides of the small houses.

The dirigible landed about a mile outside of the center by the looks of things, but even this far out, the place was bustling with people carrying baskets of food, managing unruly children, hanging washing out to dry in the morning sun, and tending to their vast gardens.

"Oh, wow," Meena said. "Look at all the tracheophyta and liliales." She stepped off the platform and walked up to a small garden fenced in by old wooden pickets, and she marveled at the sight. She brushed her fingers against a particularly bright purple flower. "I could not make an orchid grow like this if I tried."

An older gentleman coughed and chuckled. "It ain't that hard, miss. All an orchid needs is a good wet and dry pattern of waterin'." He gestured to the patch of similar-looking flowers surrounding it—all orchids, I assumed—and said, "See, they like breaks in between their waterin', and most folk just try to give 'em as much as possible in fear o' killin' 'em. But they'll drown if you do that."

"What about the type of food you feed them out here?" she asked, excitement buoying her every step.

"Well"—he scratched his head—"we don' have access to fancy food they feed flowers in richer cities, so I jus' feed 'em whatever dead stuff I can, miss. Leaves, leavings, and so on."

"Ah, so just natural nitrogen, then?"

He shrugged. "Guess so."

"Er . . . Meena?" I tugged on her sleeve. She looked at me, and I gestured her closer. "We need to get going." I flashed my eyes to her lifeclock.

"Right." She turned back to the gentleman. "I am so sorry, but I must be moving on. We are on a rather tight deadline."

"O' course, miss." He tipped his wide-brimmed hat and bowed his head lightly. "It's been a pleasure."

"The pleasure has been all mine, sir." She bowed her head in return and looped her arm through mine. "Come on. We should go to the town center and find this Varissa person."

The short journey to the center of the collaboration of villages took no longer than two hours, but it was two hours of walking through a totally different world. You could see where villages had developed, grew over time, and eventually merged with one another, with the occasional boundary to mark space.

"This place is so . . . flat," I whispered as we walked down another sun-filled path. "Light touches everything."

"You would like it out here, would you not?" Meena asked, curious about my fascination with this place.

"I like the endless sun. The freedom these people have." I gestured to three children playing with laughter and bruises. "But I'd quickly get frustrated with the lack of steam-powered technology."

Meena laughed, wheezing. "Yes. For without your garage, who are you really?"

"Right?" I feigned surprised hurt and we laughed for a bit before Meena had to stop as she started coughing.

She leaned over her knees, this fit lasting longer than any I'd seen. I rubbed circles over her back, hoping it might help, but I eventually made us sit on some nearby stone benches.

"You know," she said between coughs, "it does bring into question what your father was doing out here."

"Huh?"

She gestured to all around us. "This place is far from technologically capable. Why here?"

"You know, you have a point."

IoN had been suspiciously silent on our trip so far, but he chose that moment to wake up. "There could be a number of reasons, Princess. We should continue as soon as you are able."

"Right, of course." She stood with renewed determination.

"Wait." I put my hand on her shoulder. "We can rest a moment longer if needed." I scowled at IoN.

She shook her head. "IoN is right. We need to keep moving. Just eighteen days left." She frowned at the wrapped lifeclock on her wrist. "Come on."

We continued walking, and eventually the town got more modern, more central, and just when we were about to cross the line into the central township, I noticed the first sign of modern technology. "Look, a steam-powered sign!" It said *Welcome to Eto Center* in bright yellow letters on a worn-out scrap of metal that I assumed was once white. "So, they do know about steam power here."

"Seems that way," Meena said, a little out of breath.

"Come on." I guided her to a nearby rock to rest. "We can find someone to question in a moment. You should rest first."

"Ugh," she groaned. "I am fed up with resting!" She jumped to her feet and stalked forward. "All I bloody do is rest. I am sick of it." She threw her hands up in exasperation. "If I do not do something, I am going to . . ."

She couldn't finish the sentence, for her breaths had grown short and raspy and she was forced to stop.

"Okay, okay," I hushed. "We can keep going if that's what you want."

She walked ahead of me while wheezing. I jogged to catch up. Soon we walked hand-in-hand to the biggest building in the center of the valley. It was marked *Eto Valley Guild Hall*. Hopefully, someone in there could answer our questions.

We entered the guild hall, IoN whizzing by my head in silence as usual, and I stood aghast at the sight before me. Everywhere I looked stood benches, tables, metal railings, and an entire system of steam-powered technology that lit up the building like a signpost. It was so . . . "Bright."

"Yes, this place is rather . . . like home."

She was right. It did remind me of the higher levels of home, but with the charm of Mother Nature poking through every available crack in the cement.

"So," she began as she spun on the spot, "where to?"

I glanced around to take in the signs and bustle of people doing their jobs and eventually settled on a small desk in the far corner with a lovely elderly lady sitting behind an *Ask Me for Help* sign. How useful. "This way." I dragged Meena behind me and stood in front of the desk, impatiently tapping my foot. "Hello?"

The elderly lady looked up from her growing pile of paperwork. "Hello." Her accent was thick. "How can I help you?"

Meena stepped forward and undid her scarf, mask, and headpiece, letting her full face show.

The woman gasped and stood to attention. "Princess Jemeena!" She bowed. "I'm sorry I did not recognize you sooner."

Meena waved the woman's concerns away. "It is of no concern. Please." She gestured to the chair the woman had vacated. "We are looking for someone. Someone named Varissa?"

The old lady's eyes widened as she spluttered into a closed fist.

After regaining herself and brushing imaginary dust off her immaculate dress, she shook her head. "I am sorry, but that won't be possible."

Meena frowned. "Why not?"

The lady bowed her head with a sad face. "Because she is currently serving a life sentence in Vine Valley."

Meena's eyes widened as she took a step closer to the desk. In a low voice, she whispered, "Can you please tell me what for?"

The old lady leaned in, looked both ways, as if checking to see if the auditory coast was clear, and whispered back, "People say she helped murder someone." She sat back and shrugged. "I'm sorry, but I don't know much more."

"But—"

I grabbed Meena's hand and pulled her toward me. "C'mon, Meena. She doesn't want to share any more information." I gestured to her shaking hands and nervous eyes. "She'll probably get in trouble for saying more."

Meena's eyes glowed in understanding. "Ah, you're probably right." She turned back to the old lady. "I am sorry we have bothered you. Please, have a nice day." She returned her scarf and mask back to normal before turning toward the door and gesturing us outside.

In the high sun, we sat on a bench under the shade of a tree Meena told me was a sumac tree. IoN remained as silent as he had been for the rest of the day, but I had questions.

"I wonder what she was arrested for?" I looked at Meena. "Do you think it's true what people say? That she helped murder someone?"

Meena bit the edges of her bottom lip, and I found it hard to pull my gaze away. "It's just . . ." She took as deep a breath as she could manage. "People don't get sent to Vine Valley for any simple crime. It's where we send our most dangerous prisoners so they're out of the cities and towns that harbor people."

"From all over the island?"

She nodded.

"Wow." I didn't know what else to say. "That's . . ."

"For the best," IoN chirped in his mechanical voice.

"You think?" I rubbed the back of my neck with unease. "Doesn't it seem a little . . . isolating?"

"El," IoN said in his taking-no-nonsense voice I only hear him use when he's trying to school me in something other than engineering. "Just think about it for a moment. What would you do with murderers and other serious criminals? We are not talking about thieves or smugglers here."

"Yeah," I whispered. The thought of Bobby being around people like that flitted across my mind, and I instantly changed my opinion. "Yeah, I guess that's for the best." My eyes met Meena's green ones again, renewed with confidence in at least one part of our system. "It's keeping us all safe."

Meena's eyes lit with something akin to pride and delight. "It's in everyone's best interests."

I agreed, not really thinking about much more than whatever would make her happy. "So will finding an answer to your"—I glanced at the strip of golden cloth glinting in the sunlight—"problem."

"Yes," IoN said, "so we best decide what to do from here." He looked at me.

"IoN's right. We need to meet Varissa." Meena stood, a renewed vigor running through her.

"You don't mean . . . ?"

"Yes." She spun on her heel and faced me, her expression set in stone. "We are going to Vine Valley."

18 DAYS. 14 HOURS. 02 MINUTES.

Luckily for me and IoN, Meena was a princess and could get a hold of anything; apparently, even a steamer in an otherwise pretty technologically vacant muddle of villages. We set off into the desert in search of Vine Valley Prison, but I had no idea where I was going.

"IoN," I asked, "do you know the way?"

"Yes." He sat on the hood and held on using his claw-like hands. "My navigational system is up and running. You should head north for a farther ten miles."

"Roger that."

Meena chose to sit in the passenger seat next to me, rather than in one of the five seats available in the back, and even with her scarf wrapped around her head and mask covering her mouth and nose, features barely visible, her eyes glistened in the desert sun.

"What else do you know about Vine Valley Prison?" I asked when the desire to fill the silence overwhelmed me.

"It's manned by over a hundred soldiers we don't have a need for back home. It also has two dozen humans in upper management, making sure everything goes smoothly. Food is scarce out here, so the local villages provide whatever spare food items they have in exchange for other resources and money the capital provides.

"The kinds of people in Vine Valley have always made me shiver. Murderers, rapists, serial killers, terrorists . . . Do you remember that serial killer terrorizing women and children on floor four last year?"

The memory hit me. "Carmen Badaga, right? Rumor had it she used toxic steam to poison her victims in a trapped, air-tight room."

Meena's eyes darting ahead, scanning our environment. "How much farther, IoN?"

"Three miles, Princess Jemeena."

Meena giggled, the sound muffled behind the mask. "You may call me Meena, IoN."

"Very well, Princess."

Now it was my time to chuckle. "IoN, you know she knows you're . . . different. There's no need to be so stiff and formal."

"I am aware of the princess's knowledge of our secret, El." A crackly sound escaped his mouth. "But she is still the princess. She deserves some respect for her position."

"Well," Meena interjected, "it would be nice to be treated like a normal person for a change. Even if only for the next eighteen days."

The reminder of the reason we were here struck my chest like lightning. I grabbed her hand, providing comfort. Though for her or myself, I was no longer sure.

Would it have been better never to have promised her this false hope? To have said no that day she stumbled into the garage and sent her back to floor twenty-one to live out her remaining days in luxury and peace? Looking at her distant eyes now, full of trepidation and hope burning like opposing flames, I wondered if this hadn't been a huge mistake.

But I promised she wouldn't die alone.

If that meant we had to drive to the ends of the earth to make sure she died full of hope and happiness, then that was what I would do.

A half hour later, a line of buildings and drifting smoke arose in the distance like a looming answer no one wanted. But I had to know. I had to find out what Dad was doing with Varissa and why he couldn't save Mom. Or himself.

Why did he leave me?

We drove up to the front, where two bronze statues of humans jutted out of the sand and held up a steel gate thicker than the height of a person. After a long, tense look at the walls, I realized the entire prison was surrounded by a gate of the same thick metal.

There would be no escaping this compound.

"Drive up to the gates, please." Jemeena's demeanor had returned to its Princess Protocol, as I'd been calling it in my head: back straight, scarf pulled down, and a neutral expression on her face. "I'll handle getting us in."

I edged the steamer closer until I could take us no farther, and we waited for what felt like thirty whole minutes before someone came out of a small door within the left bronze statue, just above the feet.

Jemeena stayed seated, so I followed suit, allowing the guard to come to us, but when he did, he folded his arms across his chest and scowled. "What is your business here?"

Meena turned to face him, lowered the scarf covering her face, and smiled. "I wish to see Varissa, please."

A smirk crossed his face and he harrumphed. "No one sees the prisoners here. That's the rules."

Meena looked unimpressed but simply turned to the man with a neutral set to her lips. "Yes, I am aware of the law, having sat with my father when he made plenty of them." His eyes went wide as his skin paled, but she just repeated, "I am here to see Varissa."

"Y-y-yes, Princess Jemeena." He scurried back inside, and moments later a small door rose in the gates, just large enough for one of the bulkier steamer models, and IoN steered us through. Standing on the other side, the guard bowed. "Varissa is on level five. I will get you an escort."

"Thank you. That would be most appreciated."

He bowed and hurried off.

"Do you always get what you want, or is this just an on-the-road kind of thing?" I joked, nudging her shoulder with mine.

IoN sat quietly at the front, as still as a statue.

"One of the few benefits of being royal, I guess." She sounded put out, which wasn't what I meant to evoke. "But there are plenty of expectations I would rather not have to meet, if I'm being honest."

"Like what?"

"I can't be seen in public without dressing appropriately, I need to have perfect posture, I have to be able to give speeches and speak well in general, I have to be educated to the highest standard regardless of what I want to do with my life. I can never take a career or get drunk or fall in love. My life is paved for me." She looked me in the eyes and smiled tightly. "But I never have to worry about money, food, or how to provide for my family. I always have access to the best technology, endless sunlight, and if

I choose, I can just turn a blind eye to all of our city's problems. So, I am blessed in many ways."

"But cursed in many others."

Just as Meena opened her mouth to respond, the steel door to our right opened, and the guard returned with another security guard—probably our escort—and another bow. "This is Beffel. She'll escort you to Varissa, who is being escorted to a well-guarded meeting room."

"Thank you." Meena stood, dusting off her dress and readjusting her sleeves and cloth, then stepped out of the steamer.

I followed, grabbing IoN on the way.

The levels descended on a spiral hill, the cells themselves at an angle, but every now and then, a sign would appear hanging from the cement ceiling telling us what level we were on. There was no wind here, so the signs stayed stagnant, but there were unusual doors beside them. Each with a little window—as opposed to the windowless ones of the cells—with no handle, knob, or visible keyhole, and they had no frame, simply a hinge on one side.

It was only when we reached level four's sign that I realized they were meeting rooms, because Beffel merely pulled on the door and it swung open into a dark space my eyes had trouble adjusting to.

A light hung from the ceiling, illuminating a concrete room with no windows, no furniture other than a single wooden chair, and dusty walls with marks on them I'd rather not think about. In that chair was a pale-skinned woman with hair that fell in two large plaits down to her elbows. Her expression seemed warm, genuine, but the handcuffs on her wrists and ankles bound her to a large metal loop on the floor, and the brown hemp jumpsuit hanging limp from her frame had clearly not been washed in months and were covered in stains. Maybe years.

"Varissa," Meena said, standing in front of her with arms crossed over her chest. "I have some questions."

The two guards in the room looked at us with boredom in their eyes.

"Of course, Your Majesty." Her voice was frail, dry. Cracked from parching thirst, no doubt. "Anything I can help with."

Meena turned to the guards with a scowl. "Leave us."

They hesitated, glancing at each other then back to the princess. One of them said, "We are not supposed to leave you unguarded with the prisoner."

"Leave us. I will take responsibility from here."

They hesitated for another split second before bowing and exiting the room.

I flipped the bolt on both the top and bottom of the door, barring anyone from barging in.

Varissa looked at us with concern in her gaze. "What do you need from me?"

"Five years ago, someone visited you asking questions, didn't they? And you gave him the answer: herbilore."

Varissa's eyes widened, then glanced as far back to the door as possible. "You can't be here asking these questions, Princess."

"Why not?" The question was out of my mouth before I could rein it in. "Why can't we simply ask what he asked?"

"Because if it weren't for that ass, I wouldn't be here." The calm, kind expression dropped from her face, and with it, a snarl ripped forth. "He asked, basically begged on his knees, so I answered. And when it went wrong, which I told him it would, he blamed me. So he got off scot-free after meddling with her lifeclock."

"No way." I stepped beside Meena, frustration bubbling. "He wouldn't do that."

"He was angry that I led him to the herbilore plant, that the plan went wrong. He said that if I had simply said nothing, his wife would have lived another four months. But she died in days."

"No," I whispered, stepping back. "He wouldn't have . . ." Would he?

Jemeena looked at me with sympathy as IoN stayed in my hands. Her eyes dropped to him in confusion and then swept back to Varissa. "What did you tell him, specifically?"

She sighed. "I can't refuse royalty without lengthening my sentence, can I?"

"No," Jemeena said. But I got the feeling she would never follow through with that threat regardless. "And you'd be helping me more than you know."

She looked at the floor and dragged in a deep, defeated breath. "I grew up at the Temple of Seren. I've seen what the priestesses do in that temple, the gifts and curses they enact. And I also happen to know that the herbilore plant grows at the foot of the temple, because I spent years spinning those very plants into a liquid the temple would vial up and ship off to Prago City."

"They'd make . . . what? A potion?" If I sounded incredulous, it was because this was ridiculous. She was talking about some kind of spirit. Some kind of faith. Magic. "I doubt that."

Jemeena held out a hand to silence me before questioning Varissa further. "What does the herbilore plant do?"

"I don't know, but the legends say it can restore life."

18 DAYS. 10 HOURS. 13 MINUTES.

RESTORE LIFE? COULD IT BE POSSIBLE? A FLOWER THAT had healing properties. Jemeena couldn't quite wrap her head around the idea that a simple plant could have such reverent power, and that if it did, the Temple of Seren wasn't sharing it.

Or maybe they were?

Meena had never come across something like that before. At least, she didn't think she had.

Back on the dirigible, she sat at her desk with a pen in one hand and a stack of paper in the other. There was something she had been meaning to do, but time had gotten away from her.

DEAR MINING QUADRANT,

I hope this letter finds you well and that your expeditions below the kingdom are fruitful. I am sorry to inform you that upon the recent inspection of the mines below Palatina, the palace has found your safety equipment lacking, and we are concerned for the welfare of our citizens who work diligently to supply us with steam power. Please use the increase in funds incoming to supply every miner with appropriate attire, and if further troubles are found regarding the safety of Palatina miners, please send correspondence to the following address.

Sincerely,

Royal Palace

UPON FOLDING THE LETTER, MEENA USED THE RING THAT adorned her right thumb to seal it with the royal signet, then smiled to herself. She had arranged for the extra funds before departure but hadn't found the time to write to the mining quadrant. Not to worry, as she would no doubt be able to post her correspondence in due course.

A glass bowl of grapes sat beside the stationery. She popped one into her mouth and relished the sweet juices that caressed her tongue. Ever since her father had brought home grapes from one of his trips to Prago City when she was eight, he had ensured she was stocked throughout the year.

A crumpled piece of paper sat on the edge of the desk, wedged beneath the glass bowl. She yanked it out and flattened it on the wood of the desktop. At the top, scribbled in her four-year-old handwriting, were the words *My Bucket List*, and below that were various items already ticked off over the years, such as *Visit Prago City* and *Learn to Waltz*, but perhaps it was time for a new addition. She gathered her pen and pressed ink to familiar paper. *Apologize to Hera.*

She lay in bed, exhausted from the day. She tried her best not to cough too much, but the hacking raked at her lungs and throat for air, desperately pleading for attention until she had no choice but to give in. Hanging over the side of the bed, she coughed until she could cough no more and blood splattered the floor in small pinpricks.

Jemeena used to say she'd meet death with grace, as everyone expected her to, but now, faced with the very real threat of nothingness, of being laid to rest in the royal tomb as a forgotten princess who never made her mark, she knew she'd take any option she could to stay alive. If the plant could even provide just another day, she'd take it.

How desperately she wanted it scared her. How far she'd go to get it, how much she'd be willing to risk, shook her bones.

She'd do anything to keep breathing, whether on the throne or otherwise, but what would she risk getting there?

18 DAYS. 9 HOURS. 51 MINUTES.

THE PRINCESS WAS COUGHING AGAIN. I COULD HEAR IT from next door, echoing through the metal of the dirigible. She was getting sicker, and I couldn't take it anymore. Couldn't just lay there and watch her die like a withering plant, like she didn't matter, like she couldn't make a huge difference to the kids of lower levels back home—to me.

She made my insides bubble, my face light up, even when hungry and frustrated. She made fighting for her worth every second.

Just as Meena stopped coughing, I shot up out of bed in my camisole and stormed out of my assigned chambers. "Princess?" I knocked.

She didn't answer, but I heard her coughing again.

I pushed her door open and saw her hanging over the bed, gripping the edge of the sheets in pain until her knuckles turned white.

"Meena!" I rushed to her side and pulled her up into a sitting position. "Meena, sit up for me." I turned toward the door and shouted, "IoN!"

He whizzed into the room. "Yes?"

"Could you make some peppermint tea, please?"

"Of course." He flew at top speed to the tea station on the other side of the room and started pressing all the buttons needed. "It will be ready soon."

I helped her sit up, plumping pillows behind her back and yanking the sheets up to her waist so she wouldn't get cold. "Deep breaths in through pursed lips." I kept my voice calm, steady, but I was raging inside. How could she not have help? Did she refuse? Did they not bother to send anyone with her? "That's it."

Her color was slowly returning, and when she tried to say something I shoved a finger to her lips. "Don't talk. It'll just make you more out of breath. Just keep breathing."

She rubbed circles on her chest bone as she stared off into the distance, and when she finally breathed as normally as possible, she unwrapped the gold cloth on her lifeclock and looked at the time. "Same as before," she whispered. "It's never changed, but I'm always terrified it will."

IoN flew over slowly with a cup of tea and placed it on the bedside table. "There you go." Then he settled on the bed in front of the princess. "Are you feeling better?"

"Slightly, yes." She looked at me. "Thank you."

"You're welcome." I got up to leave, but she grabbed my hand and pulled me back down onto the bed.

"Stay?" She inched toward the other side, making room for me. "Please?"

"Okay." I slid underneath the sheets and pulled them back over us.

IoN settled on the bedside table as I handed the cup of tea to Meena, and she sat quietly in the evening light, sipping tea and staring off into the distance, her mind a million miles away.

"Tomorrow," she finally said after she'd set the cup down, "we're going to Prago City."

"You want to find some of that plant liquid? See if it'll help?"

She nodded. "But I also want to know why there's trade in something we know nothing about."

I raised my eyebrows.

"I know most of the trading on the island, El—it's about all I can do from bed—and there's nothing about flower liquid anywhere."

"Maybe it's called something different on the documents?" I suggested, mildly disinterested in trading paperwork but understanding the basics.

"Perhaps. But there's something not right here." She shut the light off and pulled the sheet tight to her chin before turning over and falling asleep.

IoN followed, shutting down for the night.

I was left in the dark, alone, listening to her breathing, making sure it was steady. Making sure she wasn't going to die in her sleep, and that I'd be here if she stopped breathing. Eventually, after what felt like an hour or two of listening and thinking, my eyes drooped and slumber took me.

---

17 DAYS. 20 HOURS. 38 MINUTES.

THE NEXT DAY WE WOKE UP TO A KNOCK AS SUNLIGHT filtered through the edges of the curtains, and IoN whizzed around the room making tea and dragging a chair for Jemeena to sit in when she got dressed.

I slipped on one of Meena's robes as I headed to the door, doing up the buttons as hastily as possible. I opened the door and my eyes met a familiar face.

"Oh, Cinderella," Captain Hera murmured. "I didn't know you would be here. It's the princess's room."

"Yes, we had a bit of a sleepover."

"I can see that."

Meena sat up on the edge of her bed and wrapped a robe around her, also fiddling with the buttons. Once she had done that, she turned to me and said, "I'm ready.".

I opened the door farther and let Captain Hera in. She strode over to the princess and sat in the chair IoN had not meant for her. "Jemeena, I wanted to come check on you. See how you are doing." She looked at me with distaste for a split second before schooling her features and smiling. "I didn't know you had company last night."

It wasn't a question, but the princess answered it anyway. "I wasn't aware you had a problem with me keeping nightly company."

"I . . . I don't."

"Then stop harassing my friend, Hera. It has been many years since we dated, and I—"

Hera held a hand up and silenced her. "I do not need to be rejected twice. We are just friends."

So the princess had ended things with Hera? That was . . . interesting. I wondered why.

"I just came to see how you are doing. Traveling while this ill can't be pleasant."

Meena shook her head. "It is not, but it's vitally important we keep going, no matter how ill I get. If I can't get out of bed, then keep going and get Cinderella to our next destination. If I can't talk, then follow her orders on where to go next. Do you understand?"

Hera bowed her head, clearly understanding that as instructions and not polite conversation from a friend. "Yes, Princess. Of course. If I knew the reason for traveling, I might be able to—"

Meena interrupted, silencing her. "You have asked before—twice—and I have denied you the information. Twice. I cannot tell you." Her gaze softened as she rested a delicate, frail hand on Hera's arm. "Even as a friend. I'm sorry."

"Whatever's so important, I hope it works out for you." Hera glanced down at the princess's lifeclock ticking away beneath the cloth. "I really do."

"Me too." She looked at Hera like a long-lost friend, a memory from a past she no longer had the privilege of living in. "The best thing you can do for me is get me to my destination as quickly as possible. The less time we spend traveling, the more time we spend doing."

She bowed and left, a mixture of emotions playing out on her face.

"I am sorry about her. I didn't think it would be an issue."

I grabbed a bodice and skirt from the closet, a jacket that looked like it would match, drawers, stockings and garters, skirt, and chemise, and we began the process of getting dressed. I didn't have to help her—she probably had someone for that—but I wanted to. I wanted to make sure she stayed seated for as long as possible, only getting up for sections I needed her to stand for.

"Is the corset loose enough?" I asked as I pulled the waist slack tight.

"Yes, thank you." She bobbed on her feet a bit, letting the

petticoat fall over the crinoline more evenly. "You don't have to do this, you know. But thank you for it, nonetheless."

IoN brought the princess her second cup of mint tea and placed a spread of biscuits, scones, and jams on the table to our right. "Breakfast, ladies."

"IoN," Meena scolded, "you didn't have to do that either. I like that neither of you treat me like a royal. I'm just a regular person in your company."

"A regular person who is struggling and ill," IoN reminded her. "We would do this for any friend."

"He's right. This is more about helping you than serving you."

"Then, I thank you. I'm hoping we're in Prago by the end of the week."

"We should make a plan for when we get there. It's a city, so it won't be as simple as finding Varissa was."

"You're probably right," she said as I buttoned up the jacket. "I have a necklace that goes with this jacket in the box over there." She pointed to a small jeweled box on the nightstand. "And a parasol in the wardrobe somewhere."

IoN fetched the parasol while I gathered the most exquisite piece of jewelry I had ever seen.

"This is . . ." I started, not having the words to finish the sentence, but I landed on, "beautiful."

"Yes, I know. Royal jewelers are talented people."

"I bet this costs more than everything on zero."

Meena said nothing, only looked at the floor. "I . . . I guess it probably does."

I went to say something, but I was too late, because IoN beat me to it. "Being born wealthy is not something to be ashamed of. Especially when you don't have a lot of control over how you help others."

"That'll change if we save me. I won't sit idly on a throne built from the deaths of those less fortunate." She stood, determination set steady on her face, hands clenched into fists. "I want to ask when we'll finally get to Prago City, then I can teach you how to play bridge."

14 DAYS. 12 HOURS. 28 MINUTES.

Prago City was three-and-a-half days away, and in that time, I whiled away the hours messing with the broken life-clock Dad had purchased from Green, trying to find a way to piece it all together. Even knowing it measured blood somehow, I still didn't understand what I was looking at.

"Maybe you are missing pieces?" IoN suggested across from me.

"Maybe." Turning the clockface over, I once again examined the steam lines behind it. "I understand the clockface, and I know some of these lines connect to the back, but then what? Where do they connect? Straight to our bloodstream?"

"But then how does it convert that to time?"

I chucked it onto the bed beneath me with a grunt. "Magic? I don't damn well know."

IoN flew into my lap, and I rubbed familiar circles across his head. "El, it's okay if this takes more time. You don't have to get it straight away."

"Time is something we are running out of. She's running out of," I whispered.

"I know." He sounded sad, and I got the feeling he'd sound sadder if he had the ability to do that with his voice.

"When this is done, I'm putting everything I have into upgrading you. I'm done messing around with nonsense. I want to focus on what's important."

"If that is what you want."

Meena walked into the room, slower than usual and mildly out of breath. "Come on. We're nearly at Prago City."

"Right." I shot up off the bed, IoN in my arms, and we followed Meena toward the disembarkation deck. "Er, Meena?"

"Yeah?" she asked as she wrapped a scarf around the lower half of her face, keeping the dust from agitating her lungs.

"I was thinking that maybe we should find a wheelchair once we're there." She went to politely tell me to go to hell, I could see it in her eyes, but I interrupted. "I don't want to agitate your condition, and to be quite frank, we're running out of time. The last thing we need is to have less of it because you're running around everywhere."

IoN wiggled in my arms. "They have steamers with wheelchair access, don't they?"

"Of course they do." She did not sound happy. "I just didn't think I'd ever need one. Or rather, I hoped."

"You'll be more comfortable, and we can get around faster, and—"

"Yes, yes, I understand. Fine." She turned to me just as the platform descended from the dirigible. "On one condition?"

"Mm, yeah?"

"You let me take you out tonight."

"I . . ." My cheeks burned and my chest squeezed. "Of course. I'd be delighted to."

THE ENTRANCE TO PRAGO CITY WAS NOTHING LIKE BACK home; it had no gates to speak of, just a wooden fence guarded by armed men in white cloth that wrapped around their faces and chests in many layers. Bare arms showed tattoos of intertwining lines patterning down to wrists and across hands.

"Prago City is under military control," Meena explained. "Since the royal family can't possibly be in two places at once."

"Who oversees the military?"

"The Temple of Seren."

Meena walked up to the guards, and they bowed, then let us through the fence into a city leveled nearly as high as Palatina. Only, this city had light shafts flickering all across the ground floor in various colors.

"The lifts are a little different here," Meena explained as we walked into a line for a glass tube system that seemed to take people up the levels. "The tubes take you all around the city, not just up and down."

"They go horizontal too?"

"Yes. They're ahead of us in technology, but then they always have been."

IoN said from beside my head, "Prago City has some of the strongest inventors on the island, and some of the best schools."

"Zime Industries has a headquarters here, since Zimeon is particularly fond of the city." His name left her tongue like fire, but she was otherwise neutral.

"So Zime Industries has two HQs?"

"Yeah, but he prefers to spend his time here. Hence why he has a council running things back home."

"Why does he prefer things here?"

She looked at me with raised eyebrows. "Are you using me to get information about your teenage crush?" Hand on heart, she feigned hurt. "The audacity."

"I'm just curious," I mumbled.

"I'm just teasing. You'll see why he likes it here. I think you will too." Getting to the front of the queue, we entered the glass tube by stepping onto the platform, sitting in the seats, and strapping ourselves in. "But seriously," she said while yanking her scarf down a minute, "I'm better than him."

IoN sat on her lap this time, a green light lighting up his face. "Of course you are, Princess."

"See?" She smiled at me, then coughed.

"We'll find a wheelchair on the upper floors," I suggested, hoping she'd know how to do that because I sure didn't.

Once we climbed to level twelve—there were only fifteen in Prago, compared to Palatina's twenty-one—we exited onto a path where various colored stones made pictures on the floor of people dancing. Gold hair flowing as dark stone held a woman up, red dress ruffling.

Looking up, I couldn't help the small gasp that left my lips at the colored buildings all around us; some were solid red stone while others glittered in some kind of weird dark green metal I'd never seen before. It stopped the moment you looked up to where the buildings on top of us glittered in different colors, so the entire city looked like a higgledy-piggledy rainbow.

"It's . . . beautiful."

IoN hovered beside me in silence, but he spun in circles taking it all in, clearly as surprised as I was.

"I told you you'd like it."

"You were right." What would it be like to live here? To be surrounded by so much color and light every day? I tried not to let these upper levels fool me too much—the lower levels were probably not this grand. "We should find a wheelchair from somewhere."

Every level on Palatina had an information desk near the entrance to the elevator buildings, so you could ask for directions and amenities. Maybe Prago had something similar? I spun on the spot, looking for anything that might look like it, and luck was on my side because a stall made from white wood and brass cogs was a few meters to our left.

"Let's ask him." I pointed to the man running the stall. The white tattoos lining his bare face and arms reminded me of the soldiers at the fence. "Maybe he could help."

I slowly guided us over, and the man bowed the moment he saw Meena on my arm. "Princess Jemeena. How may I be of service?"

"I require a wheelchair and was wondering where we might procure one?" she asked, just a hint of embarrassment tinting her voice, but she was her otherwise poised self when interacting with the public.

"Of course, Princess." He bowed before turning to a clipboard with a small stack of paperwork secured to the top. "If you could wait here, I will fetch one for you." He gestured to the stools on which we could sit just beside us.

"Okay, go on. Ask away." She placed a hand on my knee. "I know you have a million questions."

"Where do the different colors of stone and other materials come from?"

"They dye them. Well, most of them. That green metal is mined beneath the city. It's unique to Prago, I think."

"Dying stone?"

"I have no idea how they do it. Sorry. I've never thought to ask. But we can go see the factories on some of the lower levels that do it, if you'd like."

"We can?" I asked, gleaming at the prospect. How did they dye stone? And with what? I knew we bleached stone for the upper levels back home, getting it as white as possible, but this was something else. "Only if we have time. We're here for another purpose."

"A more important purpose," IoN said quietly from the princess's lap. "Where will we be staying while here?"

"The palace," Meena said. "We have a palace building here too, though it's not as grand as the one back home."

You could usually see the palace buildings from anywhere in the city, but here in Prago I wasn't sure which one it was. "Which building is it?"

"It's behind the building behind us."

The building behind us was made of yellow stone with white marble lightning throughout, and it towered all the way up to level fifteen, so I couldn't see beyond it.

"What about the patterns in the floor? How do they do that?"

Jemeena laughed, but only just, as she got out of breath quickly. "I asked that very same question when Dad first brought me here. I was maybe six years old and jumping on all the patterns, pretending to be the dancers." She stared at the one in front of us, the one where several ballerinas twirled in a line. She looked stuck in the past. "They carve them separately and then lay them into the concrete. It's a slow process, which is why Prago City is shorter than Palatina, because the levels take longer to build."

"Oh, wow." They really took art seriously here. It was about more than just form and function; it was about the way the environment made you feel. "I like it."

"Me too. I summered here once for eight weeks. It was an amazing time."

"How long ago was that?"

"Three years. I haven't been away from Palatina much. Father liked to keep me close, hoping for a cure. But he gave me more freedom last year. I think he knows how much living life means when you're dying." She fiddled with the gold cloth on her wrist. "But there's no point, of course."

"Well, maybe we can find an—"

"Princess!" The man returned with two things: a wheelchair and an assisted steamer for us. "Here."

"Thank you very much." She hopped off the stool and stood beside the wooden wheelchair with several cushions and blankets stacked on top, as though its very existence offended her in some way. "That's all we require."

"Very well." He returned to manning his information stall where a small queue had formed while we had waited.

Meena arranged the cushions and blankets how she liked and then sat down with a heavy sigh. "I hate this."

"I know, Princess," IoN said as he joined her on top of the many blankets she had piled on herself. "But this will help us traverse the city faster."

I wheeled her into the steamer and latched the chair into place, then took my seat in front. Hands on the driving stick, I said, "Where to first?"

We started with the palace so we could make sure our things had arrived and that we had a place to sleep. The building wasn't as grand as the palace back home, according to Meena, but it was still larger than anything I had ever stepped foot in. The stone used was pink with purple marbling throughout, which I couldn't even begin to imagine how they had achieved, but it was the bedroom set aside for the princess that blew me away.

I wheeled her inside, through grand white doors with golden handles, and watched her get to her feet and place her bag on the largest bed I'd ever seen. Sheets made from the same silk as her cloak that first day I met her, dozens of cushions, and drapes made from materials I didn't have names for. "It's . . . wonderful."

"It's gaudy. I never used to think much of it. I knew I was lucky, but I didn't realize quite how much." She looked around the room as if seeing it for the first time, seeing how large and grand and expensive it all was. Gaudy, sure. But beautiful in a way that we on floor zero didn't have the mental understanding for. It was as though whoever designed it had a specific feeling in mind while creating it. "But the space does make being wheeled around easier."

"Have you used a wheelchair before?" I asked.

"Dad makes me use one in the palace all the time. I hate it."

"Oh. Sorry. That sounds annoying."

She shrugged. "It is what it is." Sitting back in the chair, she wrapped herself with blankets and settled IoN on her lap. "Okay, we need to visit the exportation offices. I think they're on level ten here. I have some questions."

I wheeled us back outside, into the steamer, and then drove us back to a different tube that took us down two levels. Level ten didn't look too different from level twelve, but there were some interesting buildings down here that looked like various markets. What they sold, however, was beyond me.

"Level ten is the merchant floor. Well, one of a few merchant floors. This one specializes in materials for luxury items, like fabrics and precious stones."

The patterns on the floor once again took my breath away, but this time they showed people in fancy dresses, cutting fabric, setting stones into bracelets, and doing other things that might be done here on this floor. "So each floor's pattern represents the level's function?"

"Yes." She looked to the left, then to the right with furrowed brows. "I think we need to go left."

"You think?"

"It's been years since I've last been here. Cut me a little slack."

"Once we find the merchant office, maybe we could ask them for a map. Or find another information desk."

I steered us left, hoping the princess's memory wasn't something affected by her illness, or we'd never find anything. Just fourteen days left. Then she wouldn't be here—she'd be dead—and it would be partly my fault.

We took another left, then a right, and we eventually came across a group of office buildings for official business, like merchant paperwork.

"Let me do the talking," Meena said, clearly wanting to stand up.

"You have to stay in the chair. That's the deal. And I will take you anywhere you want to go."

She huffed a breath of frustration but remained seated. "Fine. But remember that I'm taking you out tonight."

"Right." Except, I was sure I didn't have anything to wear. "What are we doing this evening?" I wheeled her into the building, having left the steamer on level twelve.

"It's a surprise." She pointed to a reception desk a few meters away. "There. Excuse me?"

The receptionist's head lifted and a practiced greeting graced her lips. "Princess Jemeena, hello. How can I help you?" Her brunette hair swayed as she stepped in front of the desk, her dress bustling with the movement.

"We need to see whoever is in charge of Prago City's imports and exports. We're looking for some paperwork to double-check something."

"Of course, Princess." She bowed her head and shuffled away, her heels clicking on the marble floor.

"Glad you're here with me. I could never have gotten so much cooperation." We both laughed, and IoN's mouth lit up green in happiness. "Hopefully this won't be difficult."

"I doubt we're going to be that lucky. Merchants work outside the purview of the palace. So long as they work within the law, we leave them alone."

"Oh." Great. This was not going to be fun.

The receptionist came back with an escort, who guided us to an office space not far from the entrance. "Mr. Peel will be here soon." She left as quickly as she had come.

The office in question was a drab and dreary place, nothing more than a desk, some shelves, and a rug thrown over purple stone to keep the cold out. Clearly the person who worked here either didn't care for the aesthetics of Prago City or simply didn't spend a lot of time at his desk.

After a few minutes, a large man with a small gray beard and beady eyes plodded into the room and took a seat behind the desk. "Princess Jemeena, what can I do for you?"

"I assume you keep a record of everything coming to and going from the city?"

"Of course." He flicked his gaze to me suspiciously, his hands resting purposefully in his lap. "They're extensive. Is there anything specific you're looking for?"

"Yes, actually. We're looking for everything coming into the city from the Temple of Seren."

For just a fraction of a second, I swore his eyes widened. His fingers fidgeted, but he calmed them. "Of course. I'll be right back."

"I'd like to come with you to collect them," I said. "I assume the princess will be okay here for a few minutes?"

He bowed his head and spun on his heels. "Come along, then."

I turned to Meena. "I'll be back. IoN, stay here."

"Yes, El." He settled in Meena's lap, and she smoothed a calming hand over his head as she often did.

I followed Mr. Peel out of the door and sped after him, trying to keep up with his surprising speed. "Where are the records kept?"

He turned to me with a confused scowl. "In records."

We made more silent, tense turns, then scurried up a small set of stairs that spiraled upward and passed through a door that looked old—older than I reckoned this floor probably was. Inside was shelf upon shelf of folders in carefully labeled piles that were sectioned, then dated.

"We need these ones." He walked to the corner of the room and gestured to a shelf with a small stack of folders. "We don't get much from the Temple of Seren, just what excess they make or grow." He grabbed the first pile, placed them into my arms, then grabbed the second, smaller pile. "That's it."

I looked around, noticing another small pile beneath. "What are they?"

"From the outlying villages up near the Pental Coast. We don't get much from them because it's too far to travel and they don't have steam power."

They didn't? Wow. What did that even look like? Eto Valley had some steam power but not a lot, but what would life be like without? Did they have some other kind of power or did they choose to remain in older ages?

We traveled back the way we had come and sat down in the office where Meena and IoN waited patiently for us.

"Did you find what we needed?" she asked Mr. Peel.

"Of course, Princess." He bowed and placed his pile on the table. "These are all we have for the Temple of Seren, going back the last ten years. We shred them after ten years."

"Thank you," she said, then looked at me.

I placed my pile down, then sat next to her.

Mr. Peel left after asking if there was anything else he could do. Something told me he didn't actually want to do anything else for us.

"Is this really all of them?" she asked me.

"I think so. It was the only folders in the section for the temple. Unless they have another records room, this is it."

"Then I guess we should dig in." She yawned and stretched before opening the first folder. "Should have packed a lunch."

"If you're hungry, I can go find us something."

She waved my suggestion away, instead choosing to look through whatever record she was perusing. "This is just leftover cotton from their sheep."

"This one"—I waved the folder in the air—"is just a stone they purchased for some repairs." After flicking through, I realized I had the importation folders, which meant Meena must have had the exportation ones.

IoN helped Meena, scanning faster than we could and quickly racking up a done pile. There wasn't much here, so it didn't take long to reach the last couple of folders. So far, no mention of plants. But we did learn plenty about the Temple of Seren's financial status, which was not great. They were clearly struggling.

"Maybe we should be funding them better," Meena suggested. "I didn't realize it was this bad."

"Maybe you'll be able to tell your father when you get back."

She didn't acknowledge me, her eyes remaining on the paperwork in front of us. She flipped to one of the few folders she had left and opened her eyes wider. "Here. It mentions a plant juice when describing the item, but it's listed under water."

"Water?" IoN asked. "Plant juice contains water, I suppose."

"It's not even well hidden," I complained. "What does it do?"

Meena shrugged. "No idea. But we'll find out. The paperwork says a Red buys it. No idea who that is."

Red? I'd heard that name before. "I think she's an underground parts dealer. I've heard of her before."

"Then she's going to be on the lower levels, I assume. We can go tomorrow. Tonight, we have a date."

14 DAYS. 10 HOURS. 18 MINUTES.

BACK AT THE PALACE, IoN RESTED ON MY ARMOIRE WHILE I placed my bag in my room, which was conveniently a few doors down from Meena's. Then I took out the only nice thing I'd brought with me, but it was gray and drab and missing a button and I—

A door swung open as an elderly woman burst through. "You must be Cinderella?"

"Yes, ma'am."

"The princess sent me to help you get ready." Some assistants wheeled in a long clothes rack with various dresses, followed by various boxes I assumed were filled with shoes and jewelry. "She thought you might feel out of place without my help."

I breathed a sigh of relief and sagged onto the bed. "Thank you."

A laugh slipped through her thin lips as her eyes crinkled in the corners. "Come on, young lady. Let's get you ready to escort the princess."

Escort the princess? I hadn't given it much thought until now, but I had been on her arm this entire time and didn't really look the part, did I? Should we have purchased better clothes before we left? Yeah, right, El. With what money?

"What kind of dress did you have in mind?" I asked as I brushed past all the wonderful colors. "I'm not used to wearing anything with any real color. Not really a thing on the lower levels at home."

"Here, even those on lower levels wear color. It's a Prago City staple, dear." She pulled a dark yellow dress from the rack and held it up to me but frowned. "Nope. Not that one." Then she carefully placed it back onto the hanger and took out another one. Red this time, but with a deep, curving neckline I was sure would expose more of me than has ever been seen.

Holding it up to me, she beamed. "This one. This is the one. It's perfect."

"It's a little . . . revealing."

"Young lady, you are a beautiful woman in her prime and deserve to feel adored. You're . . . How old are you?"

"Twenty."

"You're a beautiful twenty-year-old lady. Trust me, dear, the beauty only lasts a couple of decades, so make the most of it."

I looked her over, taking in her slim, cinched waist and her sharp shoulders and high cheekbones. "I doubt you've ever been anything but beautiful your entire life."

She chuckled as she gathered corsets and cages and various undergarments. "Remind me to show you some of my childhood photos."

We put on the stockings and garters first, then the drawers. She slid a pair of beautiful red pumps with kitten heels onto my feet, then threw a chemise over my head and tied it up at the back, and grabbed the corset she thought would best shape me.

"I'm just going to tie this, but let me know if it's too tight." Her delicate fingers made quick work of the strings. "There. You're looking like a proper lady." She sounded almost excited, like I was a pet project or something. Then again, I bet she was used to dressing ladies and royals who were already beautiful with all their creams and baths and things that helped them look proper.

Next came the cage and bustle, accentuating my hips and shaping the dress into whatever design she had in mind, and when she was done with tying those into place, we covered the corset with a camisole and placed a few layers of petticoats in various materials to help cover the cage and bustle.

It was already so heavy I wanted to sit down, and we hadn't even put the outerwear on yet. We didn't wear quite this many layers on zero.

"We can take a break, if you'd like," she suggested, clearly noticing my fatigue. "There's a jug of water on the dresser." She gestured behind her.

"Yes, please."

One of the assistants poured me a glass, and I gulped it down. "Thank you."

"Are dresses not this complicated where you're from?" she asked as she grabbed the skirts of the dress off the hanger.

"No, not really. I'm from level zero," I mumbled.

Her eyes widened. "Oh, so this is all quite new to you, then?"

I nodded, shame sending my eyes to the floor.

"Never mind, we'll have you looking fit for a princess in no time." She winked and asked me to raise my arms, then shuffled the material onto the petticoats as I bounced to settle them into place. "There we go, dear."

The bodice came next, and we spent a good half an hour tying it into place, making sure my curves sat right and that it flowed into the shape of my corset. When we were done, she stepped back and looked at her work as though I were a doll for display, a project she'd spent the better part of an hour on.

"You are . . . stunning." She clapped at the assistants.

They scurried forward, placing various accessories on my body, from gloves that reached my elbow to a necklace heavier than any jewelry I had ever held, and they finished it up with a tulle shawl around my shoulders, dipping behind me to my elbows.

"There. Now we just need to make your hair shine and your face all pretty."

The assistants spent the next hour curling, pinning, and styling my hair into what I could only assume was a style to match the grandeur of Prago City, then spent another hour covering my face in uncomfortable creams and powders and colors that made my skin heavy and my face itch. When they were finally done, they spun me around to face the mirror, revealing my reflection. Other than the dress being red with a plunging neckline, I had known nothing of what was being done. It was for the best, really, because if I had seen this in progress, I would have run away screaming.

I looked like a lady. A real, honest-to-Seren lady. You would have no idea I was from a lower floor had you not asked and had I never opened my mouth to speak.

She handed me a fan and winked. "You'll need that in this heat tonight." She left, leaving me to look at the unknown reflection in the mirror, the lady I didn't know existed.

This was what it meant to escort the princess somewhere. Somewhere official, I assumed, or else there would be no need for the dress whatsoever. This was a complete contrast to our usual, easy-go-lucky friendship where we were both ourselves and could relax in front of each other. This was prim and proper. This was nothing I knew anything about.

I hoped I wouldn't embarrass myself.

IoN had been silently sitting on the bedside this entire time, not getting involved, but just before I left, he flew toward me with a green mouth. "You look beautiful, El. Have fun tonight. Forget about everything else and just remind the princess what it means to be alive."

I waited in the lobby for the princess, a large marble room that echoed my every step, the heels marring the peace. At the sound of wheels on the floor, I spun around to face not my friend Meena but Jemeena, Princess of Clepsydra and heir to the throne. She stepped out of the wheelchair, clearly leaving it behind for the evening. Her purple and gold dress fell to the floor in layers that dragged behind her while she walked.

"El." Wonder laced her voice as she looked me up and down, bewilderment dusting her lips as a sparkle lit her eyes. "You look . . . I'm not sure I have the words."

"I don't think I have ever worn so many layers of fabric in my entire life." Lifting my skirts, I walked closer to her and offered my arm. "It's heavier than I thought it would be."

"Some of the royal jewelry, especially crowns and tiaras, are really heavy and can only be worn for a few hours at a time."

"Really?" With her gloved arm tucked into mine, I walked us out the door. "That's crazy."

Waiting outside was a steamer made from that shiny green metal, but it went all the way over a long vehicle, forming an enclosed space, rather than being open.

"We're riding in a stretch steamer?"

"Of course." She waited for the driver to open the door before she slid inside, leaving my hand at the final moment.

I followed, doing my best to shuffle my skirts and the cage inside, but I was sure it did not look elegant. Eventually, I huffed onto one of the seats opposite Meena. "Sorry, that was not very graceful of me."

She giggled, covering her mouth with her fan. "It's okay, I didn't expect you to be perfect. I asked *you* on a date, not some noble lady."

"Right." I looked at the floor. "Where are we going?"

"It's a surprise. But it's nowhere I'll care about what you look and act like, though you do look beautiful." She looked out of the window with glassy eyes. "Maybe if I make it back home, I'll invite you to a ball. Then you'll get to really show off that beauty."

I leaned over, grabbed her hand, and rubbed circles between her fingers. "I will get you home."

"I know you'll try." She shook her head gently, her curls flowing around her face. "Let's try not to dwell on all that. Tonight is about living. And I want to go on one amazing date with you before I die."

The steamer came to a stop, and I pulled her toward the door. "Then let's have fun."

I wasn't sure how to have fun, but I would try for Meena. Apparently, the look on my face when we exited the steamer was enough amusement for her, though, as her laughter sent her into a coughing fit and I had to guide her to the side of the enormous building to catch her breath.

Blood welled in spots on her handkerchief, which she tucked back into her sleeve before anyone else saw. But I noticed.

She was doing well at hiding it, but her illness was progressing, and I had to spend the night ignoring that fact. Somehow.

This was for her. This night was something she wanted, and I was the one who told her to spend her final days doing something she enjoyed, so if going out with me and showing me Prago City was what made her happy, then I'd ignore her illness and the job and the weight of the kingdom's future on my shoulders for a few hours.

"Are you ready?" I offered her my arm.

She threaded her arm through mine and slowly led us to the front doors of the grand building. There was a golden rope barrier forming a queue, but she walked us up to the doorman.

He bowed and let us through, unclipping the rope. "Have a nice evening, Princess Jemeena." He grinned as he looked at me. Not polite or tight or a wow-she-looks-poor smile, but a genuine, real smile.

It might very well be the first of my life from someone other than a friend.

Inside, the building loomed impossibly tall, the ceilings higher than what they logically should be for this floor, but the decorative stonework patterning all the walls detailed scenes from ballets, plays, and various other productions—famous ones, I assumed. I wouldn't know, I'd never been to one. The floor was made of frosted glass, and the sound of everyone's heels clicked and clacked through the cavernous room.

"The ceiling is made of mirrored glass to give the illusion of high ceilings," Meena explained when she noticed me looking. She pointed to a decorative piece of stone that showed a prince catching his princess high in the sky. "That's from *The Prince's Rose*." She pointed to another piece, one of three young girls skipping in a circle. "And that's from *The Ever After*."

I pointed to another—this one detailing two women kissing—and asked, "And that one?"

"*The Princess and the Frog*. She kisses a cursed frog and it turns into a princess she falls in love with. It was the first time two women in love were presented on the stage." She laughed, high-pitched and elated. "I remember when it came out. I was maybe four years old, and all the noblemen scoffed and wouldn't stop complaining about it."

"Is it considered okay for a princess to not like men?" I'd never thought to ask before.

We walked up a grand staircase, taking it one step at a time.

"It's not favorable, but no one ever says anything. I think if I didn't have two brothers who regularly dated women, it would be more of a problem."

Eventually, we made it to the top of the stairs, and an usher guided us to a set of silk curtains he opened and tied with an equally elegant rope to let us through. Behind them were four plush chairs and a table filled with food, some kind of liquid in a glass jug, and glasses waiting to be filled.

"Welcome, El, to the top theater in Prago City. And welcome, equally, to the royal box." She sat in one of the front seats and patted the one next to her. "Come, sit."

"What are we watching?" I asked as I took my seat. I filled up a glass with whatever the red liquid was for each of us and grabbed a small plate of fruit and crackers.

Meena turned down food but took her glass. "It's called *Love in the City*. A play about two people from different classes falling in love." She looked at me and grabbed my free hand. "I thought you might like it."

"I'm sure I will."

In truth, it was a terrible representation of living in the lower levels of Palatina, but then maybe things were different here in Prago, who knew? The love story was, however, more sensational than I expected, more emotional than I knew how to handle, and the acting was superb. It was like it was real, happening right there in front of me.

Meena kept my hand in her lap the entire time, squeezing whenever something made her cry. Watching her watch the play was a delight I would never forget. The way the candles highlighted her lips, the way her tears ran down her cheeks, and the way her hand rubbed circles over my thumb made something in me bubble. Something I had never felt before.

As the final scene was closing and the curtain came down, I turned to face her. "Meena . . . thank you for bringing me here. It was wonderful."

She squeezed my hand once more. "You're welcome, though you spent more time watching me than the play, so I don't know how you can have any opinion of the story itself."

"What I saw was beautiful." I met her eyes as the words slipped from my lips, not entirely intentionally, and a blush crept across my face.

She had the decency to look embarrassed, maybe slightly flushed, but she held my gaze nonetheless. Something in her green eyes fizzled under the candlelight, a heat I didn't expect to be burned by. "Come on," she whispered. "There's something else I want to show you." She guided us outside and stopped to take a breath. "We should take a steamer there. It's a bit far for me."

I grabbed one for rental from the queue around the corner, our earlier stretch steamer having been dismissed, and drove it back. "Hop in."

She strapped herself in next to me and rested a hand on my knee as she tightened her shawl around her shoulders.

"Are you cold?"

She shook her head. "I'll be okay. This is going to be worth it." She drove us toward a larger elevator tube designed to take steamers and we went up to the top level of the city—level fifteen. From there, she took me across three bridges and around more corners than I could keep count of until we came face-to-face with the tower near the back of the city. "It's used for security purposes, but it has the best views."

We got out of the steamer and headed inside to find an elevator to take us up to the top.

"I got lost on this level when I was eight, and I was crying so hard the guard who found me didn't know what to do, so he brought me here while he alerted the palace staff."

The elevator climbed the few meters to the top in a matter of seconds, and we exited to a platform with a small wall around the outside and no roof. Two guards stood on either side, binoculars in hand.

One of them strode toward us. "What is your business here?" he asked before he noticed the princess. "Sorry, Your Majesty. Is there anything we can do for you?"

"No. Please, return to your business. I'm just using your wonderful watchtower to impress my date."

The guards chuckled and turned back around, ignoring us.

She led me toward the side that overlooked the city. The sight took my breath away. Lights lit up every centimeter, like little stars buried in the earth instead of floating in the sky. They were all different colors. You could see down the levels, past the crisscrossing bridges that made up the floors, but the farther down you looked, the fewer lights you could see.

"Everything is so beautiful up here."

Meena squeezed my hand again before letting it go, and for a second I missed it, until she stood behind me and wrapped her arms around my waist and rested her head on my shoulder. "It really is."

"Is it like this back home too?"

"Yes, but the lights are all the same boring color and you can't see down as far." Her hands linked at the front of my chest, holding themselves in place. "It seems more beautiful here, somehow. Less oppressive. But it might just be that I don't have to run this city one day. At least not while living in it."

"Hate to ruin your parade, but technically the royal family rules every city and village on the island."

"Not true, actually. We don't rule anything beyond the mountains, including Vakt Port and the Pental Coast." She coughed a little and then rested her head back on my shoulder. "They're part of the island, of course, and we regularly converse and trade with them, but they're ruled separately."

"I always just assumed the royal family of Clepsydra owned everything."

Her small laugh brushed up against my skin, like candlelight in the cold. "Our politics are not that simple, but we don't really tend to inform the public of things they don't need to know." She took as deep a breath as she could. "But I think knowledge is power, and if we empower our people, then we empower our city."

"That's very wise of you. I would be happy with you as my queen." The fact that it would likely never happen hung over our heads like a cloud, and suddenly, the beauty of the night wasn't enough to keep the moment alive. "I'll do everything in my power to make it happen."

The trip back to the palace in the stretch steamer had me trying not to stare at her beautiful emerald green eyes that reminded me of the leaves on the old apple trees we used to grow on floor zero—and I found myself hopelessly failing in that endeavor. She was like a magnet, the light my wings flew me toward. Her smile was something I liked to swirl around my head whenever I wondered what the hell I was doing here in the middle of Prago City trying to look for a cure to time. Then I'd look at her, and I'd watch her lips turn and laugh, watch her talk about strengthening the weak and supporting those who needed it, and watch the way she fiddled with the gold cloth wrapped around her lifeclock, and I'd be reminded that it was her. She was the reason I was here trying to cure death. Trying to do the impossible because she was worth every second of frustration, every ribbon of grief I wrapped myself within.

I had to save her. No matter the cost.

She belonged in the light.

"What are you staring at?" she asked, closer than I remembered her being.

"How beautiful you are." I couldn't stop the honest words escaping my lips, so I stared at those emeralds and held her gaze, begging her to shut me up.

Her gaze dropped to my lips, then darted back to my eyes, before she leaned in and gently brushed her lips across mine. Testing. Tempting.

Grabbing her hand in mine, I pulled her farther into me and kissed her back, slightly harder but still gentle. Her breath molded into mine as her fingers gripped tightly, as though she was trying to hold on but the kiss was pulling her away. When her tongue snaked along my lower lip and I opened to let her in, she gasped and sucked in a deep breath before plunging her tongue into my mouth and scouring her hands up my sides.

"El . . ." She broke away, catching her breath. "I want to live."

The misty gaze that penetrated mine snapped me in two, broke something within me I didn't think I'd ever find a cure for.

Tears spilled down her cheeks as silent sobs shook her shoulders, and she fell into my arms.

I didn't know what to do. Helpless, useless, I did nothing but sit there, rubbing circles on her back and being a cushion for her to cry into. But it wasn't enough. It wouldn't keep her alive.

But I wanted it to be.

When her sobs had lessened and she could breathe right again, I took her chin in my hand and looked her straight in those tear-stained eyes. "We still have time." Grabbing her wrist, I unwrapped the golden silk and showed it to her. "See. Still fourteen days to go."

She looked at her ticking clock, her time written perfectly for her to see, and I thought, for the first time, that I understood why some people kept theirs covered. Knowing how long you had left to live wasn't always a blessing. Sometimes, it was a curse.

She steeled herself like a princess: deep breaths, tissue wiped across eyes, hands ruffled across skirts, and a gentle smile placed back onto her face. All as though she hadn't been broken a mere ten seconds ago. "Okay. Right. I'm good."

"You sure?"

She looked at me with a brokenhearted kind of strength and nodded. "I am dying. But just because we probably won't succeed doesn't mean I won't try. In the meantime, I'm going to spend my spare moments living." She grabbed my hand and squeezed. "Ready to retire for the night?"

"We have a lot to do in the morning, so yes." A yawn escaped me as though to demonstrate my answer. We got out of the steamer, still holding onto each other's hand, and headed back inside.

My room was down the hall from Meena's in case she needed anything. As I walked her to her door, she turned around and leaned up to me, her lips pursed and her hand squeezing mine. She placed the gentlest kiss on my cheek, barely a whisper.

I grabbed her by the back of her neck and turned our faces together so our lips locked. Her gasp of surprise brushed against me, and I took the opportunity to step closer and press her body to mine, running my hand up the side of her dress. "Is there anything you need, Princess?" I asked, breaking away for a moment to let her catch her breath.

She smirked at me and laughed. "I bet there's plenty you can give me."

Red burned across my cheeks as I stumbled. "I meant help getting undressed or . . ." I wasn't helping.

"Uh-huh. Help. Sure."

"Seriously, I wasn't . . . well, I mean, I wouldn't mind . . ." Crap. What was I thinking? I turned around to go back to my own room, embarrassment quickening my steps.

"Wait! I can't walk that fast to stop you."

I stopped but stayed with my back to her.

"I would love some help, in whatever way you're willing to assist." She wrapped her arms around me and buried her face in my neck. "Even if that is just getting ready for bed and then cuddling."

I turned back around to face her, my face still burning red. "I've never . . . umm. I mean—"

"That's okay." Her hand cupped my face. "It's just living, right?" She led me gently by the hands into her room, as though afraid I might bolt at any moment—which was a well-founded fear because my heart raced and my chest constricted as my stomach tumbled in on itself. Then she lowered herself onto the edge of the bed, where she looked up at me. "But I really do need some help getting out of these clothes."

That snapped me out whatever trance she had trapped me in. "Right." I lifted her back onto her feet and spun her around so I could undo the ties to her complicated dress. "Seriously, how did you get into this?"

"I had help."

"You've never had to consider how difficult something is to get into before, have you?"

She shrugged. "Not really. The lady's maids are trained to do all of that, so it doesn't matter in my life, but I can see how you might have to think about that if you don't have a lady's maid."

I finally had the outer layers untied. I shimmied them down her body and asked her to step out of them. "You're lucky my stepsister has had some seriously difficult dresses before now, and that I was made to dress them."

"Did they dress you too?" she asked as I loosened the corset.

"I haven't had many chances to wear nice dresses. I do rather like this one though."

"You look stunning in it. You would make a beautiful lady, if you so choose."

"I think I'm better suited to being a mechanic, but thank you." She was in her chemise and drawers but still had her shoes on, so I sat her down to take them and the stockings off. "Besides, I don't think balls and parties and dates are in my future."

"You never know. There might be a wonderful man or woman in your future, and you might enjoy it. Someone who's willing to kiss you when you're greasy from having worked all day and who loves IoN as much as you do."

Someone. But not her. Because she was the princess; even if I saved her, it wouldn't be her. I was just a dalliance. That was all it could ever be.

"Maybe. But I'm okay on my own." If it isn't you, I didn't think

I would want anyone else. But I didn't say that out loud. "Come on, let's get you into a nightgown."

She chuckled and turned, then removed her chemise, drawers, and garters so she stood in front of me naked with a smile on her face that I wasn't sure was innocent nor one that had any inkling to put on nightwear. "Or maybe I could return the favor." She spun her finger at me, gesturing for me to turn around.

I did what any decent woman would do when asked something by a royal, I followed orders.

Her fingers brushed against the many layers of skirts and tulle as she expertly untied each and every one, lifting them over my head. Next came the top half of the dress, then the crinoline, and before I knew it, I was standing with my back to the princess in nothing but my underwear and corset. Her fingers deftly loosened the laces, and then I could feel the heat of her fingers run down the chemise beneath, a single layer from my bare skin. So close. Closer than anyone had gotten before. Then went the shoes and stockings, before she turned me around and looked me in the eyes. "If you wanted to retire for the night, I wouldn't be upset. Or if you'd like to remain like this, we could cuddle in bed while ordering all the desserts from the kitchen."

I grabbed the hem of my chemise and lifted it over my head. "Desserts sound good, but maybe later." Then the drawers and garters came off, and I stood just as naked as she was, taking in the gaze that raked up my body.

My eyes finally wandered down past her shoulders, her bare arms loose at her sides. Her breasts were on display above her tight waistline and hips, and then my eyes trailed lower than they'd traveled on anyone and landed on thighs I wanted to grab in my hands. Instead, I wrapped my hands around hers and guided us to the sheets that I moved aside and climbed under, dragging her with me.

Lips pressed to mine, hands roamed my body, heated skin lit every nerve on fire, and I drowned in her presence. Drowned in the waves that held up her soul, the very essence of who she was. There was nothing anyone could say to persuade me that this was a bad idea.

"Live with me," she whispered against my ear as her tongue licked down my neck and then she caught a nipple in her mouth.

I arched off the bed, my hands gripping her hair as her fingers delved into me, her lips seared my every breath, and her eyes stole the sanity from my soul. She worked my body like it was her personal instrument, like an expert in her field, and I rose and fell like the sun in waves as we found our rhythm. As I came down from the high, I flipped us over and got the chance to explore every beautiful inch of her sun-kissed skin, taste every delicious part of her, and yet it wasn't enough.

I could spend a lifetime exploring her, and it wouldn't be enough. But I wouldn't get a lifetime so I'd make sure the time we had counted, that every second created memories.

"El . . ." She lifted my head up and dragged my body up hers so we were chest-to-chest. "I . . . thank you." Her lips closed against mine, and I drank her in.

"I'm not done giving you life yet."

Her small laugh crawled down my body and across my heart. "No?"

"No. Not unless you need me to stop." This was vigorous, and I didn't want to aggravate her lungs.

"No, no, no. It's okay."

"You sure, Princess?"

She cringed, her brow furrowing. "Please, call me Meena

when we're in bed together at least." Her eyes rolled as she folded her arms across her chest, annoyed.

"Are you sure you don't need a break, Meena?"

Her eyes met mine with something in them, something real so I knew she was taking her own health seriously. "No, but I'll tell you if I need one."

"Good. There's no rush. We can take our time." I grabbed her face in my hand and tilted her chin up, smirking at those flushed cheeks and parted lips. "There are still things I want to try."

"I am happy to be your experiment for the night." The bubble of laughter that popped across the room exploded as she rolled us over and pinned me to the bed with spread thighs and wandering hands. "But you should get to experience me too."

Her lips kissed every inch of my body—places I never imagined someone tasting—and her fingers expertly explored every crevice, stoked every ignored cinder into a roaring flame. She took longer in places that excited me, went slower with words of encouragement in places that trembled my nerves and stole my breath, and eventually found a rhythm that made my hips rock and my mind forget about anything but the feel of her skin on mine and the pleasure she wrought.

Sweat trickled onto sheets, breaths panted into the air, and hands wandered across skin as we lived in the present. She taught me to live that night, and I didn't think I would ever forget the pleasure on her face and in her voice for as long as I existed.

13 DAYS. 21 HOURS. 48 MINUTES.

Her bare skin glowed under the shaft of morning light that landed solely on her. She was radiant. She made me shine bright. Just some drab girl from floor zero with no prospects and no money to her name, but when I was with her, I was someone. Not another nameless face the shadows didn't show, but a person. A hope.

Today we needed to find some answers, not another breadcrumb. Hopefully Red would help us find it.

"You're staring," she mumbled from beneath hair and duvets and pillows.

"Yeah, I guess I am." I moved the hair from her face. "Want dessert for breakfast?"

She crawled up to sitting and smiled brighter, her eyes dancing in the light. "Of course I do." She pointed to a radio on the wall.

I got out of bed and ordered a dessert spread to be brought up to the princess's chamber, where we lay in bed and giggled excitedly, neither of us wanting the electricity to end.

We both yanked on robes before a servant knocked on the door, and I'd never felt more ridiculous, wearing a fancy robe with lace all down the sides and white fur from who knew what animal. But the servant said nothing—didn't even look my way—before he turned on his heels and left.

"Guess it wasn't a big deal. Probably could've answered the door naked."

Meena laughed again, a sound I was becoming more and more used to every day. "They're well trained, but I promise they gossip like children in the servants' quarters."

"Will people not say something about finding a nobody in bed with the princess?"

Meena shrugged as I spread the plates out on the bed. "Probably, but it's fine. No one really cares that much."

Spoken with experience, it sounded like, but I didn't say anything. It was a stupid thing to be jealous of. I should be focused on giving her more time rather than on changing the time she had already spent.

I turned to ask her about Red, but she held out a hand as she swallowed a small pecan pie. "No, don't. I know that face. It's your let's-get-some-stuff-done face. Can we just enjoy breakfast in bed for a little while before we have to face the day?" She grabbed my hand and looked at me with pleading eyes. "I'm not ready for it to be over."

I got back into bed, wrapped the duvet around our legs, and we ate the largest selection of desserts I'd ever seen for breakfast—a concept unheard of in my life until this point. But I figured what the hell, sounded like something I'd want to do one day before I died too.

By the look of childish glee on her face as she bit into some kind of pastry, I'd hit the nail on the head. "I have never had sugar for breakfast before," she mumbled around white powder. Swallowing, she continued, "It's always, 'Jemeena, you should eat well.

Your health matters. Everything you do should exude grace and elegance.'"

"And here I am living a life covered in grease and dirt every day."

"Sounds genuinely blessed." She cringed, realizing her mistake. "Sorry, I know your life isn't great on floor zero, I just meant—"

"It's okay. I know what you meant. It's a privilege to have found something in life that makes me feel complete." Only, I didn't know if I was talking about engineering anymore.

---

13 DAYS. 18 HOURS. 42 MINUTES.

IoN WHIZZED ABOVE MY HEAD AS I STROLLED US OUTSIDE, happy to be on another adventure, no matter how critical. We did stay holed up in a dank garage most of the time, and it was no adventure, unless you counted searching for business as our X on the map. Somehow, I didn't think that would be half as interesting as this.

"So, we need to find Red, right?" I asked, my hands fiddling with the material of the skirt I'd chosen for the day. "And given they're likely involved in black-market dealings, they probably aren't from up here?"

Meena shrugged in her wheelchair as I pushed her forward. "You know, I'm not entirely sure about that. Sometimes, the best position to run an illegal enterprise from is right under everyone's nose."

"There is genius in that," IoN said quietly. "And I think this will likely be more complicated than we think."

IoN hadn't questioned why I didn't come back to our room last night, and for that I was thankful, but he seemed distant, focused. Maybe this had his cogs turning more than I originally thought.

"But they would have better access to customers and areas of trade, surely?" I argued. But I knew nothing about living on higher floors, and although Prago City was different from home, it still ran with the same basic principles. "Surely being a little freer would be better for their sanity?"

IoN settled in Meena's arms as he did his best to whisper, "But they would have larger clients up here, customers with more money to spend. You are thinking of a small operation, like Green. But what if it is not small at all?"

"That's a concerning thought," Meena said.

"So where do we start?" I asked once the nearest elevator tube was in sight. "Down or here?"

"We are more likely to get information from those below us, I think," IoN surmised. "They have needs easier to be filled, such as money or status."

"IoN is right." Meena didn't seem happy about it, though. "I can probably just pay people to give us the right information, but if we try that up here, the favors I would owe would be far greater and more difficult to accomplish."

"We don't have time for difficult." I found a tube going down and soon we were in a familiar, albeit more colorful, area of town.

The sunlight didn't quite reach this far, but artificial light bounced off the colorful rock that every building was made from, so it wasn't dingy. It was like a rainbow in the dark. While we didn't have the colors, we could definitely use a system like this back home. Something to bounce a light off so the beam could illuminate an entire street.

Meena was looking up when I came back to the here and now. "What was your genius mind thinking of?"

"Huh?"

"Whenever you're thinking about new things you could invent or getting ideas, you get this wistful look on your face, like you're somewhere else entirely. I was just wondering what it was you were thinking of?"

"The way they've bounced light off the reflective stone is a good way to illuminate dark areas without using too much artificial light we can't afford. If I could use something like mirrors but cheaper, I could light up the lower levels." I looked sheepishly at the floor, my idea probably not one worth explaining to the princess, but it just tumbled out of me.

"Cheap materials? Maybe you could buff up sheet metal? You could probably find some in the scrapyard."

"Then if I angled everything right, I could use specular reflection to bounce the beams off each building."

"I love your mind," Meena said before turning back to the street in front of her with a deep breath. "You're going to do great things one day, and I hope I played a part in that. Even if that's just showing you new places that inspire you."

"Stop it," I scolded. "I am going to save you." Because I didn't know what would happen if I couldn't. I started this journey understanding that it probably wouldn't happen, but she swept me up in her waves, and now I was riding them with as much foolish hope as she was. "You're going to live long enough to watch me try."

IoN shook his head at me before he turned to face the street. I moved my hands back to the handles of the wheelchair Meena really didn't want to be in, but with her condition worsening we didn't have a choice.

The tissues she shoved into her handbag were covered in red splotches—she tried to hide them, but I noticed. I always noticed. Her coughing fits were getting longer, and she was struggling to walk more than a few yards without getting out of breath. It would be hard to hide her condition at this point, and I was sure the public had photographs and the papers were talking about it.

She was dutifully ignoring it all—the gossip, the talk as we strolled by, and the glaring eyes that didn't know how to be polite, even in polite society—and her strength never wavered. At least not in public.

"There's probably some kind of information hub, right?" she asked, a little out of her depth down here.

"If it's anything like home, there will probably be a market square we might be able to glean some information from."

A passerby had clearly overheard us and looked us up and down. He'd gotten out of the elevator beside us and looked like he knew where he was going. "You looking for the market?"

I nodded, a hopefully nondescript look on my face.

"It's over by Pally's to the east. That's the nearest one, anyway." He walked away, not even staying long enough for a thank you.

"He just . . . gave us the information," Meena said incredulously.

"Well, yeah, why wouldn't he help?"

"But he gained nothing?"

I chuckled, trying not to sound too condescending. "When you have nothing to give, people have nothing to gain."

IoN's crackly voice further explained, "Not every social interaction has to be a bargaining chip, Princess."

"There's always a price." The smoke exiting a house we passed forced her to stop talking and take a moment to splutter her breath back. When she could breathe freely, she said, "No one wants anything to do with you if they don't gain anything from it."

That reminded me a lot of Phyllis, but I didn't dare say that. She wouldn't appreciate it. Meena was not Phyllis's biggest fan.

Eventually, we found the market square, which looked similar to the one back home, except, as with everything in this city, the square was more colorful. Bright blues gleamed off a smithy, pinks and purples glinted off a bakery on the corner, and I was pretty sure that specific shade of orange on the dress shop was hard to come by in Palatina.

"So, where did you want to start?" Meena asked.

I looked around at the various open shops and the people wandering in and out of them and cringed. I wheeled her around a few corners until I found an alley with shabby-looking shops whose only sign that they were establishments at all were the wooden boards barely hanging on over the door. "Here."

We walked past what I thought might have been an elderly woman selling her handmade pottery and an older black-haired man selling scraps and nothing of much use, but it was the young gentleman sitting on the front step of a small shop with fancy metalwork in the window that caught me off guard. He was an unusually large size for a lower floor and of a curiously young age for someone with his own shop.

"You make all of them?" I asked.

"I sure do." He stood and dusted himself off. "My dad made them, and he taught me how so I could follow in his footsteps." He gestured to the shop around the doorway he was standing in. "This was his shop."

Meena looked at me with an unreadable look on her face

before turning back to the man and smiling sweetly. "I'd love to look around."

He frowned and stopped suddenly. "I'm afraid I don't have wheelchair access. I'm so sorry." He looked genuinely apologetic for a moment until Meena stood and straightened her dress.

"Not to worry. I can walk. It's just a lung issue." She sounded so blasé about her condition, the one killing her, the one we were hundreds of miles from home to find an impossible cure for. "Can we come inside and have a look?"

Who could say no to those beautiful eyes? I knew I couldn't. It seemed he couldn't either because we were soon gestured inside with a sweeping arm.

IoN stayed in my arms in silence, knowing better than to speak around others, but his eye lights were on, so he was taking stock of our surroundings and conversations. He might have some input later.

The small back-alley shop was quaint, cleaner than I expected, and littered with metal sculptures on every available surface. They ranged from animals to little families and images you'd find in any populated place, but it was the abstract ones that caught my eye. There weren't many, but the ones that he had on display were so curious and weird that I couldn't help but stop and stare at the twisting angles and spinning circles.

Meena slowly walked around, feigning interest until she stood in front of him, arms crossed below her chest. "You have such an interesting collection here."

"Thank you." He looked her up and down, taking in her dress and the jewelry she didn't bother to hide. "Sorry for asking, but who are you?"

"Nobody," she responded vaguely. "I'm interested in how this works?"

"How what works, ma'am?"

She gestured widely to the shop around her. "All of this. How do you keep the customers coming in when you sell things that aren't of necessity. It's not like people have the funds down here."

He shrugged, avoiding her piercing gaze. "I get by."

"But it would be easier on a higher level, no?"

His eyes snapped to her, assessing, calculating. "Sure, but I have no status, no prospects, so why would I even try?"

"Could you not apply to the Creative Guild Grant for moving assistance?" I asked, knowing they had that here, since it was where Palatina got the idea in the first place. Rich people liked art and unnecessary shit, so they paid to have those creators on easier-to-access levels. "I'm sure you'd get through the selection process with pieces like this." I gestured to the stunningly intricate sand gazelle he must have seen on a trip outside of the city—larger animals like that didn't venture close to people often.

He shrugged. "This is my home. Why would I want to move?"

I choked the snark down as I took a second look around. The wood of the shelves was of good quality—clean, polished, new—and the colored windows had three layers to keep the heat out, something most people on lower levels couldn't afford. In addition, he wore finer clothes than I would expect for someone of his social status.

Someone was paying him to stay here.

I'd bet good money that someone was connected in some way to the black market—and possibly to Red.

"Do you take information requests?" I raised an eyebrow as I sealed the lock on the front door and flipped the sign to closed.

He eyed me suspiciously, his gaze darting to the bolt I'd just locked. "For the right price and an assurance of safety."

"We're not going to hurt you," Meena said. "We're not those

kinds of people. We just have some questions we can't ask more official channels." She opened her purse and showed him the small handful of gold inside. "We can pay whatever you want. There's plenty more where that came from."

"If you ever wanted a transfer to a different city and a higher level, or just up the levels here, she could probably make that happen."

His hands stopped fiddling. "Really?"

"Yes." She knew we had him. We had found what he wanted. "If you want a free ride to Palatina, I can take you back with us." She shrugged. "It's not a problem."

"And we can get you the official paperwork once there." I looked at Meena, who probably didn't think of that factor, and tried to look reassuring.

"You really are important." He took a second look at her, an I-knew-it look on his boyish features. "I recognize you, but I can't think from where."

Quickly moving him on, I asked, "So, we're looking for someone, but we're pretty sure they won't want to be found."

"You gonna get them in trouble?" he asked.

"No," Meena said. "If anything, I need their help, and keeping them in business helps me more than snitching does."

"Who you looking for?"

"Red."

Before the single syllable had even left her lips, he threw himself toward the windows and shut the blinds. "Are you insane?" he hissed. "Do you have any idea what that nutjob would do to me if they ever knew I'd ratted on them?" His eyes were crazed, his hands clenched into fists.

"So a worthy trade for a new life, an easy escape, and more

money than you would ever earn here." My lips upturned as I leaned against the wall.

Meena didn't look so calm, but that was okay. I held his attention for now.

"Besides, aren't you sick of it?" I looked at the floor, at the blinded windows, and back at the wooden door I was sure led to a bedroom or a workshop. Maybe both. "This is the only chance you'll ever get."

He followed my gaze, evaluating his circumstance, then his shoulders slumped in defeat as his eyes shifted to his feet. "And you're sure you can get me out of the city safely?"

"I'll escort you to the dirigible myself," Meena said, confidence lacing her tone—confidence I knew she didn't feel. "Immediately, if that's what it takes."

He held his hands up. "No, no. Morning would be better. I have some things to take care of if I'm going to leave the city."

Meena handed him a pouch of gold, her face full of subtle pride. "Then consider this a down payment. You can have as much as a new life costs when we get you to the ship."

I got the feeling more money was on the ship or possibly back at the palace. Either way, we were about to get our information. Red. Potentially holding a black-market cure for Meena's time issue. This could work.

We stared at him expectantly.

He whispered, "She has a warehouse below the old church building, but she doesn't deal with business there herself. I've never actually met her, just Lorcan, her associate. But be careful." He looked at the way Meena leaned on me for support, then back at me with questioning eyebrows. "What do you want with Red anyway?"

"The less you know," Meena answered before I could, "the better."

I gestured widely to the shop and to his clothes. "What operation does she have you running here?"

He smirked as he met my eyes. "The less you know the better."

I didn't know enough about Prago City—I didn't know anything, actually—so I didn't know where to take us next after leaving the alley. He said underneath the old church building, but I had no idea where that was. Guess I could go back and ask him, but I didn't want to arouse any more suspicion than needed.

We used him.

Manipulated him.

Offered him everything he could dream of and more, and now there was a very real possibility of peril for us all. Whoever this Red was, she was dangerous. I didn't want Meena anywhere near her.

Especially now that she couldn't walk more than a few meters without getting out of breath and would have to remain in the wheelchair. It was a vulnerability anyone could exploit.

"I really don't think we should—"

"I'm going." She held tighter to IoN, as though prepared to take him hostage.

"Go without some guards." I looked down at her with a raised eyebrow. "I wouldn't have left you behind." My hands tightened on the handles as I squinted under the rising sun. "But you can't run away and anything could happen, so we should take some undercover guards or something."

Her gloved hand reached behind her shoulder and rested on mine. "Of course. If it'll rest your mind."

"It will."

"Back up we go, then."

We spent an hour or so having some food and rest while Meena arranged for two undercover guards to join us. She also put less fine clothes on after all the looks we got this morning. I, however, put my regular clothes back on, shifting comfortably under the familiar fabric that rested in all the right places, tied where I was used to it tying, and moved exactly as expected after having worn them for years prior.

The guards in question were dressed down, looking somewhat comfortable, but their hair was still gelled in the style of the higher levels and they held themselves a little stiffer.

"Lose the hair gel, and slouch a bit but not too much."

They looked at me like I'd stolen the sun, but Meena agreed, a slight curling of the corner of her lips you'd only catch if you knew what to look for.

They ruffled their hair and dropped their shoulders forward, then looked at me for approval.

"That's better." I looked across their bodies, checking for weapons, but I didn't notice any. "Follow us closely, but don't draw attention to yourselves."

They still looked at me like I was a stranger, like I had no right to give them orders, and I guess I didn't, but this was Meena's safety we were talking about and I wasn't about to hold back for the sake of social propriety.

"And," I continued, "don't talk to anyone about this. If someone asks here in the palace, just say you were escorting the princess around town."

Their eyebrows pinched together, but they nodded nonetheless.

"To be clear," the one with the weird mustache said, "we're

here to protect the princess." He looked at her like she hung the sun, as though she was the most important person in his world, and maybe she was.

"Then we're in agreement."

13 DAYS. 15 HOURS. 18 MINUTES.

I drove Meena down the pipes that lowered us to the bottom floor, having left the steamer on level fifteen in favor of fitting in, and the guards stayed behind, following a few minutes later. I did my best not to look back at them, not to check they were still there, but it was hard.

I didn't trust this Red, nor should I.

My lifeclock was its usual self, so I was pretty sure we weren't going to die doing this; but that didn't mean we weren't going to get injured or imprisoned or tortured or any number of things while still alive.

Some people viewed the lifeclocks as though they were their saving grace—the knowledge of when they going to die keeping them at peace—but I thought it was a burden. There were other things that could go wrong. Other things to watch out for and avoid in life. But no one ever talked about those.

"Stop panicking," Meena said as we walked back past the cracked fountain in the center of the shopping district on level zero. "I can hear the wheels turning in your head from here."

"Wha—? I'm . . ."

"Whenever you're silent, you're working out that big brain of yours by either puzzling out how things work or worrying. In this case, I assume it's worrying. Give your brain a rest, El."

"When you've figured out the off switch to allow me that, please let me know."

"I certainly figured it out last night." She snickered.

My eyes rolled of their own accord, a blush burning my cheeks. "I'm just worried this will go wrong somehow. I have a bad feeling."

"I know." Her hand rested on mine on the handle. "Me too. But this is the closest we've had to a lead all week."

She was right. Of course she was. But that didn't stop the worry from rocketing across my brain like a pendulum, swinging from one concern to the next.

Meena thought she knew where the church might be, given where the it was on the higher levels, but I wasn't so certain. Not everything was lined up like that here in Prago City. Sometimes it was a shop, then on the level above it was a cluster of small houses, and above that it was a barber shop. In Palatina, things were always stacked on top of each other according to what the columns of buildings were. It would be a shop in that position on every floor. Except for the palace, which had royal embassies below it; of those, all below level fifteen had, apparently, been abandoned long ago.

Meena led us through the streets, past the sellers that lined a whole road, their wares laid out on patterned rugs on the floor, some with makeshift canopies overhead to keep out the overbearing sun.

To think of that. Keeping out the light here on zero. It was different here, but there was no doubt an endless list of different troubles to go along with that.

We walked through a tunnel that seemed to serve no purpose at first. It opened into a shabby stone court with a well in the center. People milled about carrying umbrellas seemingly made for shade and wearing brightly colored dresses over bustles that bunched behind them to enlarge their rears.

"I think it's around the corner from here." Meena looked up with wide eyes and mouth agape. "There are no buildings on top of this section. It's just . . . open sky."

I followed her gaze. Just as she had said, they met the sun. The real sun. No wonder people seemed happier here.

Meena turned in her chair to face me, a small smile on her lips. "What do you like best about Prago City?"

"I . . . it's so bright and colorful."

"Maybe one day you can move here, set up a new garage and start afresh." She stared ahead as she said it, a carefully placed mask on her voice, but I caught the crack at the end and the single tear sliding down her cheek before she brushed it away along with a wayward strand of hair.

"Maybe."

The corner she had pointed at earlier came into view, and what stood beyond it took my breath away. The church was stone as white as any I'd seen, streaked with teal, and it spiraled so high, it was a wonder it all fit onto a single floor. It no doubt didn't. The church, like the one back home, likely extended to all the floors. It seemed endless from here on the ground. An endless white building that held many secrets.

Around us I expected people or shops, or even a courtyard, but this was a dingy corner surrounded by houses, the white stone the only light in a dark crook of a place. So sharp in contrast to the courtyard of light mere moments away. Someone closed their shutter a few houses away, and a mother pulled her child into a building behind us, frowning and shaking her head.

The guards slowed to a halt behind us, following at a distance. Even silent, they were a reassuring presence. No matter what happened behind those doors, the princess would be safe.

That was all that mattered.

"I think it best we find a side door," Meena whispered, though I didn't know why. "Maybe we can find more information if we aren't seen."

One of the guards took the right side of the building and told us he'd be back shortly, and after a few minutes he returned from the left, having done a full circle around the building. "There's a locked backdoor and two side doors, both of which are open."

The other guard looked at us again with that confused brow and said, "I hope you know what you're doing, Princess. This doesn't seem like the kind of place you should be."

She frowned at him and uncurled her fist with a deep exhale. "I know. But it's important. Which door do you think would be best?"

"The left had fewer sounds coming from behind it, so that one."

I wheeled her chair onward, taking a left. Meena's lifeclock caught my vision, sneaking out of its usual golden cage as the cloth slipped. It ticked thirteen days.

The door was a haggard old thing made from some kind of dark wood—it barely stayed on its hinges, much less managed to keep people out—but it swung open with minimal noise, only a slight shuffle against stone.

Once inside, darkness engulfed us, but none of us dared light a lamp.

"He said the basement, right?" I asked Meena. "So we should find a way down below ground level."

Taking one of three paths—the one without a door—we made our way around the building, hoping we didn't see anyone or bump into anything that might give away our presence. The only thing going through my mind the entire time was that I was thankful Meena had hired a good wheelchair, because any squeaks from lack of oil would have echoed throughout the cavernous stone hallway. Eventually, after a couple of dead ends and a few turns, I found a set of stairs.

The guards stepped in, one taking the princess and the other taking the wheelchair, as I led us down an even darker corridor of stairs that spiraled to the floor below.

Eventually, when I thought we had been climbing down for so long we would exit at the center of the earth, I came upon a door.

"Careful, El." Meena's voice echoed, and she quickly sealed her lips.

"I know," I whispered.

The door was barred with a lock the size of my fist, with a gloomy keyhole that stared at me as though mocking my skills. I whipped out a set of pins from my belt and got to work picking the tumblers one by one. A tricky endeavor with this lock, as it had a few corners to navigate and some rusting that made some of the tumblers hard to unlatch, but eventually a click echoed through the air and landed upon our ears.

"Not so terrible now, are you, lock?"

I swung the door open with a loud squeak that made me wince, then sat Meena in her chair as quickly as possible before entering and finding a store cupboard to hide in just around a corner.

"This place is nothing but dank corridors and confusing

corners," one of the guards complained. "What are we actually looking for?"

"A warehouse," I responded, hoping to shut them up.

But they just asked more questions.

"A warehouse containing what?" the other asked.

"Nothing that concerns you," I snapped.

When it was clear no one was coming to investigate the suddenly unlocked door, I let us out of the room and took a real look around. The dusty corridor was spacious and had various shelves littering the space. I took a step back, examining the whole, and I realized it wasn't a corridor at all.

"It's a workshop," Meena whispered seconds before me. "Do you think it's Red's?"

I shrugged. "Take a look around before someone comes in here and we have to explain ourselves."

Meena spent a good while searching through papers at the desk while the rest of us rifled through bottles of things I didn't recognize and jars stuffed with various rocks and plants and strange liquids I couldn't identify.

"Even if some of these are what you're looking for, I wouldn't be able to tell," one of the guards said. "Do you know what it looks like?"

We didn't answer, and he groaned under his breath.

"He's right, Meena." I wiped an exasperated hand over my forehead. "Some of this could very well be what we need, and I'd look right over it."

"Here," she said, pointing to a paper in her hand. "We need this."

In her hands was a diagram of an unassuming plant with tiny leaves on a long, winding stem that looked for all the world like it could have been a weed growing among the moss back home, and

I wouldn't have taken the slightest interest. On the back of the paper, however, was a detailed list of all the times someone had ordered some and at what cost.

It seemed the Temple of Seren was much richer than anticipated.

"Where did you find that?" a strange new voice asked.

Fiery red hair and a strange accent graced my senses, and for a second I didn't understand that I was looking at a person of this island, let alone this city. But here she stood. "What are you doing?"

The hood of their cloak came down, and more red hair spiraled in long locks around her face and down past her waist, her blue eyes hesitating on mine. When she clicked a gun in our faces, however, I shook my stupid brain free of its shock and held up my hands.

The guards, however, raised their own guns and were now in a stalemate with what I assumed was the owner of this workshop.

Her red cloak shined in what little light her oil lamp gave off, but the clothes beneath seemed less clean, as though it had been a while since she'd had time to get around to the task. "What are you doing in my workshop?" she asked through gritted teeth. "And where did you find that paper? I've been looking for it." She didn't move, but she did consistently dart her eyes to the piece of paper in Meena's hand.

I was reluctant to hand it over, but I would if it kept Meena safe. Meena, on the other hand, only gripped it tighter, and I had to repress the frustration that lodged in my throat.

"We," Meena began, "stumbled in accidentally while getting lost in the church."

"Sightseeing," I confirmed.

"I see," she said as she lowered her weapon. "And on this tour, did you manage to see everything you wanted, Princess?" The surprise on our faces forced a chuckle from her lips. "Did you honestly think I wouldn't know who you are? And there are no ways into this part of the building from the church above us. Only through a side door and then a locked cellar door that was curiously unlocked when I came upon it."

She took a deep breath and walked up to Meena, placing the gun to her head. "Hand that over, and I won't blow your brains out here and now."

Meena gripped the paper harder, but I snatched it from her and handed it over. "Here."

"El!" Meena whined.

"It's not worth your life!"

She stood from the chair and scowled at me, fists clenched tight. "It's the only chance I have at a life!"

The woman standing in front of us changed her expression and lowered her gun, defeat evident on her face. "Princess, I'm afraid I cannot help you."

"But—" she started.

"I know what it is you seek, but in all the years my predecessors and I have searched, we have yet to find the answer."

"So," I began, "when my father came looking, he didn't find the answer either?"

Her eyes met mine in a hazy fog of recollection, and the moment the dots connected, surprise crept across her face. "You're Preston's daughter?"

I nodded, my eyes darting away from hers.

"He was a great man. If anyone could have figured it out, it was him, but he couldn't help me. Nor I him."

My brow furrowed in a silent question she answered before I could speak. "He had a daughter at home who needed him, so he couldn't stay and help me discover the answer." She stepped in front of me, her feet almost silent on the stone, and she lifted my chin so our eyes connected once more. "I never understood his decision back then. But looking at you now, I get it. He chose you."

My cheeks blushed crimson, and I didn't know what to do with the attention now searing at me. Luckily, Meena did, because she grabbed my hand and cleared her throat. "Excuse me, but can we get back to the task at hand?" Her irritated scowl amused me. "After all, it's my life we're focused on."

I rubbed small circles on the back of her hand and squeezed gently. "How far have you gotten?" I asked.

Running a hand through her long locks, Red grabbed the piece of paper out of Meena's hand. "I've been looking for this for days." She held it up and pointed to the plant. "This is a plant that grows in the blessed sands, and it has the ability to alter someone's state of time, but our lifeclocks are complicated, and no one seems able to work with them properly."

"It's forbidden," I reminded her, "so no one has ever learned how." My hand fiddled with the broken lifeclock in my belt pouch, the one from Dad's old stuff. "Do you have some herbilore with you?" I rushed to the desk and laid the old lifeclock pieces out, lining them up and trying my best to put them together. But just like before, I didn't really know how some of these pieces—several of which I had never encountered before—fit. The outer pieces weren't a problem, but the internal mechanism was like a puzzle inside a maze, and I couldn't see up from down.

Red placed a vial of dull green liquid beside me, no bigger than my pinky finger, and I grasped it. Red's fingers, however, didn't let it go. "My father and his father and his father before him tried hard to figure out how to apply this medicine to a lifeclock, but no one got anywhere, and I inherited the problem." Her fingers let it go. "I don't have much, and it's very expensive stuff."

"What happens when you just simply drink it?" Meena asked.

"It kills you in seconds," she responded off the cuff. "The plant is poisonous."

The guards had been silent with their guns by their sides since Red had holstered hers, pretending to ignore the information in front of them, but it seemed their ability to do that had come to an end, because one of them asked, "So, you've been looking for a cure to time?"

"Princess," the other asked, "why are you looking for this?"

"I'm afraid I cannot tell you that."

He only had to look at her wrist and the wheelchair she sat in to put the pieces together, and his face smoothed out intentionally as a solid picture formed in his mind. The truth, I imagined. He didn't seem the stupid sort.

Instead of more questions, he pulled her blanket up farther and stood back, grip tightening on his gun, but he was silent.

"While I can use trial and error, I really won't know if I have done it right until I've tested it on someone." But I couldn't do that, because what if I killed someone?

"And you see the problem," Red said, her voice half snark, half defeat. "Every time I come up with a potential new idea, I have to test it."

Everyone's eyes flitted to hers, accusation in them.

"Oh, get off it. Of course I've tested it." She gestured around the dark stone room with her gun. "Does this look like the lair of a sane person?"

I stepped closer to Meena while I worked, placing myself between her and Red, and tinkered faster, aware of the eyes on me and the time-sensitive nature at hand. But no matter how I placed the pieces, how I connected what to what, I got nowhere. "I'm missing something."

Meena snatched the piece of paper back from Red and scowled at the writing on the back. "You get this from the Temple of Seren, yes?"

"Yes," she said as she rearranged bottles on the shelf opposite us, again, not turning back to look at us.

"So maybe we need to take this to them?" she asked. "Maybe they have answers they don't want to share."

"But they might share with you?"

"Being the princess does have its privileges."

13 DAYS. 12 HOURS. 37 MINUTES.

"Meena, there's something I need to do before we leave the city."

She looked at me with raised eyebrows.

I slipped the envelope Lapis had handed me out of my cloak pocket and handed it to her. "Do you know where I can find this address?"

She looked it over and frowned. "Sorry, no, but hold on a moment." She turned to beckon one of the guards still trailing behind us and handed him the letter. "Could you please escort us to this address?"

He stared at the writing for a moment and paused in thought. "Please, follow me."

We followed the guard down a few levels, twisting and turning in the elevator tubes, until he found the green- and blue-stained street that matched the address. "It's the property with the green door over there." He pointed to a door in a dark shade of green that seemed to shine under the sunlight. Purple flowers hung from small baskets pinned to the wall on either side of the door.

Standing outside of it, I took a deep breath and used the heavy knocker in front of me.

A familiar man with a short beard and a dark red top hat greeted me with wide eyes. Faryl. "Cinderella! How lovely to see you. I was not aware you were traveling to Prago City."

"Yes, it was a last-minute arrangement. May we please come in?"

Faryl looked at the princess and dipped his head. "Lovely to meet you. I'm Faryl." He lifted his top hat in greeting and sat us down in a lounge with lots of heavy drapes and a large fireplace I didn't understand how he used in a city this warm. "As lovely as it is to see you again, I have to inquire as to your intentions."

I pulled the envelope out of my pocket with a frown, unsure if I really wanted to be in the middle of whatever was going on with my stepsister and this man. "She begged me to stop by and deliver this myself, to make sure you received it." Not entirely true, but he seemed to buy it.

He wiped a stressed hand down his beard and took the letter from my hand. "I have tried explaining myself, but she doesn't seem to understand the need for me to provide her with a good life."

"I'm not an expert at love, nor do I know the ins and outs of your relationship with Lapis, but sometimes love grows fonder when you face the hard times together, rather than pushing her away and trying to do everything on your own."

We sat in plush armchairs adorned with more cushions than were reasonable and sipped toffee and tea while I played love guru for my stepsister—a role I was ill-equipped and under-experienced for.

"She deserves the world, Cinderella," Faryl said with a certain wistful tone I had come to associate with Meena and her garden.

"I can't give it to her just yet, but I will. I'll give her everything she deserves."

The honesty momentarily took my breath away. I didn't know what anyone would see in Lapis, but clearly he saw her as a diamond. "Did you know she designs dresses?" His eyebrows rose. "She's been shoving the pages down the side of her bed for as long as I can remember. She likes to draw ones with high necklines and short sleeves that match the individual she draws them on. Sometimes I'll wake up in the middle of the night and hear her scratching away."

His arm rested atop the armchair as he crossed an ankle over his knee. "She always talks about the dresses in the shop windows and gives me an analysis of every dress of every ball we attend and tells me which one won her favor that night."

"I think, if given the chance, she would make a great designer." I smiled at him, trying to infuse confidence. "But I don't think she can do that from back home. But look at this." I gestured to the room around me in wonder. "You live here, working on your own apprenticeship, in a location in Prago City she might have a shot at living her dreams in."

"Maybe," Meena added, "instead of pushing her away, you could bring her with you and work on your dreams together."

After tea and chatting about what he had been up to since moving here, we left, and Meena insisted she had to pick the shopkeeper up herself before heading back to the dirigible, so I found myself once again on the ground level of Prago City browsing items in a store I'd walked into just for Lazuli, looking for her stupid hair dye. The lady helped me choose a color or two, and Meena paid, of course. The colors in question were lavender-violet and an ocean teal I thought would look nice with Lapis's favorite cloak, since I couldn't find a red that would work with her already dyed hair.

Seren, what was happening to me? I was thinking nicely of my stepsister.

She might have been an annoying pain in my butt once upon a time, but nowadays she'd grown out of the hate. She'd kept a number of my secrets over the past two years, even if those were just so she could use the garage as a rendezvous for her and her lover. Maybe they would get married. Maybe they would move here to Prago City, where he lived.

That'd be nice. She'd like that.

Phyllis would not.

And I did not plan to be home during that conversation.

We left with the hair dye and a new golden comb that had a butterfly on the handle I particularly liked, so Meena had purchased it for me.

"That was far too much to spend on a comb," I complained as we strolled around the fountain and found a shaft of sunlight to sit in.

"But you like it, don't you?"

"Well, yes, but—"

"Then quit complaining." She took my hand in hers and met my gaze. "I'd buy you a house and a life if I thought for a second that you'd let me. At least let me buy you a comb." She tucked a wayward strand of hair behind my ear. "This way, if you find yourself in a spot of financial bother in the future, you have something to sell that might help."

I didn't have the heart to tell her I could be freezing on the streets, starving to death, and I would still never sell that comb. Instead, I placed a gentle kiss on her lips and leaned my forehead against hers. "Thank you."

We fetched our black-haired metal worker a few minutes later, and we separated in a hurry—well, I separated in a hurry, Meena seemed not to care.

"I hate to be a bother," the shopkeeper said, "but if we could move quickly, that would be great."

I started pushing Meena's wheelchair toward the nearest lift tube, and we took a few lefts, a couple of rights, nearly got lost down an alley I didn't like the look of, until our new passenger, Billary, got fed up of following us around and took charge, quickly leading us to a set of lift tubes that could take a wheelchair.

Meena and I took the wider one we'd fit into while the others took the individual ones next to us, and eventually we shot up the pipes and landed on level twelve, not too far from the royal embassy. Thankfully.

As we stepped out of the tube, however, red hair flashed and a sharp grunt echoed from beside me. Billary's panicked eyes darted around, trying to figure a way out. But he was stuck behind Red's knife.

She smirked and pressed the knife to his neck tighter, drawing a little blood.

Billary whimpered.

"Well, well, well," she cooed. "Look who ratted me out to the princess of the realm. Billary, dear, you know the rules."

"No, please," he mumbled. "I'm sorry. Th-they offered me a new life. A fresh st-start. I . . . couldn't say no."

"Hmm," she considered. "Not a bad deal. Shame what they're looking for is something I've been searching for my whole life." She stomped on his foot, and he howled in pain.

"Let him go!" Meena shouted, panic lacing her face. "Let him go, and you can come with us." She looked taken aback by her own suggestion, but it was out in the open now.

Red's eyes lit up, and she lowered her knife with a maniacal grin. "That, Princess Jemeena, sounds like a deal." She sheathed the knife and stood behind us, gesturing ahead. "After you."

With Red an ever-threatening presence by our side, Billary a nervous wreck anywhere near her, a tired and mentally exhausted princess, I was anything but cheerful when we did finally make it back onto the dirigible.

Red and Billary were placed on the other side of the ship, in similar rooms to ours, so when we finally settled in and had a minute to ourselves, I exhaled loudly and slouched into an armchair in Meena's room.

"I don't trust her," I said.

Meena, lying on the bed and staring up at the ceiling, flitted her eyes my way and then back to their post. "Me either, but we do not have a choice. Hopefully, she will just . . . return here after we visit the temple, and we can all go our separate ways."

7 DAYS. 10 HOURS. 15 MINUTES.

Six days later, and Meena was quiet. Even sitting in the steamer with a scarf around her face, where she could breathe okay and avoid the sand, she was almost silent. She only answered questions with short sentences, not engaging in full conversation.

"Have you ever been to the Temple of Seren before?" I asked, once again trying to snap her out of her thoughts.

"Once or twice when I was young."

"What's it like?"

She shrugged her shoulders. "I don't remember much, just lots of stone walls and women in white."

Red butted in, answering my question instead. "The women in white are the priestesses of Seren, and the temple is the only place they reside. The cities are where they send the priests. The priestesses educate young acolytes, maintain the temple, which is the oldest structure on the island, I believe, and apparently have a secret anti-aging plant they've been denying me and my ancestors for hundreds of years." The last part was said through gritted teeth, but she kept up the pretense nonetheless.

Maybe we should keep her away from the priestesses, or at least make sure she wasn't alone with them.

The guards from our trip to Red's lair sat beside her, but others trailed behind and in front of us in two-person steamers. More guards than I was used to Meena using. We left Billary on the ship. There was no need for him to be in the way here. IoN sat in Meena's lap, like he often did.

The distance was nothing but sand for the better part of an hour, and I found myself wondering why we landed so far away, but I didn't bother to ask Meena, because the moment I looked at her, I found her staring into the distance with deep thoughts in her eyes and her hands running familiar circles on IoN's head.

After a while, when I was wondering if we would even get there before nightfall, something angular peeked over the horizon in the distance. The point grew in size the closer we got.

"Is that it?" I asked, leaning as close as I could get to the front of the steamer.

"Yup." Red fiddled with one of the belt loops in her pants and followed our gazes. "The Temple of Seren." She seemed less than pleased, and I couldn't figure out if it was a good thing she was nervous because it meant she was worried about whatever scheme was brewing inside that crazy head of hers or if I should be worried by whatever had gotten the confident maniac on edge.

Either way, though, I was apprehensive, and I got the feeling it was going around. Meena seemed to fiddle with the rings on her fingers faster the closer we got, and even the guards kept looking from left to right with increasing frequency.

The building loomed larger in the distance until I could make out a gate barring entrance to many buildings that were all connected to the massive temple in the center, which stood proudly, seeming to grow toward the sky. I had to look up to even see the roof.

"It's huge," I whispered, the atmosphere tense.

"It's the largest temple in the world." Meena stood as we came to a stop. "And it's where the inhabitants all stay until they complete their education, unless they are women, in which case they stay there a lifetime."

"You're allowed to leave if you want to leave the holy service," Red said blankly.

We stared at her, but she had her back to us, having already stood to follow the princess's movements.

The gate was a rusted set of metal spikes that dug into the ground and stood twice my height, but someone was on the other side in moments, waiting for one of us to exit the steamer.

Meena went for the steps, opening the door, but I got there first and helped her down. I tucked her arm around mine, ready to be leaned on if needed, and guided us toward the person dressed in white from head to toe.

"Princess Jemeena," she exclaimed upon seeing us close up. "What an honor. Had I known you were coming, I would have arranged rooms and a feast."

"That will not be necessary," Meena said, straightening her back. "All we require is your time."

The lady bowed her head and unlocked the gates, signaling the young guards, who were probably acolytes, to open them. "Welcome," she said after we stepped inside, "to the Temple of Seren."

With the princess in a wheelchair she clearly hated but wearing a strong and purposefully neutral look on her face, we all stepped onto the temple's grounds and were taken on a tour through the front gardens, which became more of an oasis the farther in you went, as though the sand itself was repelled by the might of Seren. It started with small shrubs with barely any leaves growing randomly out of the ground and ended with luscious palm trees and bright pink flowers with spikes on their long stems.

The doors to the main temple were the largest I'd ever seen, with ornate carvings of old on the front depicting what our guide said were the origins of the women in white. "The early texts say that three women found themselves in the desert, starving, near death, and they happened upon three white dresses and headscarves in a pool of water. After donning the material and drinking their fill, the ground split apart, and out of the desert's core rose the Temple of Seren, the first of three to rise over the course of their lifetimes."

"Are the original three temples still here?" My fingers played with the hem of my collar, my mind racing.

The woman grinned as she looked at me, her gentle face at ease in the heat. "Yes, but we don't use them often nowadays for fear of the old structure falling apart." She looked at Red for the first time, their eyes meeting in an exchange of knowledge, as though they shared a secret. "But they're still used for certain rituals."

Red's face fell to the floor, a fury of crimson crossing her cheeks as her fist clenched and unclenched at her side.

"Would you like me to make up a room for you and your companions, Princess?" she asked, looking down at Meena.

Meena considered the question for a moment but shook her head. "I would like to speak to Lady Lorelai first, Serena, then I'll know how long we might be here."

Serena bowed, a puzzled look crossing her brow for a mere moment, then she gently rapped at the doors. "It takes a moment to open these doors, I'm afraid. The mechanism is old and must be worked by hand."

Meena waved her concern off, acting the perfect royal guest, but I could see the frustration bubbling beneath the surface. She wanted to speak to this Lady Lorelai as quickly as possible, and I didn't blame her.

Red, however, seemed to feel the opposite. She continuously turned her gaze back to the front gates as often as possible, standing as far away from Serena as polite society would allow. She was a mystery, this woman, and there was a part of my brain that wanted to unravel it and gaze at the depths of what made this woman the murderous criminal she had become. But I restrained myself. However dismayed I might have been to be associating with someone like her, she was not a puzzle for me to solve, she was a person.

The doors slid open on massive bronze runners embedded in the dark stone floor, the sound rumbling like thunder. If I thought the doors were beautiful, it was nothing compared to the opulence inside the cavernous space. Columns the size of small houses stood in rows of twelve and soared into the ceiling that was so high, I couldn't make out the details etched into the stone. The floor, made of the same stone as outside, had patterns of the same flower etched onto its surface over and over again for as far as the eye could see. I grabbed the pieces of paper from my pocket and shuffled through them until I found the one with the plant drawing and held it to the floor tiles.

They matched.

That was the plant we were looking for.

Fires lit the edges of the circular space one by one in large alcoves until the dais at the back center lit up in orange flickers.

"This is the main temple used today," Serena said, waving a

hand over the space in indication. "It is where we hold daily sermons and teachings, and it's the first space the acolytes are permitted to use without instruction."

"Forgive me, Serena," Meena said, "but I would love to see Lady Lorelai first and take the tour after. It's of the utmost importance."

Serena's gaze flickered to Meena's wrist and the edges of the golden cloth cover, her eyes squinting with suspicion. "Of course." She bowed her head and rushed off, gesturing for us to follow.

Red was suspiciously silent throughout the journey down a series of alleyways and hallways until we reached a narrow staircase the wheelchair wouldn't fit through even if we could carry it. "Looks like you'll have to be carried up, Princess."

Serena looked at her with sympathy. "Can I call for some acolytes to help?"

Meena shook her head and stood, determination etched on her face like the drawings in the temple's stone floor. "I can make it." She had a look I knew all too well.

She might need help, but she didn't want it from them.

I wrapped my arm firmly around her waist, prepared to help lift some of her weight, and we crawled up the stairs, taking a break every four or five to let her catch her breath.

"I am sorry for your health, Princess," Serena said. "Is there something that can be done?"

Meena shook her head once she reached the top. "They do not even know the disease, let alone how to cure it."

"I am sorry."

Even Red looked at the floor, a sympathetic expression crossing her eyes. "I, too, am sorry." I frowned at her, but she interrupted whatever thoughts crossed my mind. "What? I can't be sorry a kind princess is sick?"

IoN made a small sound from beside my head. No one noticed, but Meena and I both looked at each other.

Serena knocked on the door, and another woman in white answered, looking at all of us with a confused scowl on her face. "Why would you disturb Lady Lorelai at such a holy hour?" she asked our guide.

"The princess requires her advice."

Meena bowed her head and muttered, "Serena, I am grateful for your service and thankful for your duties. If it's not too much trouble, I would like a private word with Lady Lorelai."

Were they both called Serena? Seemed unlikely.

Red answered my unspoken question in a whisper. "It's a title, not a name."

Oh, right.

I should have paid more attention during holy lessons, but instead I spent the time hiding small textbooks on steam engineering inside the larger holy textbooks. If I had known I would need the knowledge to save the princess's life one day, I might have taken heed.

Both Serenas bowed and stood away from the door, gesturing us inside. The room was small—more of a cupboard with shelves on every available space, displaying more books and trinkets than I'd seen in my lifetime. There was a couch at one end beneath a small corner window that overlooked the beautiful desert, and a desk and chair were in the corner by the door. On that couch, bare feet resting on the small table in front, book in hand, sat a lady with hair that trailed in ringlets past her shoulders and chest.

"Lady Lorelai." Meena bowed low, the lowest I'd seen her bow to anyone. "It is an honor to meet with you."

Both Red and I followed suit, bowing low and greeting her with honorifics.

She looked up from her book and raised a single pierced eyebrow. "Princess Jemeena, please have a seat." She gestured to the space next to her on the sofa. "I was just giving a private lesson, but I have time for you."

"Thank you." She walked a few paces to the couch and breathed heavily, mildly out of breath from the task. "I am grateful you could move things around for me."

"Of course." She placed the book written in a language I couldn't decipher on the table and looked at me with a strange flitter of recognition and then at Red, a scowl deepening on her face. "You can wait outside, Redower." She gave the girl no further thought and looked straight back at Meena.

"Actually, Lady Lorelai, I am accompanying the princess today and must stay." She bowed her head slightly and smirked beneath the social mask.

Lady Lorelai huffed but said nothing, instead placing all her attention on Meena, who looked between the two as vexed as I felt. "What is it I can do for you today, Your Highness?"

For the first time since I'd met her, Meena looked as though she didn't know what to say. I presumed there were no social lessons or graces that could be applied that would weaken the outcome anyway. It seemed she came to the same conclusion. She merely edged her sleeve up and untied the golden cloth. "I am dying."

Lady Lorelai took her wrist in hand and inspected her lifeclock. "Lifeclocks have been known to change when a cure to an illness is found. They are not entirely set in stone. There is still hope."

Meena shook her head. "Not mine. I have been destined to die on the day of my twenty-first birthday since the day I was born. Mother says I was born cursed, and Father likes to pretend as though it's not a problem. They employed the best healers across the island, even sending envoys and letters to other countries to see if anyone could help. But no one knows what is wrong with my lungs."

"And it hasn't moved a single second since the day you were born?"

She shook her head, eyes casting to her lap, then to me. "The papers, El?"

"Oh, right, of course." I fumbled them out of my pocket and handed them over.

Meena placed them on the table one by one, creating a collage of findings from the record room at the exportation office, Red's notes from her and her ancestors, my father's notes, and then mine. "We are searching for something . . . something that might cure me."

"And how do you think I can help with this search?" She hadn't taken her eyes from the drawing of the plant. "This cure you are searching for, it's for your lungs?"

Meena looked at me, then back to Lady Lorelai, and shook her head. "I have spent a lifetime searching for that cure and gotten nowhere. No, I'm looking for a cure to time."

Lady Lorelai shook her head and looked away from the papers. "No, I can't help you—"

"My father came to you once," I said, "years ago, asking for help. I know he didn't find answers, but what he did find has been erased from his notes entirely. Please, what did you tell him?"

Her brown eyes pierced me with such intensity, I had to hold onto the table to stop myself from toppling over. "Many have come looking for answers, but few find the one they are looking for."

"What did Preston find when he came looking for answers?" Meena asked.

"That the answer was not what he was expecting, and I'm afraid the information may have done more harm than good."

"How?" I crouched beside Meena, my hand on her lap.

"IoN," Lady Lorelai whispered, "you have much to share with your friends." She looked at him hovering in the air. "You need not hide your true nature from me, for I helped create you."

Lady Lorelai stood on her bare feet and exited the room. We followed down the stairs we had come up—quite the task for Meena, as she was still recovering from coming up them—and round so many twists and turns I wouldn't be able to lead us back out again if needed. But eventually, she rounded a corner that led to a grand door similar to the one we had entered earlier.

"Lady Lorelai?" Red asked. "Is that . . . ?"

"The original temple, yes. It was where IoN was created, and it's where the princess will find answers."

Red looked taken aback, as though she was surprised this place even existed, much less that we were about to set foot in it.

"Lady Lorelai," Meena said, only slightly out of breath after resting in the wheelchair, "would you prefer I leave the chair out here?"

"That's quite all right, Your Highness. I wouldn't want you needing medical attention this far into the temple. It would take us a while to get a doctor to you." She didn't look at her as she said it, but sympathy laced her tone. She took a moment to collect herself before opening the doors into a place older than civilization itself.

Records didn't even go back this far—a thousand years before steam power was invented, and barely anyone knew what life was like when people roamed this temple. It was like stepping into the past. I could feel the importance reverberate within me, through me, as though I were simply a part of a system greater than a single person.

Surely there were people who were more important, like Meena, who could change people's lives forever, shape nations, and lead the next generation into the future. Surely, she was important.

Lady Lorelai glided along the floor, and we followed, Meena's chair doing its best to catch on every piece of rubble along the way and us trying not to damage anything older than our city.

Red, however, was dazed as she looked around in awe and inspiration. "Is this really where Lady Galatria founded the ladies in white?"

Lady Lorelai turned around. "It's where Seren saved her and her sisters, and together they forged a whole new world, yes."

"It's amazing." She looked at Lorelai as though she was once a friend. "Why does no one come here anymore?"

Lady Lorelai didn't answer. Instead, she held up a finger and guided us to the center, where a statue of a flower dropping water onto a field of houses stood. "Because it holds knowledge we, as a society tasked with safeguarding Seren and all we know about Him, decided we don't want the general populace to know."

"When you say 'we?'" Red asked.

"I mean my ancestors, yes, but I agree with them." She knelt at the foot of the flower. "It's for the best."

IoN hovered above her head and asked, "How did you create me? I cannot seem to recall that information."

"No, you won't be able to. We made sure to erase it from you before allowing you to wake." She finished whatever prayer she recited inside her head and turned to face him. "IoN, you are a unique specimen that I have always questioned whether I should have helped create. I've wrestled with the idea of it being the wrong choice for many years, but now I see that it was Seren's plan all along." She looked at the princess. "Without you, she wouldn't have made it here."

IoN turned to the princess and his mouth lit up green. Then he turned to me and said, "Anything to make El happy."

A single tear slid down Lady Lorelai's cheek, and she quickly wiped it away. "Cinderella, when your father came to visit me, he was looking for a cure, as you know, after having tried many times to transfer time from himself to your mother, but to no avail. It didn't work because he didn't have all the information about our lifeclocks. When his time was coming to an end, he came to see me, seeking answers so he could live long enough to give his daughter a chance at a better life.

"Red, your ancestors couldn't find the answer because you were also missing information. Information I was careful not to reveal to you while you were here with us as a child."

Red's gaze fell to the floor, her cheeks as bright as her hair. "So, it didn't matter. Everything they've done, everything they've sacrificed was meaningless?"

"People are not meant to cheat death, Redower."

"Why tell us now," Meena asked. "If this is such a secret, why tell anyone?"

Lady Lorelai smiled gently at the princess. "Because some people are worthy of the knowledge." She looked up at me. "Just like your father."

I squinted at the statue, and the recognition flashed through my mind like lightning. "It's the herbilore plant!" I pointed to the statue and then looked at Meena. "It's the plant Red buys from the temple."

Lady Lorelai scowled, then looked furiously at Red. "You are a menace to this world."

Red flicked her hair over her shoulder. "I try."

"But yes," Lady Lorelai said, "it's a plant we call herbilore today, but in the old tongue it was called *gracious*. It was used during the grace ritual to keep the sisters healthy. They performed it every morning, and the texts say they lived hundreds of years and only passed upon their choosing."

"Is it true?" Meena asked. "Can it really extend life?"

"Not quite, no." She looked at me with sadness in her eyes. "It can transfer life from one being to another."

"Just like Dad was trying to do."

Red furrowed her brow. "But how were the sisters able to live long lives if they had to trade years between themselves?"

Meena's eyes pinged open and she gasped. "They didn't transfer years between each other. They took them from their followers."

"It's an old way of life we don't subscribe to anymore, but yes, I'm sorry to say the sisters took the lives of their followers—often willingly given, but sometimes not. They did great things for this world, but they were troubled, and the older they got, the more troubled they became."

Meena frowned up at me. "El, I can't do this. This isn't the answer we've been seeking."

I frowned, not understanding. "You're one of the most amazing and important people in the country."

"I can't steal someone else's life just so I can sit on a throne for the rest of mine." She looked at Lady Lorelai and apologized. "Take me home, please."

I turned the wheelchair around, but IoN flew in front of us. "El, you have been wanting to understand your father's steps for years. You have this opportunity right in front of you, and you won't even consider asking questions?"

"I apologize, El. Of course you should stay and get the answers you seek. I'll wait for you." She looked at the lady in white, who stared at her in shock. "Is there anyone who can wheel me to a room I might reside in while I wait?"

Shaking her curls, Lady Lorelai replied, "Of course, Your Highness. I'll summon someone now."

Red shook her head. "I'll pull the cord. You stay." Red disappeared outside for a while, and in the meantime, we both turned back to the plant statue with solemn expressions.

"I am sorry," I whispered.

Meena rested her hand atop mine on the wheelchair's handle. "It's quite all right, El. It was always meant to be this way."

"But it feels so wrong."

"Death isn't supposed to feel right."

Yeah, but this feels like something that could be prevented. Something with an answer on a silver tray in front of us, but we're too afraid to take it.

Red returned several minutes later, a little out of breath after exclaiming there weren't servant cords anywhere near here—whatever that meant—but I ignored her. Instead, I traveled around the room, looking at the statue and how the steady flow of water dripped into a pool in the center of the houses, which then flowed around a river through those houses, watering everyone.

It was intricate and beautiful, but nowhere I recognized.

"Some of our best scholars think this is supposed to represent the village that once stood here. There are still remnants of it behind the temple, where the Serena and acolyte quarters reside."

"You do not agree?" Meena asked, curious.

"It's my job to pass down knowledge to those I see fit to hold it, to oversee the teachings of the ladies in white, and to ensure our line is never broken, but it's an awfully dull job, to tell you the truth. I spend a lot of time poring over texts and diary entries and anything written down by long-forgotten ancestors who also resided here. And what I have found, among lots of other important thoughts and theories, is that the people who lived here four or five hundred years ago thought this temple held the power to create towns and entire cities. That that was where Palatina and Prago City came from. That the statue represents what could be, not what has already passed."

"Could it not just be metaphoric?" I asked. "That the sisters truly believed they were feeding their people life, that the herbilore plant kept themselves and therefore everyone else alive?"

"Possibly," Lady Lorelai said. "Others have suggested as much. There are as many theories about this one statue as there are carvings on every temple's walls, and all of them could be the answer. So to answer your question, Princess, I am unsure what its original intent was."

"How does it work?" I asked tentatively, worried I wasn't really allowed to ask. "How does one transfer time?"

"It's really not that complicated, but if you try doing it without the plant, it doesn't work. We are unsure why. We ladies in white believe, of course, it's because Seren doesn't allow it. Herbilore is His plant, His gift to us. Without it, we are cheating His will."

"But others believe other things?" I asked, curious.

"Some scholars think the plant might act as a buffering agent, like a stabilizing mechanism that enables the transfer of time. That without it, the lifeclocks might destabilize and start to erode, therefore eroding a person's time with it."

Meena gazed at me knowingly.

It sounded exactly like what Dad had described: Mom's years disintegrating before his eyes.

IoN asked, "Why did he make me?"

Lady Lorelai turned to him and said, "To provide El with a friend, so that she might always have love, even after he'd passed."

IoN settled in my arms and wrapped his around my wrists. "So El is my purpose?"

"She always has been, and I think you already knew that."

Another lady in white bustled through the door moments later, and she bowed at both the princess and Lady Lorelai, then wheeled the princess away, asking her what kind of food she preferred and whether she wanted anyone to gather her things from the dirigible.

"Do you have any other questions, Cinderella?"

"I feel like I have more questions than words in the dictionary, Lady Lorelai, but for now, I think I'd prefer to just absorb."

"I do." Red stood next to me, fists clenched. "I have many questions."

I should have left—it was rude to eavesdrop on someone else's conversation—but curiosity got the better of me, as it often did, so I shrank into the shadows.

"I know you do, Redower." Lady Lorelai ran a frustrated hand across her forehead. "When your parents abandoned you on our doorstep, I didn't know what to do with you."

"So you knew?" She knelt in front of the statue and clasped her hands, folding her fingers together.

"That you were here to provide information to your parents as to the properties of the herbilore plant? Of course I did. Both of our ancestors have accounts of each other. Why else would you have been here?"

"To learn, to be guided?" Red didn't open her eyes or look at

Lady Lorelai, but the hint of amusement in her voice was evident. "Maybe my parents thought I needed Seren's guidance."

Lady Lorelai let out an undignified snort that sounded erroneous coming from her, then knelt next to Red and placed a hand on her shoulder. "Red, I am sorry for how things turned out. It is, in part, my fault for how you were shunned out of the temple."

A single tear slipped down Red's face. She opened her eyes and met Lady Lorelai's gaze. "It was supposed to just be a mission, to find out your secrets and then leave, but the temple was my home. Something I didn't know I needed, and you threw me out of it for something I couldn't control."

"It is still forbidden to fornicate with a lady in white, to taint Seren's purity. It is instant banishment."

Red's head fell onto her shoulder as hiccuped sobs echoed across the chamber. "I . . . needed . . . you."

Lady Lorelai wrapped her arms tight around her, and a few tears slid down her face before she hid them in Red's hair. She mumbled something I couldn't hear, but then she pulled herself back and raised Red's chin to meet her face. "For what it is worth, I forgave you a long time ago, and I eventually came to realize that you didn't need my forgiveness at all. That everything you did was consensual."

7 DAYS. 8 HOURS. 33 MINUTES.

I slipped out after that, feeling guilty for intruding on such a moment. When I eventually found a lady in white to guide me to the prepared rooms, or at least point me in the right direction out of this maze, I found my way to a small corridor of chambers.

"The princess said that you have a room next to hers, if you wish to use it." She gave me a small curtsy and hurried off.

Did Meena really think that low of me, that I would stop cherishing her the moment we couldn't find an answer? "Pfft." I made my way to the widest door, assuming she would be in there, and turned the knob to the sound of sobs and the sight of her tangled in sheets with makeup trickling down her face.

I rushed to the bed, kicking my shoes off on the way, and yanked her into my arms. I didn't say anything. There was nothing I could say, nothing that would detract from the fact that she was going to die in a matter of days.

"It's not fair," she mumbled into my shoulder.

"I know it's not."

She spilled a lifetime's worth of tears onto my shoulder, and when she calmed down, she stayed there. "I'm scared."

I didn't know what to say. Words seemed little comfort in light of such a time. "Is there anywhere you'd like to go? Anything you'd like to do?"

Meena looked up at me and smirked. "Well, I can certainly think of something I'd like to do right now."

"In the Temple of Seren? Really?"

She shrugged. "I don't have much time left, so I'd like to spend it doing things I love." She stared into my soul, her eyes still glassy from the now dried tears, and leaned into me. The kiss was tender, soft, but with an undercurrent of desperation that swept me away on a boat of soft skin and a breeze of gentle moans.

We took our time removing each other's clothes layer by layer, and I made sure to touch every inch of her skin as I peeled her open like a rich sunrise, paying particular attention to her neck, the space between her shoulder blades that made her breath hitch, the soft skin of her breasts, and the ticklish underside of her feet that I rubbed into relaxation. She lay sprawled out on the bed beneath the waning candlelight, the moon shining through the window on a cloudless desert night, and she gazed down at me as I peppered kisses across her inner thighs, slowly rising higher and higher.

Her head fell back on the bed in a moan as I wrung pleasure from her. I explored every depth, used every idea I had ever dreamed of, tried to mimic what she had done to me, and did my best to make one of her last nights a pleasurable one.

We had to stop multiple times for her to get her breath back, so I tried to keep her as relaxed as possible, eventually lowering her into a steamy bathtub filled with all kinds of salts and scents

—most of which I had never seen before—and continuing to run my hands over her soapy skin.

"I want to pleasure you too." She stopped my hand from delving below the water and kissed me, driving her tongue past my lips and tangling it with mine. "I want to watch you fall apart."

After pulling me into the tub alongside her, she took her time bringing me to release as often as possible, and after my skin had pruned and my eyes couldn't stay open a moment longer, she guided us back to bed, where she lay in my arms and made herself breathless kissing me.

---

6 DAYS. 19 HOURS. 42 MINUTES.

MEENA DIDN'T LOOK HER USUAL SELF IN THE MORNING, already sitting up in bed reading an ancient tome by candlelight when I opened my eyes. "How long have you been up?"

"A while." She didn't look up from the book, poring over every line. "Did you sleep well?"

"Better than I have in ages, actually." I smirked, and a small chuckle slipped across her lips in response. "Is there anywhere you wanted to go today or something you wanted to do?"

Meena pulled out a slip of paper from her nightstand and handed it to me. "It's my list."

"Your list?" I asked, but upon opening it, I needn't have asked because the answer stared me in the face. It was her list of everything she wanted to accomplish before she died.

Some of the things she had already crossed off, especially the ones at the top of the list in untidy handwriting, obviously having been written when she was just a child. But there were a few left at the bottom:

43. *Stay in bed all day and eat nothing but dessert*
44. *Run naked in the sunlight*
45. *Apologize to Hera*
46. *Fall in love*

"Well," I started, "I'm up for staying in bed all day, unless you'd rather go home first."

Meena shook her head, closing her book and looking down at me. "The crossing from here to Palatina will take a week." She unwrapped the cloth on her wrist. "I only have six days."

I looked at her lifeclock and felt the ticking deep in my bones, echoing so loudly it was as though the last few days of her life screamed at me. "I promised you wouldn't be alone at the end, and I have no intention of letting that promise be false."

Her smile lit up the world, the candlelight bouncing off her beauty like the sun, her kissed skin a marvel I wanted to run my hands over, even now, when she was paler than ever.

"Reckon they'll make us dessert for the whole day?"

"If I ask, they probably will," she replied as she bent her head and kissed my forehead. "There's a servant cord at the end of the corridor."

The end of the corridor led to some stairs we had come up earlier, and dangling from a golden panel in the ceiling was a red rope, which I tugged.

Less than a minute passed before a lady in white hurried up the steps and bowed at me—which was still an odd experience. "Is there something I can do for yourself and the princess?"

"Yes. Could you bring us lots of dessert?" She looked confused for a moment before blanking her face and nodding. "And make sure there are some apple tarts in there. They're the princess's favorite."

She bowed and got halfway down the stairs before I thought of something. "Actually, there's also something else."

She hurried back up, and guilt grasped me for a moment after seeing her mildly out of breath. "Yes, my lady?"

Lady? Shaking the question from my head, I said, "Could you send IoN out to our dirigible for Hera. The princess would like to see her friend this evening."

"Shall I bring her to her room, or would she prefer to meet her somewhere more formal?"

"Er . . . Her room will be fine." That way she could truly stay in bed all day.

Meena was resting when I returned, having finally fallen back to sleep. I sat at the desk situated in the corner, hoping the extra candlelight wouldn't wake her. It turned out Lady Lorelai had delivered some old texts while I was sleeping this morning, and that was what Meena had been reading.

I sifted through them, hoping for something I could use as a distraction. I came across a diary entry from an ancestor of Lady Lorelai's only a hundred years ago. This was around the time we were inventing steambotic technology and the great Averice Sellion made the first of what we would go on to call a steambot. It seemed this lady thought that one day we might be able to place life into steambots using the same practices the three sisters used, but even I scoffed at that thought.

It was impossible.

No one could put life into a steambot—they were all instructions and cogwork, not people.

Just before I could think further on the subject, a knock sounded at the door and Lady Lorelai entered with a wheeled tray.

Pain in her eyes, she looked at the sleeping princess, who turned over in bed in a disgruntled version of sleep. "I'm sorry I couldn't be of more help yesterday," she whispered. She left the desserts by the bed and sat on a chair next to me, her hand resting gently on my knee. "I am sorry for your pain, Cinderella. Truly."

"I promised her I would try." Tears slid down my face. "That I would try to find a cure, but I failed. The only cure I found can't be ethically used." I looked at her sleeping face, peaceful and in another world. "She's going to die in six, and there's nothing I can do about it."

"You can give her the best last days you can. You can make someone, who has known their entire life that they wouldn't get long to enjoy being an adult, happy enough in their last moments that they forget entirely about their fate."

I grabbed the list from the nightstand and handed it to her. "She made it when she was young and has been adding to it ever since."

Lady Lorelai stared at the paper with some level of astonishment and internal struggle. "I wish I could help. I wish the help I could give was a viable option." She looked at the paper with tear-stained eyes and said, "You can use the grounds of the temple for whatever you wish while here. I recommend using the gardens in the back if you want to be naked in the sun." She got up and left, her hands shaking.

I was left in a dark room watching the princess slowly die while she got a few hours of being alive without worry in her dreams.

6 DAYS. 9 HOURS. 51 MINUTES.

Meena could feel Cinderella watching her as reality slowly took over from slumber, and as the fog faded, she remembered why her lover might be doing that. The first thing she heard was the ticktock of her lifeclock. *Thrum. Thrum.* It beat despite the knowledge of every last hour she had. After all, she'd been counting them down since she learned basic numeracy.

They had failed.

Meena would never again be able to dance at a ball or sit beside her father on the throne or be in any of the annual family paintings. She'd never get to love again.

She was safe here, in her last moments. She could fall apart, and she knew El would be there for her.

"Where's IoN gotten to?" Meena asked.

"He stopped by earlier before leaving to get Captain Hera."

Meena shot up too quickly, coughing and spluttering into her handkerchief. "El?" she choked out.

"I don't know what your past is with that woman, but she is on your bucket list, is she not?"

"She is." Meena opened her mouth to explain, to offer something to the beautiful woman now in her life, but she kept drawing a blank. She settled on a simple, "Thank you."

"I can leave you two be, if you'd like?"

Despite El's careful demeanor, Meena could tell she didn't want to do that. She was jealous—had been from the start. Meena couldn't help but find it sweet. "No, that's all right. It's nothing you can't hear."

"Are you sure? I don't want to impose."

Meena made her way across the small space and sat on El's lap, facing her. "There's nothing in my past you can't know about. Besides, I don't want to be alone." She wouldn't be with Hera there, but that wasn't what she had meant, and hopefully El knew it. She didn't want to spend a single second of the time she had left without her.

Just as they were kissing, a knock sounded at the door and Meena stood back up, a groan escaping her. "One moment," she tried calling, but it wasn't loud enough.

El repeated it louder as Meena put on pants and a robe, readying herself as best she could for the visitor behind the door.

The door swung open, and Hera stepped through, as chipper as ever, if a little confused as to why she'd been summoned to the temple. IoN, however, flew in after her without a care in the world; or rather, she assumed it was without care, but reading his emotions was something only Cinderella was skilled at.

"You summoned?" She raised an eyebrow at the word, clearly finding the summons hilarious. "It's been a while since you summoned me, Jemeena. You usually just barge through my front door as though you own the place."

"I do own the place."

Meena had purchased the house and the dirigible her friend resided in long ago as a birthday gift, so she'd be free from working hard. That knowledge brought new hurt to the surface—a different one to the recent pain.

Meena had ended things poorly with Hera, and she needed to apologize and explain herself now she was free to do so. "For such a long time, I wasn't allowed to speak of my illness. My parents forbade it for fear of inciting panic and rumor among the citizens, and for that, I am sorry. I'm sorry I kept it from you, but most of all, I'm sorry I let it be the reason I hurt you."

Hera sat down, dumbfounded for a moment before asking, "Is this really the moment you're choosing to have this conversation?" She looked at Cinderella with a small scowl but said nothing about her being here.

"I don't have enough time left for it to be anywhere else." Meena carefully unwrapped the gold cloth that had become a permanent feature of her life but had been removed so often of late she was increasingly aware of it tightly winding her wrist every second.

As it fell free and she turned her wrist up so Hera could see, a single tear fell from Hera's eye and drove a lonely path down her cheek and off her chin. "I . . . I didn't know. I always assumed it was a chronic illness you'd just have to live with. I didn't realize you were dying?"

"I've known for as long as I can remember that I would never reach my twenty-first birthday. Nothing anyone has ever done has changed the numbers."

"Nothing at all?"

Meena just shook her head.

"But you're royal. You have the best healers and doctors money can buy."

"Father even sent for doctors from distant lands, hoping they might know something we don't." She shook her head again, her eyes resting on her lap. She couldn't bear to look anyone in the face. "Nothing worked."

"I tried," El added. "I tried to find a cure to the lifeclocks. A way to extend her time." El looked at Hera's crying face, the same look in her eyes. "But I couldn't do it. I'm so sorry."

"It's okay, El," Meena said. "You tried, even knowing it was illegal, punishable by death. And you still tried for a complete stranger."

Something shifted on Hera's face, and she looked at Cinderella as though through new eyes. "Is that why we're here, at the Temple of Seren?"

"We thought we found something," Meena said, "but I can't use it now. It's too late." She shook her head again, as though it were the only action she knew how to perform in the moment. "I'm so sorry I didn't let myself love you, and I'm sorry I used the love you had for me for my own gain. It wasn't fair."

It was why Meena had bought her the house and the dirigible, because she felt guilty and wanted her to have a money-trouble-free existence, even if that was all she could offer.

"Shhh," Hera whispered, grabbing Meena's hand. "It's okay. It was a few years ago and I've come to terms with it. Don't let the guilt destroy your final days. Not for me."

They spent the last few hours of the evening reminiscing over old times, the trouble they got up to in their youth, and eventually, when the light was beginning to fade, Hera left. It was a teary goodbye, and Meena didn't know how she felt about it, but she knew one thing: She wanted El to know how much she was loved.

5 DAYS. 17 HOURS. 03 MINUTES.

Meena didn't wake up the next day. She was still breathing, but her brow had broken out in a cold sweat and I couldn't wake her. "Meena!"

IoN whizzed into the room, shoving his metal frame into the door to open it. "El?"

"I can't get her to wake."

IoN left the room for a moment, pulled the servant rope, and rushed back. "It's okay, El."

"This isn't okay, IoN. It wasn't meant to be this way. She still has five days left." Tears streamed down my face as my hands shook, but I managed to tuck her hair behind her ears and button her shift to retain her modesty. "I was meant to save her."

Ladies in white rushed into the room and threw the blanket off the princess. They rolled her onto a stretcher they had brought with them, clearly expecting the call, and rushed her out of the room and down the stairs as quickly as they could.

I didn't know what they were going to do, but in that moment I didn't care. I simply followed, my brain on autopilot. I wore nothing but a robe that came with the room, and slippers, and the only sound other than hurried feet and Meena's wheezing breaths were the slap of those slippers on stone matching my heartbeat.

They took her to the same temple we were in the other day and laid the stretcher at the feet of the statue in the center, where Lady Lorelai rested on her knees, one hand on her heart and then the other on her stomach. She was praying.

"Is . . . is there anything we can do?" I whispered, knowing the answer and yet still being afraid of it.

After muttering something under her breath, she turned to me and shook her head. "No. I can make her passing more comfortable, let her pass in the hall of the sisters, but I cannot save her. I am sorry." She turned back to the statue and rubbed water over Meena's forehead, whispering more words in a language I only recognized as the one Minister Farro sometimes used in church.

Like this, unable to wake and her every breath labored, her illness was all I could see. I couldn't separate her from it.

"She's going to die?"

Lady Lorelai shed tears as she said, "Yes. I'm sorry."

"But . . . we came all the way here."

"You did your best, El," IoN said, "but sometimes you cannot win. Some things are too powerful to fight against."

"No . . ." Meena's hand was limp in mine; she hadn't even the strength to hold my hand. "No, I have to do something."

"You cannot." IoN sat beside me, also touching Meena. "And that is okay."

"Nothing about this is okay!" I snapped.

Silent sorrow. Grief so thick I couldn't breathe, choking on its edges with every inhale I forced into my lungs, shoveling air into my body by force, against its instinct to cease living.

I had no idea how much time had passed, nor could I recall a single thought from the hours I spent crying beside her dying body, until I could finally utter a sentence. "She's such a beautiful person." It was barely a breath, the words a whisper, but it was all I had.

"That she is," Lady Lorelai said. "She is magnanimous in every way." Her white dress was slightly less white today, as though she hadn't changed it since yesterday. She kneeled at Meena's feet, washing them and preparing her for her next journey. Her next adventure.

IoN had moved into my lap at some point, silent, but his presence was like a weight keeping me from floating off into the empty space of grief.

Tears fell freely from Lady Lorelai's eyes, and she looked at me with such sadness I didn't know how to respond. "Are you going to remain here until she passes?"

"Yes." Turning to face Meena, I whispered, "I'm sorry I failed you." I didn't take my eyes off her body the entire time, waiting with bated breath for the moment she stopped breathing. "I promised she wouldn't spend her final days alone. I promised she wouldn't die alone and afraid."

Lady Lorelai unwrapped the princess's lifeclock and checked her time. "You have another few days left, Cinderella. You should go and rest. It's been a long day."

The day had passed, and I hadn't noticed. Tiredness was taking the edges of my vision.

"Go," she said. "I'll stay."

I looked at Meena, then at IoN on my lap, and nodded reluctantly. "I'll be back in a few hours."

---

4 DAYS. 14 HOURS. 23 MINUTES.

. . .

I WOKE A DAY LATER TO THE SOUND OF CRINKLED PAPER beneath the pillow my head rested upon. No matter which way I tossed and turned, I couldn't get rid of the offending sound. Finally, stressed and tired, I threw the pillow off the bed and yanked the piece of scrap paper from underneath. Only, I recognized this piece of paper, and it wasn't scrap. At least, it wasn't to Meena. It was her bucket list. I unfolded it and laid it flat in my hands, seeing the last two items she hadn't gotten around to completing, but something wasn't right. She had crossed off *Apologize to Hera*, as expected, but she had also crossed off *Fall in love*.

"She loves me?"

"Of course she does," IoN said. "Just as you love her."

She loved me. Somehow those words sunk deeper than I had expected them to. Finding love wasn't on my bucket list, but somehow I'd found it anyway, and I wasn't going to let it go. I crumpled the paper in my hand and shoved it on the nightstand, storming to my feet. "Then I can't let her die."

Moments later, or maybe minutes—my time seemed frozen as hers ebbed into death—I stormed back into the chamber, toolbelt in hand. Ignoring the scowl from Lady Lorelai, I cradled Meena's lifeclock in my lap. "Lady Lorelai, the herbilore plant serum, if you please?"

"Cinderella, I can't let you do this."

"I wasn't asking for your permission; I just didn't want to fight with the Lady of Seren. Now, the herbilore plant?"

"The no wasn't a suggestion for you to ignore, engineer. It was an order." Lady Lorelai hovered over me with a bitter stare, her hands clenched to her sides. "I want to save her too, but this isn't the way."

"This is the only way. Don't you see that? Do you not understand what is happening here?" I gestured to Meena lying at my feet. Her breathing stuttered, and we all snapped our heads to watch her regain her unsteady rhythm. "If she dies, the lower levels of Palatina will die with her." I turned to Lady Lorelai, aware I was speaking treason. "I apologize for my words, but I must speak them, regardless of the consequences." Hands clenched into fists, tears streaming down my face, I said, "She has such vision for us. To make the levels equal, to reinstate trade to level zero, to provide us an education and fair rations, to give us the opportunity to be great again. If she dies, that'll die with her." Under my breath, I added, "I'll die with her."

IoN spun in a circle behind me, grabbing my attention.

"What?"

"El, I don't think this is a good idea. I love how happy she makes you, but sacrificing your life, even for a princess, even for someone as lovely as Meena, is not the right choice to make."

Ignoring him, I wiped the tears from my face and unscrewed all the bolts and tiny filaments that sealed the top of Meena's lifeclock. I unwound the coil and pulled it out. Just as I went to grab the screwdriver to undo my own, IoN yanked it out of my grip and chucked it a few feet away.

"What are you doing?"

"Ensuring you don't die for a love you've only had for a month." He threw the screwdriver across the room and wound Meena's coil back into her lifeclock. "I know you don't want to lose her after losing your mother and father and feeling as though you have no one, but this isn't the way."

I went to grab something else from my toolbelt, but it wasn't there. "Where's my toolbelt?" I spun around, scanning the dim space, and noticed it dangling from Lady Lorelai's fingers. Her gaze could cut glass even with the tears leaking from harsh pity falling in small rivers down her face. The scream that left my throat didn't sound like me when I caught its echo, but it continued to rip from my throat nonetheless. "What are you both doing? Why would you . . .?" My knees gave way, and they slammed into the stone below me as I fell to the floor.

Something sharp pinched my arm, but I barely felt it, and the tears blurred the world around me until I saw nothing.

5 DAYS. 8 HOURS. 42 MINUTES.

NOT ABLE TO FULLY COMPREHEND EL'S BODY LYING IN THE bed, IoN had watched her chest rise and fall like a hawk. "Oh, El. You have lost so much."

He couldn't let her sacrifice her life when she had so many days left to live: 22,254 to be exact. She was supposed to keep running the garage, show Phyllis her worth, create something out of the ashes between her and her sisters, and demonstrate to the world why she should be as revered as her father.

Lady Lorelai sat beside him, her head in her hands. "I'm so tired."

"It's a heavy burden you carry, and I am sorry it sits on your shoulders. I am sorry I made it heavier."

She shook her head, her eyes not removing themselves from Cinderella. "You did what any father in your shoes would have done."

"You will tell her afterward?"

Her head spun to face him, and for a moment he was caught by the pain in her eyes. It was always her. She held the sole responsibility of anyone who came here looking for answers on how to stay alive. Every sick person, every single parent, every lovestruck fool—everyone with a story, a worthy reason as to why they should not be allowed to die so soon. But none were ever granted.

Until him, of course.

"What I did for you was unprecedented, and quite frankly, some nights I lay awake under the desert stars wondering if it was the right thing to do."

"I understand, but the longer I have spent watching El and Meena, the more I have come to terms with the idea that this was meant to be."

"You think you were always meant to be here, to give your life for hers?"

IoN laid his arms on her shoulders and made a crackly sound that was supposed to be a sigh. "I have always denounced the idea of a god. What's the point in believing in some revered entity who never answered a single call for help? But I have come to realize that it is not His help I have been seeking, but my own. My choices shape who I am. And this is my final choice."

"You would die for her?"

"I put my consciousness into a steambot and lived a shell of a life for a decade for her. She is my daughter. I would do anything for her."

23 DAYS. 21 HOURS. 17 MINUTES.

Meena. She was my first thought the moment my eyes peeled open. Her name scraped up the dry walls of my throat. "Meena."

"She is in the hospital wing at the moment."

That voice. I recognized its soft cadence. "Lady Lorelai?"

"Good afternoon, Cinderella." There was the clink of china placed onto the nightstand and the stir of a metal spoon in liquid. "Sit up when you're ready. We have much to talk about."

"Hospital? So she's . . . still alive?"

Lady Lorelai looked at the floor and then dragged her gaze to me, a few tears leaking down her cheeks. "IoN gave his final days to her. This way, you get to live your happily ever after together."

"He . . . what?" IoN was dead? No, that couldn't be. He wouldn't have left me like that. Not without saying goodbye. "I don't understand." My head was full of half questions—why did IoN have a lifeclock, why did he give his life for my happiness, what was he—but I voiced none of them when I realized I was asking in the past tense. That was all he was now. A piece of the past.

"I'm so sorry for your loss, Cinderella. You have endured much in the last few days and over the course of your life, and I'm afraid the truth I have to tell you will not ease the burden of grief."

I didn't know the words coming out of her mouth. Although I recognized the sounds and syllables, I could not form them into meaning and I couldn't write them down, even if I had tried. It was as though the voice now echoing in the stone room made my brain freeze so nothing else could be processed. Why didn't it sound like a real sentence? Why were the words not sinking in?

"IoN was created by your father so he could extend his own time and not leave his daughter before she was ready to be fatherless. When he transferred his time into IoN, the mere days he had left turned into years. He programmed himself so he couldn't tell anyone but me, so the technology could never be used by anyone else."

"I was . . . with my father this whole time? Did he know? Was he aware of who he was?"

"I don't think that question has an accurate answer, I'm afraid. He seemed aware last night, when he was talking to me."

Had he known and not told me because he couldn't? Or was he not aware until he saw Lady Lorelai again? Had he been suffering in silence while I did nothing but complain? Seren, I was so stupid.

"But this means, Cinderella, that Meena is alive."

Meena's survival hadn't clicked in my brain yet either, the ice taking its time to thaw, but the moment it did, I rushed to the small hospital they had here on bare feet, forgetting how hot the sand would be outside.

With burned feet, breathless lungs, eyes sore from fresh tears, and hands shaking from the possibility of a heavily-paid-for miracle, I threw the doors open. There she was. Sitting up in a bed with empty beds and white sheets on either side of her. She was staring out the window into the desert, a pensive look on her face, while drinking tea, just like she usually did first thing in the morning. When she finally stopped staring out the window and looked toward me, her lips curled and her eyes widened.

"Meena?"

"El . . ." She dropped her gaze to her lap. "I'm so sorry."

They'd already told her then. I was hoping I could be the one to do it, to soften the blow somewhat, but it seemed I was beaten to it. Sitting on the chair beside her bed, I pulled her mug away and placed it down, then wrapped her cold hands in mine. "You have nothing to be sorry for."

It was, after all, his choice.

"But you'll never get to work with IoN again. You'll never—"

"He was such an important part of my life, but he was living in a silent pain I never even knew existed. He was my whole world growing up without my parents." I frowned, a correction almost leaving my lips but I held it back. "And I'll never get over him." My tears seemed dried up for now, as no more wanted to shed. "Honestly, I'm not sure his death has sunk in yet. But I'm not alone anymore, so the grief won't feel so heavy."

Her lifeclock was once again covered in her golden cloth, but after a lifetime being stuck with its numbers like a curse, I didn't blame her for not wanting to waste a second longer worrying about when she would one day die. I stroked my thumb back and forth over its smooth surface, feeling the clockface beneath.

"Hey, Meena?"

She met my gaze again, another sad but hopeful smile gracing her features. "Yes?"

"You never did get to run across the sand naked." I gestured to the wheelchair on the bed's other side with a suggestive eyebrow raise. "Want to have some fun?"

16 DAYS. 13 HOURS. 02 MINUTES.

THE FOLLOWING WEEK WAS SPENT GETTING MEENA BACK on her feet and prepping for the journey home. Surprisingly, Red was still here, skulking around and getting up to goodness knew what, and on the day we were due to depart she paid me a visit while Meena was writing yet another correspondence to her parents.

"I cannot believe you pulled it off, to be frank," she said as she settled into the chair at the desk in our chambers. "I thought for sure the princess would die." She fiddled with a pen until it plopped onto the wooden surface with a metallic ping.

"Is there a reason you're here, or am I supposed to simply guess your villainous motives?"

Our relationship over the past week had not improved, and I doubt it ever would, but at least she had stopped with the flirting. That, at least, made talking to her more comfortable.

She pulled two vials out of her pants pocket and placed the green things onto the surface. "Take these with you, in case you ever need them again."

I didn't know what to say.

"Don't look so surprised. I am not as villainous as some would believe."

"You put a knife to Billary's neck and finagled a way on to the royal dirigible, then proceeded to hassle Lady Lorelai for the past week."

She shrugged. "Perspective, dear." She turned in the chair to face me, a wicked grin ear to ear. "I would say that I alleviated the princess from irksome tattle-tales, ensured her safety on a voyage of dangerous discovery, and then spent the week ensuring you were both free from your hostess's words of wisdom."

I got the feeling that last one wasn't true, given her inability to hold eye contact through the words and the way she fiddled with her belt loop, but I wasn't about to suggest it.

"Anyway," she continued, "take them." She gestured again to the herbilore vials on the desk. "You'll make better use of them than me."

I still wasn't sure how the procedure worked or how Dad had managed to transfer himself and his time into a steambot. I had been so caught up in the back and forth between grief and relief I had forgotten to ask Lady Lorelai about it.

"Thank you, I guess."

Hands slapping her thighs, she stood. "For whatever it's worth, I hope you two get your happily ever after now. I've never met someone who deserves that fairy tale ending more than you, Cinderella." She walked out the door and down the corridor, and I got the feeling I would never see her again.

I would say that I was sad about it, but out of the numerous things to be sad and confused about right now, that wasn't one of them. My life would be simpler without that criminal in it.

I scooped up the vials and placed them inside my toolbelt before wrapping it around my pants' waist and buckling it into place. There were many things I now had to take good care of, but these were the ones that posed real danger.

The door opened and Meena walked in, full of life and color. She grabbed my hand before placing a gentle kiss on my cheek. "Are you ready?"

I looked at the bed the ladies in white had stripped earlier and to the lifeless steambot that lay on top. "Just need to transport him to the ship, say goodbye to Lady Lorelai, and then we can go."

"I'm so sorry," she whispered again. It was probably the thousandth time she had said those words whenever IoN came up in conversation.

"I know you are, but I didn't have the choice either. I couldn't have stopped him, I couldn't have made the choice for him. He wanted to save you." Given I had planned to do the exact same thing the day before him, I wasn't about to begrudge his sacrifice. "It's so sad he's gone. And I don't think I've processed it yet. But it was his choice, and I won't belittle that by letting you live in guilt." I wrapped my arms around her shaking shoulders. "He wouldn't have wanted you to feel sorry for him."

"I can't . . . help it." Her tears stained my tunic, but I didn't attempt to calm her down. I merely let her lean on me. "He's gone, and I wouldn't be watching the love of my life grieve if I had never met you both."

"Lady Lorelai told me that IoN . . . Dad believed we were meant to meet. That's why Lady Lorelai felt obliged to help him when he came looking for answers she had denied everyone else."

She pulled away and looked at me pensively. "You think Seren intended it to be this way?"

I shrugged. "I've never really been much of a believer in Seren. Neither was Dad. It's hard to believe in a god when you live in hunger every day. But if he believed that it was some form of fate, whether willed by Seren or not, then I'm inclined to believe him. He was the smartest man I knew."

"I wish I had known him before IoN."

I picked up IoN's body and carried him out of the room, the princess following behind me.

Over the last week, Meena had focused on regaining her strength and enjoying her newfound freedom, eventually walking without hesitation so long as she could take regular breaks. But that was more from malnutrition than breathing. I hadn't heard her wheeze or cough once since I went to see her that first day in the hospital. It seemed her lungs had gotten better the moment IoN had transferred his life to her.

I didn't understand it.

For the first time, really, I was faced with something I didn't think was understandable. That maybe the answers to time and how our lifeclocks worked were not something we were ever meant to discover. It nagged at me nonetheless. The number of unanswered questions continued to build every time I mulled over the events.

Did IoN really have Dad's consciousness, or was he just a clone of Dad's remaining time? Why wouldn't he try to give me clues or hints over the years, even if he did prevent himself from saying the words? Did he not trust me? Why didn't he help more with the garage?

The more I thought about it, the more I disbelieved that IoN was truly the same as Dad; that maybe they were similar and he had parts of him inside, but there was no way every part of Dad's consciousness ended up inside IoN.

Even if it did, how did one go about transferring consciousness? Was it just a side effect of transferring time? Or did our lifeclocks mean more than what I believed them to?

"You're thinking too loudly," Meena said when she finally reached the front door to the temple. "I can hear the wheels turning in your head."

"Sorry. I was just thinking about everything that's happened. It's unbelievable."

"Yes, it is," said Lady Lorelai from the chair beside us that was in part-shade, part-sun, as though she'd had a lifetime to perfect her lounging placement here at the temple. "Which is why I hope you won't tell anyone else what you have learned here."

"I won't tell a soul, so long as you answer a single question." I folded my arms across my chest, doing my best to stand firm.

"I knew you would not be satisfied leaving without answers," she said. "Go on then. Ask me your single question." She lifted the glass of milky-white liquid to her lips and lay back down, content to simply listen it would seem.

I could have asked how Dad's consciousness had been transferred to IoN, but something told me that I needed to ask something else. Something more important. "How does the procedure to transfer time work?"

She opened her eyes and lifted an eyebrow. "In the grand scheme of things, I do not think telling you will be a problem." She sat up and rested her head in her hands. "Although it's against protocol to give the information out, I will tell you because I feel you of all people deserve to know." She looked at Meena, her lips turning down almost immediately. "You need to inject the herbilore serum into the tube inside of the lifeclock, then connect them and turn the dials of the person receiving the time."

"That's it?" Meena asked. "Is it that simple?"

Lady Lorelai shrugged her shoulders. "Well, we have a more complicated procedure involving ladies in white, Seren's holy blessing, and a temple, but yes. Essentially, everything your dad did before he came to me was right; he just didn't have the final piece of puzzle."

"Herbilore."

She nodded and went back to closing her eyes and lounging in the half sun. "Now, if you don't mind, I have important duties to attend to." Only, she didn't move anywhere, and I think, by the time we had made our way down the front steps, she had fallen asleep.

"You could have asked anything, but you asked that?" Meena asked as we were escorted to the dirigible a few miles north.

I shrugged off the question as if it were nothing. "It's what I was most curious about." Something flickered in the back of my mind. Some kind of blinking light that told me something wasn't right here.

The journey home was filled with surprise reunions, many tea parties, and taking the time to stare at the sunset over the desert horizon as Meena talked endlessly about her life in the palace and all the things she wanted to share with me once we were home. It wasn't until we passed the gates to Palatina in the distance that I realized we weren't going straight home.

I looked at Meena with a furrowed brow.

She handed me Dad's notes from the final days of his travels. "It's the final place he went before going home. You deserve to finish his footsteps."

"Vakt Port?"

"In a few hours, yes," the captain said with a smile on her face. She seemed less frustrated by me the more time we spent together, but I think the conversation she had with Meena was largely to credit for our new amicable friendship. "I can't land too close to the town since they don't have any place for me to make port, but I'll get you as close as I can."

"Are you coming with us?" I asked, curious. Did she always stay with the ship?

She shook her head. "I'm not comfortable leaving the ship. It's a high-profile target, after all—a known royal vessel. Maybe one day I'll get to travel as a passenger."

Meena frowned, unsure what to make of that information. "Is there anything you want us to pick up for you?"

"Some salted fudge, if you wouldn't mind. There's a stall in the harbor that smells amazing. You can't miss it." After we looked at her with surprised faces, she explained, "Best in Clepsydra."

"You can make me a list, if you'd like?" I asked, knowing she probably didn't get to enjoy herself very often, which was sad for a captain. "I'll pick you up whatever you want."

She clapped me on the shoulder and smiled bright, her lips a deep orange color from whatever lipstick she had chosen to don this morning. "You're a good friend, El."

The couple of hours before landing were spent in the captain's deck discussing Vakt Port and all the wonderful places Hera had visited before, which was everywhere, apparently.

"The Pental Coast is a beautiful sight, if you ever get the chance to go one day. White cliffs surrounded by raging northern oceans and beaches filled with green and orange rocks from the seabed."

"I've seen the paintings," Meena said in awe, her voice full of wonder, "but I've never been, since it's outside Palatina's jurisdiction."

I looked at them in confusion, not understanding why that would make a difference in her ability to travel.

"Inside the kingdom I have immunity and protection, but outside there are constant threats. I would have to take a whole team of guards and an entire entourage with me just to cross the border."

"She could be assassinated by people with grudges against the kingdom or people who want to take the throne for themselves, or she could be harmed in an attempt to weaken the kingdom or bleed it dry."

"I'd never thought about it." It was more complicated than I ever thought it would be; I always imagined the lives of the rich and royal to be ones of luxury, but there was more to it than that, it would seem. "Maybe we can arrange a trip one day. Maybe we could even leave the island and travel to nearby lands."

Hera laughed, an incredulous look on her face. "Dream big, girl. And never stop."

"You've never been off the island?" I asked.

She shook her head. "Never. Never met anyone who has, either. But I'd love to. One day."

"Why?" I'd spent my life so caught up in the here and now that I never really gave much thought to what was out there and if we could see it. "You have the dirigible . . ."

"The ocean out there is a dangerous place full of unmapped territory and unknown threats. Not many people who leave the island come back."

"Captain," Yolot, the second in command, shouted, "we're about to land."

"Got to go." She tipped her hat at us and practically jumped to her feet and into her captain's seat. "Okay, on my count, turn off flight and descend landing thrusters. Three, two, one." The dirigible jolted for less than a second before we started descending and the air pressure gradually changed. "Initiate crew landing." A clunking sound echoed from somewhere deep in the aircraft, and what I assumed was the landing platform at the back of the dirigible dropped. A few moments later, Hera said, "Radio landing crew to tie us down." She looked at Yolot and said, "Descend the anchors."

"I had no idea there was such a complicated process for landing," I shout-whispered to Meena over the noise.

"It's only when we hover," she replied. "When she lands properly it's simpler, but we can only do that safely while in a port."

Why was that? I'd have to ask her one day.

In the meantime, Hera waved us off, gave me her list, which I tucked into a pocket on my toolbelt, and told us she was off to bed so she could rest after the long flight.

We, on the other hand, descended into an empty field just outside of Vakt Port, having left the desert behind us the moment we flew through the mountains yesterday. I didn't realize things would look so different on the other side of those mountains, but it was less dry here, the air less muggy and cloying. I could breathe. Vakt Port was a cluster of buildings with neither a gate nor a wall surrounding it. In fact, it had nothing but a wooden arch slapped between the two outermost stone buildings with a sign hung from the post.

The buildings themselves were of a single story, and when we stepped foot into the town, I could see the sky from level zero, as though they had never thought to build upward at all.

"I have only been here once, when I was a small child, but it's just as I remember it." She looked around as awestruck as I felt, her eyes not quite able to fix onto one thing long enough before they were stolen by another piece of wonder. "Everything is so flat."

Everything was made of plain gray stone and dark wood, clearly from the woodland to the west, but the shutters on the windows were pastel greens and blues and purples, adding dots of color to the otherwise pristine landscape. The cobbled path clicked under Meena's heeled boots. It had wide paths, open, sunlit streets, and bakeries and bookshops and candle stores that littered the streets with signs flapping in the sea breeze. As we turned a corner, I spotted a shop selling soaps and shampoos, so I took us in.

"First item on Hera's list is a butter and sea salt scented soap," I explained to Meena. "Might as well try here first."

"Can I buy you things while we're here?" she asked. I went to shake my head, but she stopped us in the doorway and took my hands in hers. "I want to buy you things and treat you and shower you with love. Will you let me?"

Her green eyes begged as her face sparkled in the cloudy sunlight and her hair blew in the breeze. How could I say no to that? Sighing, I gave in, and she hopped in delight as she dragged us fully into the store.

Back home, we bought plain soap sparingly, making it last as long as possible so we didn't have to buy the expensive stuff more than once a year—and often families shared a bar. But here the prices were cheaper. Though Meena didn't even notice them, placing bars into my waiting arms that smelled nice. And that was before we moved onto shampoos and perfumes.

We left that shop with more items than I had used in my lifetime, much less in a year or two. But I did particularly enjoy a woodland-scented shampoo and soap set Meena picked up for me, and I was curious to try it. In the meantime, I was trying to forget what the numbers on the price tag said, but I failed.

"What is next?" she asked, clearly on a mission.

I pulled out the piece of paper and read the next two items listed, and off we went. We wandered in and out of several stores, some where she was recognized and some where she wasn't, but she didn't seem too bothered either way. We weren't in a part of the kingdom, so it was to be expected. Seeing her able to walk down the street without issue and walk up steps without pause and have long, rambling conversations without needing to be quieter than she actually was, sent a thrill through me.

She would live the rest of her life like this.

As we wound our way farther south toward the harbor, I began to forget about the questions niggling at the back of my mind and I almost forgot the reason we were here altogether. I wanted to find the scavenger Dad had met on his journey. I wanted to find the final piece of the puzzle.

The sea brushed against the wooden pier we walked down, a slow wash of salt water edging along the sides and creeping underfoot as gulls cawed in the distance. Stalls lined the pier, selling things from fish to crab to salt reserves to iron jewelry and ... fudge!

"That must be the fudge she was talking about." I pointed out the stall with the sign labeled *Sea Salt Fudge*.

Meena walked up to the stand and bought three pots, one each, filled to the brim with the sweet delicacy, and I put one into Hera's bag and the other two into ours as we carried on down the pier.

"Who was it your father met here? Maybe we can ask around?"

"A Mr. . . . . Buke? Dad's notes don't really say much, just that he had a long conversation with the man and finally decided on the parts he'd need for IoN."

"Wasn't there a Buke's Trading Post on the promenade?"

On the what?

She clearly knew what she meant, though, because she grabbed my hand and guided us to the end of the pier, up the stone steps, and to a garage-like building back around the corner we had come from. Written on that building was *Buke's Trading Post*, with the O and the S so faded they were barely legible. But here it was, the last stop Dad had made on his final journey before he came home and died a week later.

I really hoped Mr. Buke had the answers I sought, otherwise I was afraid it would remain a mystery.

The door was rusted shut, the dented metal so thin in places I could almost see through to the darkness beyond, but with a strong shoulder I screeched the door open along stone flooring. "Hello?" I called into the barely lit room. Shadows scattered across the floor like rats scurrying from the outside light, and the sea breeze whooshed our hair farther in.

Meena was the first to step through the entrance, then I followed, but I held her hand as we continued through the space.

"Can you spot a lantern anywhere?" she whispered.

I shook my head, barely able to see three feet in front of me this far away from the sun's light.

But just when I was about to suggest leaving, finding a lantern, and returning, lights buzzed overhead in a string of small gas lamps the shape of teardrops. I'd never seen anything like them before, always having relied on oil lamps and candles. They looked like something out of a children's story.

"Who's there?" a gruff, older voice croaked. "I'm not open."

"We just have some questions about some work you did a long time ago?" Meena asked, polite as ever and gentle as a mouse. "Would you care for some tea at the café around the corner, sir?"

"Can't leave. Mustn't leave. Stay, stay, stay," he mumbled, his breaths puffing in ragged gasps. "Stay . . ."

"Okay. Then is it okay if we take a seat by your workstation over there?" Meena pointed to a large wooden desk with scattered tools and a larger, unused version of the smaller gas lamps in the corner.

There were pieces of machinery and tools and wayward sheets of metal, and every now and then I spotted a random pile of assorted bolts and screws, as though they belonged to a project long forgotten. A thick layer of dust and debris suffocated the room. As I moved a steam thruster strapped to the ceiling out of my way, I realized he hadn't worked in this garage for quite some time.

What had happened here?

"Sure, I guess." The man entered the room in a mechanical wheelchair that looked steam-powered somehow, but the frown on his face when he looked at me, a glimmer of recognition fluttering in the space between us, nearly stopped me dead.

I'd seen this man before.

Not in person, but in an old photograph.

"Gabriel Forthright? It *is* you, isn't it?"

"That's me," he said as he wheeled himself to the workbench. "And who are you?"

I looked at Meena, unsure if mentioning my name would help or hinder our progress. "Cinderella. I'm Preston's daughter."

He spluttered a series of coughs into a handkerchief he fetched from his breast pocket. "I don't think you should be here, girl." He went to turn himself around and leave, but I grabbed the handle of his wheelchair and stopped him.

"No, wait. Please. Dad died a long time ago." Well, kind of. "But I have questions . . . about the Internal OxiNexus."

His face blanched white, his eyes widened, and his jaw opened and seemed unable to close again. "I . . . Please leave."

"I can't." I sat in the chair in front of him and grabbed his hands. "I know you and Dad were friends, and I know it ended badly, but he never spoke of it. He just said he couldn't come and visit you anymore because he wasn't welcome."

"Of course he wasn't bloody welcome," Gabriel spat. "What did he think would happen when he made me make that wretched contraption?"

"You mean IoN?" Meena asked. "You made him. Or rather, you made him who he was inside?"

Gabriel nodded, his brow permanently furrowed.

"You transferred Dad's consciousness to IoN?"

His gaze snapped up to mine, his dark eyes almost black in the dim light. "How do you know about that?"

"It's been a long month." I shrugged my shoulders to brush off the question, knowing Meena wouldn't want anyone gawking at her new life. "How? How did you transfer someone's brain into a steambot? I don't understand."

A calloused hand scratched his forehead. "Look, I wish I could answer your questions, but I don't really know how it works. I'm not sure we understand Seren's work enough to have the words, ya know."

"I don't understand." My eyes shifted from him to Meena to the workbench. "You're saying Seren did this? That you didn't do anything? That it's nothing more than godly magic?"

"I saw him. When I transferred your father's time into IoN, hoping for nothing more than storage while we found a solution to what ailed him, he appeared before me." His eyes filled with tears as he dropped his gaze to his lap, where he fiddled with nuts and bolts. "He told me that what had been done couldn't be undone. That I'd . . . killed him." His shoulders shook as sobs echoed in the dusty workshop. "I tried. I tried to use the backup herbilore to transfer the time back—maybe he could spend his final days with you. But it didn't work. Nothing I did made a difference." He looked at me, dark eyes even darker in the barely lit room, and whispered, "I'm sorry. I didn't mean—"

"This wasn't your fault. He went searching for answers, and he got them." I was starting to understand the perilous nature of seeking answers to questions that shouldn't have been asked. "I understand that."

His shoulders sagged and more tears fell, but this time they descended with relief, as though he'd heard something he had needed to hear for years. "Thank you."

"You know, you have some great inventions here." I gestured to his wheelchair and the lights. "Why don't you sell them?"

He laughed then, the tears having stopped with the conversation. "I don't need the money, dear, but working has become difficult with my joints the way they are."

"Then teaching, perhaps?" Meena joined in. "We have a great academy in Palatina. I could get you an interview, at least."

"Teaching, huh?" He scratched his head and beard in thought. "Not a bad idea, Your Highness."

Meena beamed at the man, clearly proud she had maybe given him an idea as to how he could put his skills to use. "Are you sure you wouldn't like some tea, Mr. Forthright?"

"Well, maybe I could swing my behind by and have a slice of Mrs. Bumble's ginger cake. Best on the island."

9 DAYS. 10 HOURS. 32 MINUTES.

THE GINGER CAKE HAD INDEED BEEN THE BEST I'D HAD IN recent memory, but I hadn't really enjoyed it with the endless swirling of questions in my head: Why would he not tell me the real answer? Could Seren be a real entity? No one alive today had ever claimed to have seen Him, but the ladies in white claim their ancestors had. Had Dad been wrong? Or did Gabriel just not want anyone knowing the technology to transfer a consciousness into a machine existed?

"Come on, El. Let it go. Sometimes you are not going to have all the answers. Isn't it enough that we're both alive and well?" Meena twirled under the flickering lamplight of the garage.

Everything was where I had left it. My rickety shelves were still overflowing with knickknacks and ideas, a layer of dust still sat over the corners and desks and piles I had neglected over the years, and my tools still hung from the wall and sat in boxes on the left, ready for use. Everything was just the same as it always had been, but I had changed.

And IoN wasn't whizzing around, causing havoc and

correcting me whenever he got the chance. Maybe there had been some of Dad in him after all.

Sometimes I had felt so alone it was suffocating, hard to breathe without someone else in my atmosphere, but after a while I had gotten used to the feeling of not quite being able to breathe; until someone stepped into my life and reminded me of what it felt like to inhale without struggle, and then the pang of loneliness stung harder, the lows from the happiness highs swung lower, and I had to sacrifice emotional stability for happiness.

Meena grabbed my hand and squeezed, not saying a word. She had this amazing ability to always sense when I was sad, when I was thinking of IoN and my mother and father, wondering what it would be like today if everyone I had lost was still around.

"I have some good news," Meena said. "I got you into the fast track program at Palon University on level eighteen. You start next month."

"You . . . what?"

"It's your payment for the job of fixing my lifeclock. Remember? It's what you asked for." She looked at me with gorgeous green eyes and glowing skin from her time in the desert sun. "It feels like underpayment if you ask me, but it's all you wanted."

"It's all I've ever needed."

She leaned up to me, brushing a wayward strand of blonde hair behind my ear, and placed a gentle kiss on my lips. Her lips were soft, like normal, but insistent, and soon she barged her tongue past my lips and we stumbled into a nearby wall. "I have to go," she whispered between fervent kisses. "My parents are expecting me. But here." She held out one of the envelopes she had picked up at the post office in Vakt Port and handed it to me.

I ripped open the handwritten letter addressed to me,

surprised to find an invitation tucked inside. *You are cordially invited to Princess Jemeena's twenty-first birthday ball.*

"Come with me?"

"Like, as a date?"

"Yes, as a date. I want to show you off, Cinderella. Twirl you around the glittering ballroom and make everyone jealous that you're mine and no one else's."

"I . . ." I was about to think up some excuse as to why I couldn't possibly attend a royal ball, but after everything that had happened in Prago City and the Temple of Seren, nothing seemed a good enough reason to say no. "Of course I'll come." Besides, she was celebrating her twenty-first birthday—an age she never thought she'd reach. If she wanted me there, then I'd be there.

"Great!" She bounced on her feet, her heels clacking on the floor, and spun around. "I love you," she said as she ran out the door, leaving me alone in the garage.

I suspected she left on purpose, giving me space to unpack my adventure and find out where I now fit into my life. Of course, I could ask Meena for anything I really needed, but I didn't want to do that. I wanted to earn it. The tuition at Palon University was technically a payment for a job well done—or a job done to some degree of wellness.

I clicked the lock on the garage door shut and yanked the shutters closed, ensuring no one could see into the building, then pulled the glass vials out of my toolbelt pocket and stared at the green liquid. Herbilore. The power to give life to another by taking it.

Would I ever get that desperate?

I hoped not.

I wanted to smash them, pour the liquid down the drain and be done with it all—but I couldn't. Something wouldn't let me pull the stopper off. My hand stilled, hovering over the vial like it held my chance at life in its fingertips.

Fine. Frustration bubbled over into grief, and tears ran down my cheeks. "Why?" Why would Dad do this to me? Why would he force me to lose him twice? I just wanted IoN back. I never told him how important he was to me, how much I viewed him as a person and not a steambot, how I would have flown off the island to save him and Meena both if I'd had the time.

But I hadn't had the time.

I couldn't have saved them both. I was not responsible for IoN's choices. He was.

Taking a deep breath, I settled myself and wiped my face clean. Instead of wallowing, I locked the vials of herbilore into a box only I had the key to, which I tucked into my toolbelt.

---

8 DAYS. 17 HOURS. 22 MINUTES.

HOME WAS CHAOS THE MOMENT I WALKED THROUGH THE dusty front door. Phyllis met me with glares and daggers and looked as cold as ice, while the twins shouted at each other from the bedroom in ever-increasing pitches.

"You can't just not go," Lazuli said. "I don't want to go alone."

"I can't hold your hand through every social event, Lazuli. One of these days, you're going to have to woman up and marry or educate yourself."

"Ah! How can you be so selfish?" she shrieked. "You're just going to leave and never come back?"

I looked at Phyllis for an answer, but noticed the puffy rings under her bloodshot eyes from a night of crying that I missed before behind all the anger. She was not happy about this choice of Lapis's either. But I guessed it was a good sign that she wasn't trying to control her or scream at her.

Our shared bedroom was a heap of thrown cushions and dress piles and torn rags, the single desk strewn with papers and pencils, as though someone had angrily swiped their hand through the usually organized materials. Lazuli stood over Lapis, who sat huddled in the corner of the bed, screaming at her sister. I had told her to tell her the truth and not wait like this.

One look thrown my way told me that she now understood what I was talking about. That I was right. She should have told her sister sooner.

"Cinderella," Lazuli snarled. "What do you want?"

Ignoring her, I walked over to Lapis. "Do you need help?" I held out my hand, offering her a way out of this mess, and maybe I could offer her the sofa in the garage to sleep on if she needed somewhere else to be.

"Thank you, but I think I should see this through. I should have told them both sooner, and it's my fault they're hurt now. I should fix it."

"You knew?" Phyllis asked, her voice hurt. "You knew she was courting someone and you didn't tell me?"

I turned on the spot and met her eyes, trying to force myself to be as relaxed as possible. "Yes."

"I asked her not to say anything," Lapis said. "I just needed somewhere to meet him where you wouldn't see us. He's from here, on level two. I knew you wouldn't approve. I knew you wanted me to marry higher and make a life for myself, but there was something about him. He made me feel seen, he used to walk me through the streets of two in total silence just to let me talk his ear off about utter nonsense. But six months ago, he got a fellowship to work with a carpenter in Prago City up on level ten. He didn't want to go originally—he wanted to stay for me." She turned to face her mother, a fierce look in her eyes. "He was willing to remain in poverty for me. How could I let him make that choice? I told him to go and to keep writing to me."

"I met with him when I was in Prago City with the princess," I added. "He has a nice-sized house on ten not far from the workshop. The sun shines there—you can see it from anywhere on that level." I also turned to face Phyllis. "It's a fantastic city, he seems like a wonderful and kind gentleman, and it's a big step up for Lapis. I . . . I think it's the right choice."

"But what about me?" Lazuli asked.

Lapis grabbed her hands and squeezed. "You are not half of a person. You are not the other side of my coin. You are you. And you deserve to find the same happiness one day. Besides, he promised me there's a spare bedroom in our house, so you're more than welcome to spend your summers with us." She grabbed Phyllis's hand and yanked her to them. "Both of you."

The three of them hugged, and without the screaming, the hurt and pain Lapis's departure was going to cause was obvious. Rather than stay an intruder, I turned to leave.

"Hey, El?" Lapis said. "How did your trip go?"

I turned back around to face them, but I didn't know what to say. It went great: I saved the princess's life, I got my educational reward, I saw the entire continent. It went horribly: I watched the princess almost die, IoN died, I lost Dad all over again, and Palatina is one of the worst places on this damn island to live. "It went okay. I start school next month as payment for my services."

Phyllis opened her mouth, her lips downturned, but I interrupted her before she could get a word out. "Don't worry. It's on a fast track so I'll be done in a year. And it's the big one on eighteen, just like Dad. This will help all of us, I promise."

Phyllis went to say something else, but I shook my head.

"No, I didn't ask for money or a house on a higher level or anything else I didn't think I deserved. I want the chance to build my life for myself, and despite the fact that you're impossible, Dad asked me to take care of you, so I'll continue doing that as best I can. And when I have earned enough to move us up the levels, I will."

I didn't mention IoN, and I hoped I would never have to, but the lack of my best friend was like an exposed wound. They'd notice eventually.

"In the meantime, here." I gave her a copy of the invitations Meena gave me. "She invited everyone."

Phyllis ripped open the envelope and grinned with large teeth. "This is perfect! Well done, Cinderella. Lazuli, come along. We have to get you fitted for a gown worthy of a royal ball. And maybe we might find you a suitor tomorrow night."

I guessed that Lapis and I had to fend for ourselves, but it didn't look like she minded, as she immediately started tidying up the gowns on the floor and placing them back into their meticulously organized structure inside the wardrobe. Then she pulled a few out and held them up to the mirror, trying to decide which one to wear.

"Did you want to borrow one?"

They wouldn't fit me, so I shook my head. But she brought up a great question: How was I supposed to attend a ball I had no attire for?

7 DAYS. 20 HOURS. 16 MINUTES.

The following morning saw three knocks on the garage door: Bobby, whose toy car had broken; Levitus, an older gentleman who volunteered at the church and gave out soup to the homeless, who wanted to know if I was free next week to look at his steamer; and Old Mags, who swung by just to say hello. We were each currently holding a steaming cup of toffee and eating a piece of the sea salt fudge Meena had bought me back in Vakt Port.

Somehow, even though it was a mere few days ago, it seemed like a lifetime had passed between now and our shopping trip.

"How was Prago City?"

I shrugged, not really sure what to say, what I could say, or what I wanted to say. "It's a lovely city. I can see why your granddaughter moved there. I love how they make their buildings all those wonderful colors."

"It's certainly a sight, isn't it?" She looked around the garage, a small furrow in her brow. "Where's that steambot that usually follows you about? It's a little quiet in here without his consistent noise."

"Oh," I started to reply, sucking in the tears and quieting my shaking hands, "he broke beyond repair on the trip."

"And there's no replacing him? No one who could fix him? I know how fond of him you were, even as a child."

I shook my head. "Afraid not."

"And the princess? How was your work with her?"

I couldn't help it. I grinned from ear to ear. "That went . . . well. We work well together."

"I know that smile, those rosy cheeks." Her gray hair shimmies down her back as she laughs. "Oh, young love. What a wonderful time of life."

"She wants to show me off at the ball tonight." The smile faded from my lips, doubt shoving its way in. "But I . . . I don't know."

"What don't you know? That you're beautiful? Look in the mirror. That you're worth her affections? Look at everything you do for the people in your life. You took nothing more than a scholarship from the princess, you provided for Phyllis and the girls, despite the fact that they deserve to rot on the streets, and you fix any broken child's toy that comes your way for free. And don't tell me you've stopped giving some of my eggs to Levitus to boil and feed to the homeless. I know you do that."

"She lives in a totally different world from me, Mags. She's prim and proper and princess-like, and I'm just me."

Mags waved her hand in the air, dismissing my concerns. "You can learn to be all of those things."

"I don't want to, and that's the problem. I want to be with her, but I don't want to sit on a throne next to her. I want to run the garage, go to school, build my brand, invent new technology."

"Have you talked to her about this?"

"Well, we haven't really had the I-want-to-spend-the-rest-of-my-life-with-you talk yet." My eyes fell sheepishly to the ground.

Old Mags sighed and put her cup down. "Seriously, you young people need some life lessons from us older folk. Talk to her. It's okay to have doubts and be scared, but you shouldn't choose to not live just because of a few thoughts in that giant noggin' of yours." Old Mags stood up in a burst of energy and held out her hand. "Tell you what. Let's get you ready for the ball, and then tonight, after you've danced the night away and you're inevitably looking for some space to be alone, talk, and just exist, tell her your concerns. I'll bet she's already thought about them."

"You think?" I grabbed the keys and locked up behind us. "I just don't want to lose her or hold her back." She's been through so much, lost so much of her life; I didn't want to be another reason she couldn't be herself.

We trudged down the street and around the corner, heading to Old Mags's house. Lapis sprinted toward me holding a wooden box almost as tall as she was. "Cinderella!"

"Lapis?"

"This arrived for you from a royal courier." She handed me the box and rested her hands on her knees, her breathing ragged from carrying it all this way. "I think it might be from the princess."

I looked at Mags, who smirked. We all turned the final corner and headed through the moss-covered door and into Mags's living room.

"Come on, then. Let's see."

"Yeah," Lapis agreed. "I want to see what being friends with the princess gets you."

Everyone stood on edge as I unlatched the box and lifted the lid. We were momentarily blinded by the bright flash of silver.

"Is that a necklace?" Lapis asked.

"It looks to be made of metal," Mags added.

"It *is* made from metal," I explained. "In Prago City, the more beading and metal elements you have, the more noble you are." I held the necklace up to the flickering bulb. "But this is made entirely from metal."

"You'll have to wear something beneath the necklace, lest you ruin your skin." Lapis had become an expert in fashion from all the pageants Phyllis had dragged her to, and I hoped one day she would make use of the sketches she shoved down the side of her bed. "I have the perfect pair of shoes to go with this, if you need them."

"Really?" I asked, surprised she would let me borrow something from her prized collection.

She looked at me and said, "Of course."

"You basically tried to gouge my eyes out every time I so much as looked at your shoes my entire teenage life."

She cringed, her eyes darting back to the necklace for something else to look at besides me. "I . . . it was wrong of me. I'm sorry." She didn't offer anything else: no excuses, no reasons, no explanations. Just a simple apology. "But you can take whatever you need."

I shook my head, not understanding why now of all times, not understanding her change of person.

"Without you," she whispered, "he would never have said yes. I'd been trying to convince him for months to marry me, that we'll find a way, but he wanted to make it big before he introduced me to his world. He wanted to make sure I had everything I could ever ask for. But all I wanted was him. He wouldn't listen, so I sat quietly and waited. And waited. And waited. Until I couldn't take it anymore and sent that letter begging him to be with me. Just one last try. I owed him that."

I still didn't understand why she was thanking me. My confused face must have given me away, because she went on to explain.

"He said that something you said changed his mind. That he wasn't putting enough value on the things in life that were important to him." She met my eyes, and her blues shined with love and appreciation—a look I had not seen on her face before—and I wilted.

It didn't matter that she'd teased me and bullied me my entire childhood; it didn't matter that her sister still hated me; all that mattered was that she was getting her happily ever after now, and that I helped make that happen for someone who had spent their life as trapped as me. But her entrapment was being locked into dresses, dragged to balls, forced to dance with suitor after suitor like a prized lily at a flower show. Maybe, in some regards, I had gotten off easy.

"You're welcome. Just remember to send me an invite to the wedding." Now, about the ball. "I still don't have a dress, though. Nothing you and Lazuli have will ever fit me."

Mags looked at me with a devilish grin and her eyes sparkled with some kind of mischief. "Did I ever tell you about my wedding gown?"

Lapis and I looked at her with puzzled expressions.

"It is the most beautiful shade of sky blue, designed by my sister when we were still young enough to do such nimble work with our fingers." She vanished into her bedroom and came back moments later with a worn box almost the length of her. "I've kept it in perfect condition all these years, hoping it would one day find another use." She unlatched the wooden box and pulled out a dress that was more tulle and lace and beading than it was solid fabric, but when she held it up to the light, my eyes danced over it. "Think it'll do?"

Once we had found enough bracelets and material to cover both arms, grabbed the necklace, found the shoes at the bottom of Lapis's closet that fit, we were all the way to creating a more formal look.

I had been through this once when Meena had taken me to the theater in Prago City, and I didn't like it, but at least then I didn't have anyone I knew bearing witness to my humiliation. By the time the dress was sitting on my figure and we had locked me into more layers than I had ever worn, though, I had to admit I looked okay in the dim lighting of the living room.

Lapis stood beside me in her own gown made of layers of white and peach cotton with silver tulle and buttons. Where her usual style was bright colors and cinched waistlines, this was more laid back, more sedated and settled but with an elegance that showed off the intelligence in her eyes and the thoughtfulness in her smile. It was more her.

Lapis tugged at my hair again, and I flinched but tried to hide it with a laugh at something Mags had just said.

"If you did this more often, you wouldn't find it so horrid. Seriously, your father left you socially feral." She curled another chunk of blonde strands with a tongue tipping beyond her pursed lips.

"I think he just wanted me to be myself and not be molded into society's idea of a well-fitted woman. He wanted me to forge my own path."

"He was a good man." She pulled another few pieces down and twisted them into the perfect curls that trailed down my back. "Do you remember when he used to take us to the empty warehouse with the tall window view of the sunset? You could see the perfect desert hues from there. It was Lazuli's favorite time of the week."

It had never occurred to me that my father had left an impression on them. But he took them in and gave them guidance in a way Phyllis couldn't. He was always kind and gentle toward them.

Mags had steamed us cups of hot milk and sat them on the table in front of us. "He was a beautiful person."

"I miss him," I whispered. I missed IoN too.

"Me too," Lapis admitted.

After they had placed all kinds of powders and colored creams on my face—only half of which I had used before and only some of which I recognized—they placed me in front of the mirror. The dress looked like feathers made out of moonlight in the dark room, with pieces of material curving over the shoulders to my back. It cinched in at the waist and came back out to curve over my hips in a way that made me look more feminine, more delicate, than I was used to seeing in my reflection. It was like a beautiful, strong contradiction.

"You look fit for a princess," Mags said and winked.

Lapis looked at me with a tilted head, confused for a second before she blushed. "Let's go get you your princess, then."

7 DAYS. 13 HOURS. 51 MINUTES.

OUR INVITATIONS ALLOWED US UP THE ELEVATOR, AND Mags waved us on as Phyllis escorted us to a level I had never dreamed I would get to see, much less experience.

Level twenty-one: The royal floor.

The moment we stepped out of the elevator building and onto the bridge that led to a central garden square, floating candlelight greeted us on small squares of metal that used steam power to hover in place almost silently. They seemed to line the way to the palace in the distance. Meena was lighting my way to her—lighting my way home. The palace was so much bigger up close than it was from a distance, and I wasn't prepared for how humungous the front doors and leading staircase would be, much less the foyer inside.

"It's bigger than I thought it would be," Lapis whispered.

"I . . . never imagined it would be so opulent," Lazuli whispered in return.

I didn't say anything. Mostly because I didn't have the words to verbalize my feelings, but also because Meena's home was nothing like her. The white walls were accented with light pinks and hues of peach that made Lapis fit in well with her surroundings but made me look like a centerpiece.

Lazuli was dressed in her usual gaudy colors of green and yellow, making her stand out like a flower in a storm—which, I guessed, was Phyllis's intentions. She would never be ignored or passed over for not having been seen.

"Lazuli, remember, dance, enjoy yourself, but be polite and your happiest self. Men do not like a sourpuss on nights like these."

"Yes, Mother," she replied automatically, like she hadn't even heard the words themselves, just that she was being directed.

There was a grand set of stairs in front of us, as well as open doors to the right that led to a ballroom filled with people dressed in all kinds of colors and wearing all manner of dresses. I vaguely heard Lapis telling Lazuli about the different styles and makeup trends, but my attention had returned to the stairs, where a smaller lady in a plain red dress hurried toward us.

"Cinderella, isn't it?" she asked with a small bow. "You are to enter with the princess. Please, follow me."

Phyllis scowled at me but said nothing, while Lapis grinned like a cat who'd caught a fish. She gestured to the lady in red who was soon halfway back up the stairs. I hurried to follow, but it wasn't easy in the dress.

"The princess is waiting for you on the royal staircase through those doors and up the stairs on your right." She bowed and hurried off, no doubt off to attend to an endless list of duties an event like this would entail.

"Thank you," I tried to call after her, but she had disappeared too quickly to hear me.

The stairs on my right were a narrow set, twisting up in an endless flight that took far longer than it should have thanks to the number of layers locking my ribcage into place. Seriously, how did women get anything done in this many layers? I wouldn't even be able to look at a steamer dressed like this, much less repair one.

Once I had finally reached the top, I glanced around the small veranda that overlooked an opulent ballroom. Meena stood in front of two guards dressed in tasseled suits and standard-issue caps. "Meena?"

She spun around to meet me and stopped as her smile froze halfway. "Wow." Her eyes swept over my body with an appreciative flare hidden in their depths. "I thought that necklace would look amazing on you, and I was right. Prago City suits you."

My hands rested in hers with some trepidation. I was one hundred percent sure of my love for this woman, but I was zero percent sure of my position by her side now that I had the opportunity to think about her future. Our future. They were all going to look at me as an attachment to her, like a purse or a piece of jewelry.

"Are you okay?"

"I'm just a little nervous. I've never been escorted to a ball by a princess before—or anyone, for that matter."

"Forget about all that this evening. None of it matters." She placed gentle lips to my cheek, her warmth flooding me. "Just for tonight, can we please just have fun? Live with me."

Her gaze pleaded with me, and under the candlelight, her green eyes twinkled and her mouth twitched, knowing how much she could get from me with just those perfect eyes.

"Of course." This was her night. One she had spent her life assuming she would never get to see. I would never ruin that for her.

She took my hand and gave a small nod to the guard by the

stairs that descended into the ballroom before placing us at the top of them. I was by her side—not one step behind her or one step in front like a show pony—her hand resting in mine. "Ready?" she whispered.

"As I'll ever be." I squeezed her hand and took a deep breath. "Let's go."

As the words left my mouth, a series of soft lights fell upon us and the music that had previously filled the air stopped as an announcement took its place: "Princess Jemeena of Clepsydra, escorted by Lady Cinderella Ferning."

Meena took the stairs one tiny step at a time, giving me enough room to ensure I was walking in the heels correctly. The room of guests and royal attendees were staring straight at us, their eyes burning holes in my dress and setting my heart on fire as it raced to catch up with the moment. I couldn't breathe. My lungs burned and my breath halted. Meena's hand squeezed mine, and she stole my gaze away from the people and held it as we descended the last few steps.

"There. That wasn't so scary, was it?"

"Terrifying," was all I managed to get out between teeth that wanted to remain clenched. "But it's better with you."

The music had started back up by the time my senses went back to normal, and Meena dragged me toward the dance floor where Lazuli was dancing with fake gratitude in the arms of a gentleman old enough to be her father. Meena scowled at them for a brief moment before turning her attention back to me and wrapping one hand around my waist and resting the other in my awaiting hand.

The music was a waltz, which was at least a dance Dad had taught me, so I could follow the basic slow-quick-quick formatting and keep up. But after a few boxes and me very obviously counting my steps, Meena leaned in and whispered, "You don't have to focus so hard on being perfect. You can stumble your way through the entire night, and it would still be perfect for me."

All I could hear was her voice and the music, all I could touch was her solid hand in mine, and all I could feel was gratitude that I was invited here. That she was here to celebrate herself. It could have been a very different evening—would have been if Seren had gotten His way. But I did it. I saved her.

"Thank you," she whispered. "For giving me this night."

"And every night to come."

Her lips glinted in the light as they neared mine, and before I knew it, she spun us in a tight circle and kissed me with a glowing ember that simmered between us long enough that it began to crackle. I wanted nothing more than for that heat to pop, a fire to be raised, and her skin to dance in its flames along mine.

"Later," she whispered again. But her eyes nudged mine and her gaze swept low to the corset holding me in place and the figure I was cutting. "Maybe a little sooner."

"Would you like something to drink?" I asked, needing a break and maybe to sit down to rest my feet.

"Ooh, yes. I ordered some punch from floor one that I'd overheard people raving about during my adventures with you. I wanted to try it." She grabbed my hand and gracefully walked us off the dance floor and through throngs of people that seemed to divide the moment she was anywhere near them.

She'd ordered punch from floor one? But why? There must have been better options farther up. I didn't understand. But politics weren't something I was up to in this heady moment, so instead I put my questions to rest—something I needed to practice frequently in the company of this mysterious woman—and simply followed.

Two glasses met us the moment we reached an ornate table with gold trim and a dark lacquer I couldn't begin to the fathom the cost of. "For the princess and her escort," a servant said. "It's so good to see you up and about, Your Highness."

"It is good to be up and about, Renault. Thank you." She bowed her head and turned to hand me one of the glasses. "It is made from a desert flower and some kind of apple grown on floor three."

They could grow apples on three? Wow.

The small fluted glass felt delicate between my rough fingers, but I held it with grace like Meena and sipped. The sweet apple and floral tastes hit me straight away, like how I imagined a scented candle would taste, but the lingering honey and floral notes made me want to drink more.

"Do you like it?" Meena asked, who was looking at the glass with a perplexion I couldn't read. "Because it's certainly unique."

"I didn't know you could grow apples that far down, but who knows, maybe they have some patches of sunlight they utilize." I took another sip and swirled it around my mouth. "It's unique in a pleasant, refreshing kind of way. It's a lot sweeter than I would normally drink, though."

"That's the third bowl we've gone through," Renault said, looking at us both. "The guests seem to love it."

Meena shot me a wide grin, pride evident on her face. "I knew it was a good idea." She waved at the entrées and hors d'oeuvres with a dismissive hand. "Everything we have for these balls comes from the upper floors, and they're beautiful, of course, but I wanted something simpler. Something that was just about taste, rather than presentation."

I suspected she just wanted to support a business on the lower floors—trying to make a difference with a small act—but she was giving herself and the people around her justification for her actions. She winked at me, and I knew I was right.

"How about a stroll through the gardens?" she suggested. "I've always wanted to show you them."

"Sure." I grabbed another glass of punch for each of us and let her guide me through the throngs of people—some stopping to greet her, others moving out of the way, and some simply staring in awe. We went out a small door in the corner of the room hidden behind a heavy red drape. "I used to sneak out of balls and formal functions as a child through this door. Since it's never locked, I assume the servants always leave it open, just in case." She chuckled to herself, probably over some private thought, and whispered, "I'd never thought about it like that before."

"They seem to care for you a great deal."

"I know it may seem strange from the outside, but they're as much a part of my family as my parents are. They nursed me, played with me, held me when I was sad, educated me." She grabbed my hand and wandered us down the candlelit path through midnight shrubs and past hanging trees. "Though we may be from different classes, our worlds collide as though we are one."

I didn't know if she was referring to us or herself and the servants, but it didn't matter. I guessed, to her, they did act as one.

"But you've opened my eyes to how much of a divide there really is. I'd never looked up from below before, but it seems so far away, doesn't it? All the royalty and pomposity?"

I rubbed circles with my thumb over that sweet little corner where our hands joined. "We just don't really think about it much. You live in a whole other world to me."

"El, are you okay? You seem . . . not yourself."

She pointed out a particularly rare species of tree with low-hanging red fruit before returning back to her question.

"I just don't know where I fit into your world." I spun her to face me, the moon the only light on her beauty now as we stood in a private garden overlooking the city. "I love you, but I don't know how to stand beside you."

She tucked a strand of wayward blonde hair behind my ear. "It must be overwhelming. I apologize for springing this ball on you. But it is only important that you are here. You do not need to act right or dress a certain way or know how to talk to diplomats and foreign peacemakers and heads of trade organizations. That is my job. One I have been educated in my entire life, even though they never thought I would live long enough to use it."

"But I don't want to make a fool of myself or you. This is important, isn't it?"

Her warm hand on my chilly face sent sparks throughout my body, and I shivered involuntarily. "Yes, it is. But you have a lifetime to figure it out." She gestured around to the world and the people and the ball happening inside. "This isn't going anywhere."

Meena chewed the inside of her cheek when she lied. It was so subtle that most people wouldn't notice, but I did—I always noticed her. And right now, she was lying.

But I couldn't tell how.

7 DAYS. 8 HOURS. 56 MINUTES.

BACK INSIDE, MEENA LED ME OVER TO A GROUP OF PEOPLE I didn't recognize except for one. His image was usually on a poster above my bed, but today it moved and smiled and charmed. Zimeon himself stood in front of me, and I didn't know what to say.

Meena, who was looking positively delighted by my social predicament, introduced me. "Zimeon, I would like you to meet Cinderella. She prefers El."

"Anything other than Cinderella, really."

He took my offered hand, raised it to his lips, kissed it, and then dropped it. "It's wonderful to meet you. I have heard all about your adventures with my sister." He leaned in close and whispered, "Don't worry. Whatever the two of you are hiding, she wouldn't share it." Leaning back, he looked at me with flushed cheeks. "And I would like to apologize on behalf of Zime Industries for trying to purchase your steambot without your permission."

I was trying to process what was happening, but too much information had entered my brain and I was struggling to process.

Zimeon kissed my hand. Zimeon apologized for his company's behavior. Zimeon was Meena's brother.

"And I am sorry for the loss of your father. I met him once when I was younger. He was a brilliant man."

"Thank you," was all I managed to utter.

Once Meena had whisked me once more to the dance floor, she laughed out loud.

"Why didn't you tell me he's your brother?"

She shrugged. "Mostly because he doesn't like it, but I will admit, your face was priceless."

We danced, we laughed, I introduced her to Lapis and Lazuli, who helped me keep Phyllis away, and Hera spun the princess around the dance floor once or twice as friends. It was lovely, but it was coming to an end. The candles were nearly stubs, the servants had tried in vain to hide a yawn or two, and the last punch bowl had emptied hours ago.

"It's time," Meena said. "I've put it off all night, but it's time I introduced you to Mother and Father."

My eyes went wide and my heart stuttered to a standstill, forgetting how its job worked. This was important. If I wanted to remain a part of her world, I needed a final piece of her sphere to spin around us. I needed her parents' approval.

"Consider yourself lucky that you don't need to do this," I said out of the corner of my mouth just as we arrived before the older couple who had been dancing all night. "Your Majesties." I curtsied and kept my gaze low, mirroring others from the evening.

"Ah, Cinderella," the king said, disdain evident in his voice. "I understand I have you to thank for my daughter's current... well-being."

"Well, I did what I could, but she saved herself really."

Meena laughed but hid it behind her gloved hand. "There's no need for that. They know everything you've done."

"Oh, I see." I met their gazes briefly, their stern eyes burning my retinas. "Then I apologize."

"There's no need, dear." The queen grabbed my hand and held it tightly. "We understand how these things work. Adventures and seeing the world and falling in love. It was inevitable."

"Yes, well," the king said, "Jemeena is back now and in line for the throne, given her time, so she'll need to pick a more suitable partner." He forced me to meet his steely gaze. Somehow, despite having the same color of eyes as Meena, his were harsh and bitter where hers were deep and gentle. "You understand, don't you?"

Meena looked at him with warding eyes, her brow furrowed low. "Father, now is not the time. I can have whomever I want in my life. I can rule a kingdom without a man by my side, thank you very much."

"Now, Meena, we've talked about this. You need—"

"You need to fulfill your promise and learn how to keep your word." She grabbed my hand and squeezed, not letting go. "You promised a civil night, an introduction, and a thank you for saving my life."

Her mother turned a strong look at her husband, who conceded in less than a heartbeat.

"Oh, very well." He faced me once more with a softer expression and grabbed my hand. "May we dance?"

I nodded, entirely too terrified to use my words or, for that matter, to do anything else. He led us to the dance floor, where a fast-paced number struck up with quick violin strokes and steps I couldn't follow particularly well. "You see, my dear, while I have nothing against you personally, my daughter needs a leader by her side. Someone she can trust to help her make decisions that will be hard for someone with a soul as gentle as hers."

We spun and I nearly lost my footing entirely, but he helped keep me on track. If I were in a different scenario, one where I wasn't being told how terrible a choice I was for my girlfriend, I would comment on his excellent dancing skills. But I wouldn't, because he simply didn't deserve it.

Meena was gossiping with her mother, excitement in her eyes as she watched us dance around the ballroom.

"Keep smiling, dear. We wouldn't want to upset someone we both care about."

"I don't want to break her heart at all if I can help it."

He swung me low, and my hair pins came loose, my hair scattered around my shoulders, and he pulled me in close, slowing us down. "I don't think that is an option. I know you care for her, and I know you want what is best for her, but what is best for her now that she must take her place in the royal succession is someone of a more practiced status."

Practiced status? What kind of dictionary did they feed kids up here? But he was right. I couldn't rule beside her. I couldn't even keep my own garage up and running, and that was when I had IoN to help. What kind of ruler would I be?

But she could run the world if I let her.

"I do care for her. I love her, and I'd love to live in a world where I could be by her side forever, but I don't think I can."

"I'm glad at least one of you sees reason." He met my gaze with questioning pride. "You have everything you need to begin school and keep yourself and your family afloat in the meantime?"

I nodded.

"Then after tonight you will never come back here. You will

leave during the nearest social opening, and you will let her live the life she deserves. Are we agreed?"

"Yes, Your Majesty."

"Good." He pulled himself from my arms as the song ended, and he bowed his head at me as I curtsied at him. "I wish you a nice life and my deepest gratitude, Cinderella."

"And yourself, Your Majesty."

Meena spun into my arms the moment he left, and I couldn't contain the wonder at her beauty or the amazement at her soul. "You looked beautiful while dancing with Father. Was he pleasant? Because I swear, I will kick him out of my palace the moment it is mine if he acts otherwise."

I chuckled, her passion seeping into her features for a moment while she forgot where she was. "He was the perfect gentleman. And a wonderful dancer."

"Yes, I know. He taught me himself." We wandered around the edges of the dance floor, eating the last of the canapés and trying our best not to wince at our heels. "We used to dance around every available space when I was young, when I was still able to breathe at least semi-normally. I used to wait for him outside of meetings, and he'd dance as politicians and trade masters left, all of them rolling their eyes at us. But he never cared."

"He loves you very much."

"I know, but sometimes his love can be suffocating."

I couldn't relate. "Dad always gave me as much freedom as he could. He never took me to balls or social functions. He never made me wear dresses or socialize with the other kids if I didn't want to. He let me simply exist. In some ways, I'm grateful, but in others I feel as though his idea of freedom has left me on the outside. I'm not free to enter the regular world now."

"It sounds like he loved you a lot too."

There were fewer people in the ballroom now, some having already left for the night, but Phyllis was still flirting with some older man in a blue tailcoat who looked bored by whatever topic of conversation she had chosen. Lapis and Lazuli were dancing together, I suspect to fend off any potential suitors Phyllis had designated Lazuli to dance the night with.

"Would you like to see my personal garden?" Meena asked. "You're here, and it would be a shame to not share it with you."

"How personal?" I asked, her gloved finger tracing circles on my wrist.

"Lock and key." She snickered as we took a walk around the public gardens and exited through a servant door no one was even looking at.

"We have a few flights of stairs to go up, but I think we should be there soon."

The palace was a maze of corridors and grand foyers and comfy seating areas that looked barely used, all ornately opulent in various golds and whites and blues. Everything looked polished to perfection, and I found myself wondering how much the palace spent simply keeping the dust off everything. Not to mention the hours spent sweeping the floors.

"My rooms are through the doors over there." She gestured to the other side of a grand staircase. "My brothers' rooms are both through the other door, which divide off into separate sections. One each." She opened the doors and gestured me inside. She threw her gloves off and laid them on a side table in the corridor lined with paintings of people, some of whom I recognized and some of whom were strangers to me. I loved the one of her and her father dancing in the midday sun in one of the palace's gardens, her mother looking on from the stone bench under a tree. Meena looked no older than five in the painting.

It wasn't until she led me through her bedroom and past the drapes covering the doors that led to her private balcony that I understood how important nature was to Meena. The entire floor was covered with moss and clover and something purple she said was called creeping thyme, so I removed my shoes, and when I stepped my bare feet on the patches carefully left to provide footing, my entire heart sang.

I was here, in her space. Not just the place she lived and spent her time, but the space she'd carved out as a living incarnation of her soul. I breathed it in and mapped it out with my eyes, never wanting to forget a single inch. From the willow tree in the corner that sat above the pond to the sunflowers growing along the eastern wall.

I would remember it all.

And I would remember how she looked as she stared out at the moon from the edge of the balcony, her fingers running familiar patterns in the wall of plants beside her. She looked like a goddess fit to be queen.

My hand rested heavily on her shoulder, her skin kissing mine, and I began unlacing her dress and removing the many layers that kept her cinched in, suddenly thankful for the fewer layers of her previous outfits, and she did the same to me. We undressed each other in silence, kissed in silence, and ran out hands over each other in silence. We didn't need to speak words for the moment to mean something. It already meant the world to me, and by the looks of pleasure in her eyes whenever I touched her just right, it meant something to her too.

She kept our eyes locked all night, making me look at her whenever she brought me to release and staring down at me whenever I was in my favorite place between her legs tasting her. Without the illness holding her back, she used me in any and every way she wanted: riding my thigh, using my fingers and tongue, even instructing me on how to use some of the things in her bedside drawer.

Eventually we were both too tired to continue, so we simply lay in the moss and clovers covering the floor and looked at each other. I mapped the way her eyes curved into her nose, the way her smile stretched from cheek to cheek, the way her chin dimpled whenever she laughed, and the way her brow furrowed whenever she was deep in thought.

I never wanted to forget a single moment of her existence.

The words haunted my breath, getting stuck in a way I couldn't force out. I didn't want to leave. But I had to. She needed me to, even if she didn't recognize it yet.

"Meena, I'm leaving."

"Oh . . . Okay. Well, I can walk you to the elevator building if you'd like, and then tomorrow I can show you more of the palace and . . ."

I turned to meet her soft green eyes, tears threatening to fill the void of mine, and I shook my head.

"You're leaving me."

"I'm sorry. I can't be in this world with you. You deserve someone who can be the left to your right, and I am not her."

"But I . . . I thought . . ." She sat up and wiped tears from her eyes. "I thought we could figure it out. That we could fight through it together."

"I'm sorry." I slipped on my shoes, grabbed the sleeves of the cloak she had given me, and ran. I didn't know why I couldn't face her—maybe I was a coward—but I needed to get away from this world. This floor. And go back to my normal life.

"El, wait!" Meena raced after me, but she was slow after spending twenty years in ill health. "Wait, please!" Her voice broke as she begged me to stay, to talk through everything. To stay with her. But I couldn't listen. I couldn't give in. The king was right: She needed someone better suited than me.

I descended out of the castle, but I lost my footing and a shoe came loose. I spun around to pick it up, but Meena shot me a hurt look, tears running down her face, so I decided to leave it. Turning back would make me stay. Turning back would force me into her arms, and if I stayed there for even a second, I didn't think I would ever leave again.

Eventually, as I ran farther down the stairs and followed the floating candles back to the elevator building, Meena's cries got quieter and quieter. She stopped running after me.

Instead, she sat on the stairs holding my shoe and weeping, which I shouldn't have known, but I did the unthinkable and looked back at the last possible second. Apparently I needed to torture myself for the rest of my time.

The ride back to floor zero was torturously slow. The time it took to return back to my regular life was simplified into a two-minute descent, but it might as well have been two years for all the distance it put between myself and the princess.

3 DAYS. 14 HOURS. 28 MINUTES.

I DIDN'T HAVE THE LUXURY OF CRYING FOR DAYS ON END and bathing in misery while lying in bed, so I did it while working in the garage instead. Well, I tried to, but work was a little dry. Instead, I spent time with my head in Dad's textbooks, refreshing my technical knowledge before the start of school next month. But at the end of every paragraph, whether I wanted to or not, Meena's crying face screaming my name washed into my mind and stuck there. It wasn't leaving.

She was permanently etched into my brain, she had forever changed my chemistry, and I didn't think I'd ever forget her. No matter how hard I tried. Her dad was right, after all—she needed someone more like herself by her side. Not some nobody from level zero who couldn't even keep a single business alive, let alone a country.

The more I thought about things, the more I wondered if I had rushed into that decision. Had I let him manipulate me? But I agreed with him. He was right. I was thinking that long before he had said anything.

Usually, I was a 'think everything through' kind of woman,

but when it came to Meena, I soared headfirst into every decision: Helping her do something very illegal, leaving Palatina on a mysterious trip, prodding for answers in dangerous places, and going to a ball as her official date. There was just something about her that made me crazy. Made me irrational and made me not think things through.

A knock on the garage door sounded, and I threw it open with a frustrated groan, which silenced the moment I saw a royal courier outside.

"For Miss Cinderella Ferning." He handed me a small box with a letter taped to the top.

Familiar handwriting was scrawled across the letter, and I took a shuddering breath. "Thank you." I shut the garage door and placed the box on the desk while I slipped open the letter.

Dear El,

I enjoyed our time together, and you are someone I will cherish for the rest of my days. I won't beg you to stay with me or force you to live a life you don't want, but I owe you the world, and that will never change. You deserve everything this life could possibly offer. Please find enclosed two things: your missing shoe and a bank account. Use it however you wish.

Please be well, and remember me fondly.

Meena

I scrunched it up and threw it onto the desk, frustration bubbling over the edges of my sanity. I wanted nothing more than to be with her, to learn where my place was at her side, but I couldn't. She deserved a practiced noblewoman. Someone her father approved of.

Days slipped by, the weather remaining the same dry heat it was most of the year, but I had become cold. Something inside of me had frozen over, the ice spreading through my soul like a disease. It had gotten bad enough that even Phyllis had stopped asking me to do mundane things. Lapis constantly asked how I was doing, neither prodding nor nosing into my personal life—which was rather unlike her—and by day three I snapped. I yelled at her to stop wondering about me, to stop badgering me over my feelings, to just leave me alone. By the end of the day, I felt so bad that I bought her a slice of apple bread as recompense.

Even the smile on her lips when she unwrapped the rare treat wasn't enough to thaw the winter inside of me. It seemed nothing could. The one person I could have counted on to listen to my woes was now dead, sacrificed for the princess I would never see again. The thing I had always wanted was right in front me, starting in mere weeks, but I couldn't look forward to it. The ice barred even the strongest threads of happiness from slipping through.

"Cinderella?" Phyllis asked the following morning, caution in her tone. "I was wondering if you'd like to attend Lord Fathom's ball with Lazuli next Wednesday. It might be a good chance for you to meet some of your classmates before the semester starts." Lord Fathom, a lanky fellow with a mustache I found rather ridiculous, owned the series of hardware stores found on every level, even ours, and Phyllis had managed to score Lazuli an invite to his annual ball during the princess's birthday party.

I had no interest in attending a ball she might also be at, so I shook my head and grabbed the toast from the grill before plating them up for everyone. "No, thank you. I have studying I'd like to do before school starts."

"Okay. Well, pass me today's newspaper then. It's on the counter in the entryway." Her hand flicked in the general direction of the door to our tiny apartment, as though I might somehow get lost in the few feet between the kitchen table and the bedroom door that makes up the entirety of our living space.

With a small sigh I tried to unsuccessfully hide, I grabbed the paper blindly and threw it onto the table in front of Phyllis, barely missing her toast. Upon sitting down, the front headline caught my eye: *Princess Jemeena on her Death Bed with Hours to Live.*

The ice inside me shattered, and days of emotions flooded into me at once, the dam bursting. Tears fell down my face in raging rivers as the butter in my hand clattered to the floor.

Phyllis looked at the article with a confused expression, and Lapis looked at me with a matching face. "I don't understand," she whispered. "Did you know she was going to die?"

"I . . ." Words failed me.

What had I missed? IoN had saved her. He had given her the last of his years. The last of Dad's days.

Days . . .

Dad only had days to live, so how had IoN lived for years? Did time change when you transferred it between human and steambot? And if so, what did Meena's time say once IoN had died?

She knew all along.

She knew she was going to die, and I just abandoned her like she meant nothing.

I couldn't . . . breathe.

I had to save her.

0 DAYS. 2 HOURS. 13 MINUTES.

My feet slapped across pebbled concrete, a shawl wrapped halfway around my shoulders, my corset only half done up as I couldn't wait for Lapis to finish tying it off. My hand clutched the newspaper.

"I'm coming, Meena."

My toolbelt had been hastily strapped to my waist, the vial tucked neatly inside. The ire at having to run all the way to the garage before sprinting to the elevator building burned through me; I should have kept the vials on me at all times. What had I been thinking?

It didn't matter now.

The building loomed closer and people jumped out of my way while I rushed past them. They shouted things like my name and "hey, stop". I barely took them in.

Once I got to the elevator building, I stopped, head bent over my knees, as I tried to catch my breath.

The desk was being manned by the usual steambot, who asked for my paperwork. But I didn't have any.

Instead, I shoved the newspaper in front of his face. "She's going to die, and I can save her. Please, let me pass." I shook my head, knowing it wasn't going to work but determined nonetheless. "I have to get to her."

"Without the proper paperwork, you cannot go any farther. Please move aside."

I lowered the newspaper and scrunched it into a ball in my clenched fist. "No."

"If you do not move aside, I will have to enforce security measures. Please, ma'am, step aside."

I grabbed a small mallet attached to my toolbelt and gripped it. "I can't afford to abide by your rules right now. Doing so will kill her." I launched myself over the countertop and hammered both eye sensors before he could press the button.

"Emergency. Emergency. Sight sensors are affected."

"Yeah, yeah, I know." I also knew I was going to serve prison time regardless of what defense I tried to give. But it was worth it. I tugged at a steam line connecting his head to his body, and he went quiet. "Sorry about that."

If everyone knew it was that easy to get past them, there would be anarchy, but I knew that was a key vein in their anatomy, and if I pulled hard enough, I could deactivate them. Usually, it just wasn't worth the prison sentence.

I sprinted past the few admin steambots and janitors, not bothering to try to deactivate them all, and instead headed straight to the royal elevator. If logic served, it would be closer to the palace than any of the others.

A few wrong turns and curses, and I was there, the golden room shining in all its dusty glory. I guessed it didn't need using as frequently as the other levels. Pulling the lever, I called the elevator down and waited for what felt like an eternity as the whirring and purring got louder.

Nearly here. "C'mon..."

Once down, the steambot manning the platform asked for my paperwork again, and I shoved him out of the way and pulled the lever myself.

"Ma'am, you are forbidden to use the elevator without a steambot's permission. Please, step aside."

His arms reached out to me, but I swung at him with my hammer as the elevator moved.

"Stop. Security has been informed."

I hammered out one eye sensor before his hand clamped around my wrist and twisted. A snap echoed.

"Ahhh!" My wrist cradled in my hand, I leaned against the central pillar and focused on my breathing.

"Stand down," he said three times, his eye flickering red. "Stand down."

"No." I swung the hammer with my left hand and took out the remaining eye sensor.

He spun on the spot, not sure where to look or what to do. "Emergency. Emergency. Sight sensors are affected."

I shoved him with my good hand, and he rolled backward, freeing up the exit just as the elevator came to a stop. I sprinted, my bad wrist screaming as it trailed behind me. I barreled through a line of steambots at the end of an elegant corridor. "Out of my way."

They tried to grab me, but I took the opportunity and continued running.

Multiple shouts rang out behind me, but not all of them were steambots; some were human law enforcers, who were, I hesitated, probably armed.

A few warning shots at my heel proved my point.

But the palace loomed outside the glass doors that now stood as a barrier between Meena and me. An invisible barricade lined with soldiers.

"Stop," one of the soldiers in the center said. "You are under arrest."

"Like hell I am!" I uncrumpled the newspaper and spread it out in front of me. "She's dying, and I can save her. Let me through." Standing my ground, I let no wavers enter my voice, no shake in my hands, and nothing but stern stubbornness in my presence. I would not yield to people who knew nothing of what was happening.

"No one can save the princess now. The king himself informed everyone here on floor twenty-one this morning."

Crap. That made it harder. I wouldn't be able to talk my way through. What did I do now?

"Let her through!" a familiar voice rang out. "She's with me."

"But Lord Zimeon, sir, she broke several laws, including permanently damaging two steambots."

"And she will be dealt with accordingly," he said, his white cloak billowing in the breeze he'd let in by opening the doors. "For now, she is needed."

Begrudgingly, and with no hiding the furious scowl on his face, the soldier signaled his men to stand down and allow me to pass through a small gap in his defense line.

Zimeon grabbed my good arm and led us away. "Come on. She's nearly gone. Can you really save her?"

"Yes."

That wasn't the right question. The right question was: What would saving her cost? But suddenly I didn't care. I didn't care about how many days I had left to live, what the knowledge of time transference would do to the world, or how the king would react to someone from floor zero being irrevocably in love with his daughter. All I cared about was saving her. I wanted to know that, even if it wasn't me, someone would get to spend the rest of their life seeing her smile. The world was a better place with her happiness in it.

We sprinted up the steps to the palace two at a time, ignoring the worried and puzzled looks on many servants' faces. Zimeon, still clutching my arm, whizzed down a few corridors and up a few more flights of stairs until we stood face-to-face with a familiar ornate door.

I looked behind me, back toward the elevator building that I could just see out of the window on my left. There was no turning back now.

"If you can save her, please." The look on his face was something I didn't think I'd see there. Something akin to grief and pain for the inevitable loss of his sister. Apparently, even if you knew a loved one's demise was coming, it didn't erase the pain of the emptiness left behind. "She deserves to live. The world deserves her rule."

He was right about that. Floor zero deserved her as queen, and I would give it to them.

The corridor was silent, and every sort of nothing echoed in my eardrums loud enough I could hear my blood rush. I expected servants to be bustling about or shouts to be heard, but it was as though everyone had accepted that she was leaving, and there was nothing to be done.

She lay on the very bed we had laid on together only a few nights ago, but she wasn't glowing under the moonlight anymore. She paled in the sunlight that used to radiate off her skin like she held the secret to life itself. She had fallen very ill in such a short space of time. Her eyes fell on me, and where I thought a frown or a tear would appear, a smile graced her lips.

"El," she rasped. "You came back."

I fell to my knees at her bedside, tears sliding down my face. "Of course I came back. I'm so sorry. I shouldn't have let fear rip me from you."

She frowned at her father, who sat in a chair beside us. "Wasn't . . . your fault."

"I should have been brave, like you. And I should have trusted you. Us." I grabbed her arm and took a look at her lifeclock, which was down to the last thirty minutes. If I wanted to save her, I needed to do it now. "You know why I'm here, and you can't stop me."

The glass vial of slightly glowing green liquid rested in my hand, and her eyes widened. "No, El . . ."

"Shhh." I wiped a gentle thumb over her sweaty forehead. "It's my choice to make. We know when we're going to die, we know what levels we can live on, and we know the quality of life we will have, but we get full freedom over how we choose to spend that time." I kissed her lips, a soft brush of love across a vast ocean of uncertainty. "And I choose to spend it with you."

I turned to the king and asked, "Your Majesty, if you could please turn around and look the other way."

He frowned at me and went to say something no doubt annoying and kingly, but Zimeon interrupted. "Turn around, Father. It's for the best. Trust me." His voice hid something that persuaded his father to turn his chair around with a huff and a complaint about intelligent children thinking they know best.

When the single maid in the corner of the room had left, I turned back to Meena and opened her lifeclock for the final time. Once both the faces of our clocks had been lifted and I'd unwound the right lines, I poured the herbilore tincture into the lifeclock and then connected our times.

"I'm sure Lady Lorelai would know exactly what to say in this moment, but I'm not as well-read as she and I don't pretend to be good with words, but Meena, I will give you a life, even if I have to give half of mine to make it happen."

The cogs spun faster than I could count, and when my clockface counted some eleven thousand days, I unconnected the lines and put everything back into place—until finally her lifeclock read 11,115 days.

She looked at it in wonder as tears streamed down her face. "I've never seen the number that high."

I'd never seen my number so low. But it was worth it to see the look on her face, the color return to her skin, and the light in her eyes shine beyond happiness. I wrapped my fingers through hers, and she yanked me to her.

"Never leave me again," she whispered, a stern edge to her gentle voice.

"You're linked to me now, Princess. Forever and always." I looked at our time and asked, "Think thirty years is enough time to make the changes you want?"

"It'll do." She grinned at me, then turned to her father and said, "I'm ready."

EPILOGUE

10,385 DAYS. 14 HOURS. 12 MINUTES.

Level fifteen was lit with oil lamps as far as the eye could see, a trail of mini-suns lining every street leading out from the university like a spider's web. They said you could see hints of them even on zero, but I thought that was egotistical gloating. The banner at the front of the university's stone steps, pinned from one giant column to the next, waved in a slight breeze as I went through the double wooden doors for the final time.

It had been a memorable two years, full of new friends, old textbooks, and getting the Tinker Hut finally off the ground. Green pulled through on his word to throw some customers my way, and word had spread of the floor-zero nobody dating the princess. That might have helped some. But really it was the confidence I had found in these very halls that finally screwed all of my bolts together and put my head on right. I'd spent years training with Dad, then a further span of time exploring what engineering meant to me with IoN, so I'd earned this day.

Happy Graduation Day was written on another banner inside the foyer, along with a detailed map of where everything was being held.

"Ella!" Tris called from the doorway to one of the assembly halls. "You made it." She trotted over—a lady never runs—and wrapped me in a one-armed hug. "Have you seen the lineup for the presentation yet?" She waved a wayward piece of paper in my face, expecting me to somehow read it while it was moving.

"No. I tried to grab a copy this morning, but they were all gone by the time I got here. Busy morning in the garage."

"Zimeon himself is giving the speech this year. Eek!" Her cheeks blushed bright red as she wiped her clammy hands on her gown. "I can't believe it."

"Maybe it's because a certain *someone's* royal girlfriend is going to be in attendance," Flare whispered from behind me, making me jump. "You know, I still can't believe you got your business off the ground, got a first-class degree, attended etiquette lessons, *and* kept your girlfriend." She blew a strand of her curly blonde hair from her face. "Such an overachiever."

"Oh yeah," Tris added, "how's the new garage on level twenty-one treating you?"

I hadn't really wanted to move Dad's garage all the way to the royal floor, but it was near-impossible for Meena and I to have a working relationship without one of us moving up or down; and since she couldn't live on a lower level, it was up to me to make the decision. Eventually, our relationship mattered more to me than memories, so I moved. Though, because of the restrictions on who can actually enter the level, I also have an office on floor ten, with a small warehouse attached. Meena swore she'd one day make me my own elevator so I could simply bring things up and down the levels, but the paperwork has been a nightmare.

"It's going great. I spend most of my time in the garage, but my assistant runs the office well. So far, I've had clients from all over using my services." I even still did business on the lower levels for a cheaper rate, something Lazuli, my new assistant, had been helping me with since Lapis left for Prago City. I think she just needed something to do—a purpose—and an excuse to escape Phyllis's clutches now that they were lined with gold. It seemed Meena followed through with her word and bought the contract for IoN originally held by Zime Industries. "I even employed a junior assistant recently, since work has been bombarding me." Bobby loved helping out, and he was a natural with the tools. "I can't wait for the Zime Industries Expo in the summer. Are you both working on something for it?"

Flare shook her head, her curls a bouncy jumble as she smiled secretively. "No, because guess who got an internship at Zime Industries?" Hand in the air, she squealed, "Me!"

"You got the only internship?" Tris asked, looking a little disappointed she didn't get it herself, but it was a competitive field. "Wow. Congratulations."

"Tris, any idea what you're doing after graduation?" I asked, knowing full well she had been deliberating while trying to persuade her grandmother it was okay for her to move to Prago City.

"I got a job as an assistant to Everlake." She didn't look happy about it, which I was about to question when she explained, "I just need to break the news to Grandma."

"She'll be okay eventually. She just needs some time to adjust to your being an adult with choices ahead of you." I placed a comforting hand on her shoulder, knowing how hard family can be.

"She still wishes I were married, so working is a little beyond her comprehension."

"C'mon, let's go find our seats." Flare grabbed our hands and yanked us into the assembly hall, where we found our seats at the very front.

The hall quickly filled up with the university faculty, parents and friends of graduating students, and, this year, the royal box attendees. Meena's security guards filed her into a makeshift seating area to the left of the stage, and she found my gaze immediately, her face warm and full of pride.

"Thank you all for coming today," the president of the university, Dr. Shelway Copperbottom—we had all made endless fun of the name in the last two years—said. The lapels on his suit were bright orange today instead of the usual bright green, and the rest of the material was a deep maroon instead of the usual indigo. "We are here today to celebrate the graduating class of this year's honor students from all of our eclectic courses of study. I hope, like many of you here do, that their futures are filled with as much brightness as their eager faces were on day one."

He went through each course one by one, starting with the sciences and mathematics, then moving on to the more active courses, like ours and production design. As he called each student's name, everyone clapped and cheered, and the student walked onto the stage with a nervous glint in their eye, shook the president's hand, and walked back to their seat. It was a repetitive affair filled with more applause than even my weathered hands could keep up with.

When he finally called my name, one of the last of my class, I wasn't nervous as I had expected to be. I was proud. I had done this. I might have gotten the fast track placement with Meena's help, but that was payment for a job well done. I earned this. This was the start of my life.

THE PARTY AFTERWARD WAS HUMID, WITH THE HIGH summer heat suffocating the room, but it didn't matter. Meena's hand was in mine, and my friends were standing next to me while we chatted with the professors about our futures.

"So, Cinderella, I hear your business is going well. You even have an assistant working the office on floor ten?" Dr. Radsbury asked. He had taught our theory classes. "That is quite impressive for someone of your years."

"Thank you, professor, and while I'm proud of the achievements, I had some help." I squeezed Meena's hand. "I couldn't have done it had Dad not left me the garage or Meena not paid for my tuition."

"Come on, now, El. We've talked about this," she admonished from beside me. "You earned that tuition."

"Also," Dr. Radsbury beamed, "it helped start the royal funding scheme to assist those on lower levels with tuition and a living pay while studying."

"Yeah, Ella," Tris added, "you've earned this. You put in more work than any of us on this course."

"Remember that time you stayed up all night to finish the essay on the history of steam combustion during our first year, all because you wanted to finish working on that job for a loyal customer? You managed to meet both deadlines and get an A." Flare huffed an annoyed breath, always hating my work ethic, but she was a good person really. "And the time you nearly missed an exam to attend Queen Jemeena's coronation day." She curtseyed to the queen, who waved her formalities away.

"What about you two? An internship in Zime Industries and a job in Prago City."

Dr. Radsbury turned his attention to the others at this news, a congratulations and a farewell all rolled into one speech about how they, too, deserved the rewards for their hard work.

Meena pulled me aside after that, made our excuses, and, with a suggestive smile, pulled me into a small courtyard with few people. "I'm so proud of you, El. You're going to be leading our technology one day, and I'll be right there to watch." The lifeclock ticked in her wrist, reflecting the sun now that she left it uncovered, and I couldn't help the glee that overtook me at the thought of living side-by-side with this woman for the rest of our time.

"You know, at some point we'll have to tell people about the engagement."

She frowned at the mere mention but grabbed my hands and lifted them to her lips. "I can't wait for the world to know just how serious I am about you, but let's not take the limelight off you today. I promise, we'll announce it in the summer."

"Just before we leave for Prago City, you mean, where your father can't berate you unless he wants to make the trip out there to do it in person."

"He'll try sending some letters, but they only bother me when I open them." She shrugged and wrapped me in a hug. "Besides, I can't wait to go back. A whole month! Think your business will survive?"

I shrugged. "It only bothers me when I open the front doors."

The End

AUTHOR RAMBLINGS

Phew. What a ride writing and producing this book has been. If you've stuck around this far, thank you so much, and if you enjoyed the book please consider leaving a review to help this tiny little author out.

I started writing this book in 2020, and I'm sat here writing this in 2024, four years later. This book began before COVID, before I'd become disabled, before I'd lost half my family, back when I was a completely different person. So you can imagine how difficult editing has been when different sections were written by completely different version of myself. Forming my brain's scramblings into some form of coherent structure and plot has been a challenge to say the least. There were so many people who helped along the way, from beta readers to the dev editor to the line editor, to my amazing Alpha team who keep me going through the thick and thin. And let's not forget my husband, who keeps me sane every day my brain decides to slip into fantasy and refuses to come home when the street lights turn on.

Writing Meena and El's journey has been as much a privilege as a burden. I loved being able to bring a small little light in the back of my mind to life, to turn the cinders into a roaring flame, but the pressure to do so with enough skill and care overwhelmed me on more than one occasion. I just knew that their story needed something, and I have lain awake many a night wondering if I had the skill to produce such a something. Maybe, hopefully, with enough wishing stars and bottled moonlight, I have done something someone somewhere will love. Hopefully I've managed to pour their story onto the page with enough love that it set your heart on fire.

If you'd like to stay attuned to ramblings and book releases, please follow me on social media:

Facebook Reading Group: Kilmari's Keep

Instagram: @AuthorKilmari

ALSO BY FREIDA KILMARI

The Fifth Horseman Saga

The Fifth Horseman

The Lost Horseman

The Dead Horseman

The Magic Horseman

For the Love of Gods Series

For the Love of Hades

For the Love of Poseidon (*coming soon*)

CINDER31LA

Milton Keynes UK
Ingram Content Group UK Ltd.
UKHW021744260824
447290UK00005B/14